HER GOLDEN EYES

First Published in Great Britain in 2020 by
LOVE AFRICA PRESS
103 Reaver House, 12 East Street, Epsom KT17 1HX
www.loveafricapress.com[1]

ISBN:
Also available as paperback

---

1.   http://www.loveafricapress.com

Acknowledgements

I would not be here without #UkRomChat and ThePink-HeartSociety.com. Thank you for wanting to include me.

Thanks too to those down the years who listened to and read my stories—from pegasi in the dorms, to medieval fanfic with pink fluffy handcuffs on the forums.

The teachers who told me I waffled and the kids who laughed at my poetry can have a hearty middle finger.

To Kiru Taye and Zee Monodee who believed in me and in my characters I am forever indebted.

Finally, apologies to all the people at neighbouring tables who had to listen to me argue with my mother about metaphors.

Dedication

To my family, especially Mum

Chapter One

There were, Sabbah knew, three things that made his position as *Muhtasib* easier. The first was that he loved his city. It was absolutely not depressing or pathetic that Marrakech had taken the place of the parents he had lost, the lovers he never had time for, and the children he had not yet had.

Secondly, he considered while settling a dispute between two old rivals: both the Arab populace and the black Africans saw kinship and neutrality in him, even if certain members of the old nobility disdained his mixed blood.

He paused and watched two of his agents come running down the street in his direction, notebooks in hand, marking his final point for him.

The third thing? At the end of the day, he could leave the mad bustle and return to order and quiet in his own home.

The sun was already high. Less than an hour, and midday prayers would be called from those minarets not being rebuilt. The little matter of constant masonry work in a perpetually rebuilding city would not stop the five prayer times each day. Sabbah smiled proudly. *I doubt even a siege would do that.* He then inwardly rolled his eyes. What a prig he was becoming!

Then he gave himself a stern shake. He would have to solve this next dispute quickly. His men reached him, one skidding to a halt as he reached the edge of the slave markets.

Sabbah paused to point out a fallen sign blocking the walkway to one of his agents, and the leavings of a donkey that needed clearing to another.

"Yes, Muhtasib." One nodded. "But please! Two Egyptians. Claiming ..." He heaved a breath, and the other took over. "They claim they were Muslim when they were sold."

Sabbah groaned, but kept his face even. Even over a tricky case which could well spill over until after Dhur prayer, a Muhtasib could not be dismayed or reluctant, as he had no need to remind himself.

More of his agents were gathered together, facing a trader and his friends while of course, there were those who had been out in the bazaar and pressing in on all sides, sensing entertainment to be had. His men sighed with relief as he approached, and he acknowledged their bows of respect. The space around them widened as they backed away to leave him with a fuming, worried merchant and an interested audience. How wonderful, he thought wryly, for them to have such faith in him.

Fortunately, he reassured himself, fighting the urge to smooth his simple but expensive tunic and check his head covering was not askew on top of his shaven head, he was no longer newly appointed. The mere fact that the problem was his to unravel no longer made his palms glisten and his knees wobble.

"They're lying!" the merchant exploded, once he had set eyes on the Muhtasib. "Egyptian Christians! Not Muslim at all!"

Sabbah scanned the pens. Men and women—mostly younger than twenty, not all comprehending and almost all ruddy-skinned Slavs, pink and with peeling skin—either glanced up for a moment or forcibly kept their gazes on the ground. Two young men stood with their arms folded and their chins high. Behind them, catching his notice as he inspected the pen, was a bold pair of eyes.

A woman with dark skin and a thatch of brown hair beneath a tattered shawl stood watching, no shame or modesty in her as she locked eyes with him.

Shock clenched at his chest and made him want to gasp for air. How uncomfortable, that sudden shift from calm to disorder, and he quickly turned his attention back to the two claiming they had been illegally sold. Nothing else but the case mattered; not the sudden pressure on his lungs or that his feet were now rooted to the paving slabs.

"We questioned them, Muhtasib," one of his men called over.

Sabbah heard the crinkling of paper behind him, clear and crisp past the blood roaring in his ears. Despite keeping his eyes on the accused slaver, he could feel that pair of fine eyes burning into him. His ears stung with heat, the urge to turn to her again a compulsion hard fought.

"They know the faith. No mistakes," his man continued.

"That is because I am an honest servant of Allah."

The slaver looked tired, not guilty, but he was a man who traded in people. Where was guilt in a man like that?

Sabbah chastised himself. He himself still owned his doorman and friend Kanto. He had no grounds for feeling superior. Certainly not when he was, for the first time in his career, completely distracted by a woman. A woman still watching him. Wasn't she? He was so sure but did not dare check.

"I have tried to convert them," the slaver continued, waving a hand vaguely at the two lads standing proudly at the front of the penned area.

Sabbah did not want this going before the judge. He and the *Qadi* had history. He could see, though, that these young men were ready to yell and shout and fuss in their search for freedom. His natural sympathy for men longing for freedom, however, faded behind his responsibility and need to restore order.

Once again, he moved his gaze over the other slaves. The black woman was still watching. He glanced quickly on, but his eyes were drawn back. A man dying of thirst might know drinking his fill would split his belly, but it didn't stop him.

She shifted, pulling herself forward like a cat reluctantly leaving a comfortable spot in the sun, and came to lean on the fence alongside the source of the trouble. She moved like silk tumbling off a table, and he felt himself focus on her. Not just his eyes, but his entire body seemed to be fixated on her. She put her chin on one of her hands and met his eyes.

Catching his breath again, he forgot all about men who made themselves fools for women. For a brief moment, he forgot that other people existed at all. He warred between the hard shock of seeing this woman and the peculiar softness her smiling eyes cast around his pounding heart.

"You need help, Important Man?"

Her voice, husky rather than smooth, had a quality that got under his skin and scratched an itch he had not realised he had.

Sternly, Sabbah tried to be logical. She was neither Slav nor Egyptian. Under all that desert dust, she was darker-skinned than he was. Unlike him, she had no Berber or Arab blood. Her accent was unknown to him, too, over the precise, musical Arabic of the marketplace. High cheekbones, curving lips, and brown eyes that caught the noon light and glowed golden.

Another jolt went through him so powerfully, he began to sway a little, just a little. He tried once more to focus on the facts, rather than her beauty; on the dirt, rather than the flesh beneath it.

"Can you give it?" he invited, and was caught by her smile again. She was filthy with dust from the Sahara and the mountains to the east. Her hair probably nested fleas, and she was a slave. But that smile, crooked by design, proved irresistible.

Sabbah smiled back, and his cheeks ached with the unfamiliarity of it. A real smile. Not a polite one. For a second, his rational mind could not exert control. She was the entire world, and nothing but a pair of golden eyes and a kissable mouth existed.

Then, all of a sudden, the brief moment was shattered.

"Don't listen to her."

It came from one of the slaves whose claim had brought him here in the first place. He shoved her to one side, and she gave an awkward, shocked cry as she shot a hand out to stop herself from falling.

Cold fury at the lack of care one man had for a woman snapped Sabbah's professional control back into place. Something ferociously protective flared.

"She's lying for him! He's probably put her there to spy on the rest of us."

Just like that, the man ruined his chance. The other boy groaned as he realised his friend's vehement rejection of a witness had betrayed them both as liars, and the slaver praised Allah loudly in gratitude for his exoneration. Sabbah looked to the woman. She lounged where she had been pushed and then jutted her chin, jerking it up in a backwards nod at him. She shrugged elegantly, shoulders rising alongside a long, graceful, slender throat.

"Just call me Solomon." She grinned, and once again, he felt his mouth mirroring that smile, responding to her. Still, her hand pressed against her wrist where it had caught the edge of the wooden pen, and there lingered a slight shake to that broad smile as she continued. "They would have silenced me, or my master. Either way, you find out who's lying."

"And if they guessed you knew nothing?" he questioned, even though he did not need to know. His involvement was over. His agents had already melted away, into the market, readying for prayer, no doubt.

"Please, Important Man," she chided, narrowing her eyes and scrunching her nose just a little. "I know everything."

He grinned in appreciation. Then her expression changed, and her eyes went wide and intent. He almost felt she was grabbing him, even though her hands were tucked on the railing.

Sabbah considered himself oddly cheated that he felt that fervent grip, but did not have it in reality, even though she had him rooted to the spot. He had the entire market to order and organise, and she had roped him about with one urgent look. He reached over the fence to check her arm, but she waved his hand away.

"You need me in your life, Important Man," she instructed him, voice low. "Buy me. I'll run your house, cook your food, sweep your floors, or shake your foundations. Whatever you want. But buy me. Because you need Tison in your life."

Her jerkily-spoken Arabic jolted him from the soles of his feet to the hair he did not have on his head. She did not seduce or plead; she merely stared him down. Her fingers gripped into the railing, but when he looked down at them, she released it, the momentary pallor about her knuckles fading.

And she had him. She had him with that demand. That order. Had she pleaded, pathetic and sorrowful, he would have perhaps sought out another position for her. Had she not been able to meet his eyes, had she not challenged him, had she not made him feel as though he were chained to her, indivisible ... Thoughts trailed into nothing.

She had him.

Soon, the call to prayer would come. He needed to be in the centre of the market where he could wash his hands and kneel in the place a mosque had stood before the Almohad conversion. A clean place amid the work and trade.

He would be seen by all the other men praying—they would know their Muhtasib was a man of faith, one of them, but also a man of focus and without distraction.

This woman was absolutely distracting. She was obviously without scruple. That offer to shake his foundations, for example, should have shocked him. No, it should have disgusted him. It *had* shocked him, and he liked it. For a few moments, he was entirely Sabbah, and the Muhtasib became his position rather than his personality for the first time in two years.

His heart was beating stronger than it ever had before. He was fascinated by the effect she had on him, that constant awareness of her. He wanted to grin at her. He wanted to find out what she would do. He wanted it to be just wicked enough to tempt him.

No. He could not think that way. If he owned her, she would be under his protection.

He turned away from the compelling woman.

The trouble was that he could feel her there. He could feel the potential of her, the 'what if' of her. Besides, he'd had a woman he had failed years before. He could not abandon someone who asked him for help, and for all her demand, all her bargaining, she was in need.

"Sell them to separate masters," he recommended to the relieved slaver, gesturing to the growling men he had bested. No, who *she* had bested. Sabbah gave in to what he truly felt was inevitability. "And I'll buy the woman who helped us, to stop them turning on her."

He winced as one of the two men continued to curse loudly but would have ignored them if their blasphemies and epithets had not been so close to midday prayers. They did not deserve to upset the devotions of others. Lying was something he had no time for, not for any reason. He turned his head and snarled, his deep voice booming from behind his teeth as he allowed his power to surface.

"If you did not want trouble, you should not have caused it." He stared them down, anger swelling, and they recoiled, looking down. He took a few deep breaths past his nostrils, forcing his usual calm back into place. "If you continue to cause a disturbance, I will have you flogged. I am Muhtasib. I keep peace in the markets, and you are disturbing that peace."

Cowed by the threat of violence at least, one man pulled the other to the back of the pen. Sabbah accepted the slaver's thanks and gave direction to his home for the woman's delivery despite the way she made his heart clench and pound. He had just finished paying for her when the wailing call to prayer soared over the city. With a deliberation that made his chest ache, he departed without looking at her again.

He reached the centre of the market in time, pulling his prayer mat from the bag at his side and managing to banish a grinning woman from his mind just as his knees hit its colourful, woven surface. Had he not needed to be always pure as Muhtasib, he might have just been late to prayer. No man would blame him but himself, just as no man would know to disdain his wandering thoughts. But he could feel the effort it took to keep her from his mind, to keep her from his focus and devotion. It was new, a distraction that could do that, and somewhat disturbing.

She was somewhat disturbing.

Chapter Two

Marrakech was a pink-gold city comprised of smells so strong and varying, Tison would guess its natives could walk about blindfolded and not get lost. For herself, she was glad for the escort of one of her new master's agents. She knew how dangerous things could be for lost slaves, by the grace of God not first-hand.

She shook herself, reminding her dazed, wandering mind to focus.

That she had been incredibly lucky was undeniable. If the Muhtasib had not spotted her, if her mind had not been reeling around ways to silence the obnoxious pair who had been plotting escape since she'd joined the caravan at Tunis, and probably before ... In fact, if they had not been so stupid that she was able to trick them, she would have been a fool and a snitch both.

She shuddered and reflexively picked at her tattered shawl. The once fine fabric was dirty and ripped at one side, but then again, it had never been meant for long journeys. *I never needed hardy clothes in the bathhouses.*

Her rescue was a fluke, but she had to be *her* now. She was going to have to be wise and strong and all-knowing. Gone was the woman whose broken heart had dominated her thoughts for years on end.

"What is your name?" she asked her thus-far silent guide.

"Excuse me?" He looked at her and then at the ground. He lacked his master's unblinking strength, obviously a sweet boy unused to speaking to women at all. So she guessed, anyway. Unless she had grown fangs without noticing. "I am Ibn Yusuf."

"What is al-Muhtasib like?" She gave him a toothy smile, hoping to create a sense of kinship, to stop him thinking of her as a woman he could not talk to and instead as a fellow. "You hear Muhtasib, you think old, fat jackals playing politics and accepting bribes."

The smile did not work. The implied compliment to his employer did.

"He is the best man in the city," he assured her, and she blinked at the sincerity in his voice. "You have a good life ahead of you. He is honourable. He has been Muhtasib for two years or so. Allah be merciful, he will be so for many years more."

Tison did not reply. She was impressed. Given what people in Tunis used to say in the bathhouse where she lived about the Muhtasib there, quiet praise from someone who worked for him was not merely impressive, but unprecedented.

She had decided not to give any master her respect until she had seen them in fury, and her trust never. The way Sabbah's arrival had melted the crowds and soothed his agents told a story louder than if it had been wailed, searing, from the minarets.

Privately, even she had felt the way his presence had changed the air. It was not just his looks, making a fool of her with those broad shoulders and melting eyes, but more than that. Something about him filled the space. Something about him made her think he could be depended upon, even though she should know better.

And he appealed for help. He heard you out and let you come to his aid. What man would do as much without then taking credit?

She had been one of the most sought-after masseuses at the bathhouse, she reflected, without smugness or pride. She had seen attractive men, had touched them, too—she knew muscle. Even the men she had worked with, the male slaves, purchased for their physical perfection, could not compare to the Muhtasib of Marrakech.

She just had the impression of strength and solid warmth.

He was, she admitted, eyes flaring as though she were speaking aloud and not immersed in an internal monologue, even better-looking than the man she had loved. A man who had destroyed her life twice. She shuddered, chastising herself for letting her memories hurt her.

Ibn Yusuf led her to the richest, cleanest part of a city that flourished from wall to wall. As they climbed the slight hill, the street widened, and Tison looked about as houses were replaced with walls ringing compounds. Here, where fewer feet trod, birds crossed from garden to garden in front of her. Red-bellied flycatchers skimmed the air in sweeping circles, and little brown birds flitted back and forth, clamouring for attention.

She breathed clean air and looked back the way she had come, at the city opening out behind her and the plains beyond. She stood still, stunned by the pure beauty of that sight. Beside her, Ibn Yusuf halted and gave her a shy smile.

"Welcome to Marrakech, Mistress Tison," he said. He seemed to have made a decision on how to behave with her. "Is it overwhelming? I've lived here all my life so I don't know, but it is perfect, isn't it!"

She gave him one of her best smiles. He was a nice boy. The world needed more nice boys.

"A little," she admitted, quickly clarifying. "Overwhelming. It is ... perfect. Wholly perfect. Tunis is big. And louder. But there is something awe-inspiring about a new place, and the rock is such a beautiful colour. Even before that blue ..."

Here in the richer part of town, she could marvel at the bright blue paint that gave the walls a look unlike any she had seen.

"You'll be safe working for the Muhtasib, at the least."

Ibn Yusuf smiled again, but it was clear he wanted to get on back to work, so she stopped staring about like a dazzled halfwit and followed him as they went on up the hill.

They approached a compound almost indistinguishable from the others. The same white and painted walls, the same flat rooftops.

The gate was closed. No welcoming braziers, and no water for travellers. Even in a city where there were fountains and funduqs, the shut gate filled Tison with a feeling of wrongness. Marrakech was still a desert town. She frowned. Hospitality was greater than God, whether you called him Allah or Yahweh or simply Lord. It was disturbing, like seeing the sun rise in the West. Marrakech might not *be* in a desert, but Morocco, Tunisia, Egypt, and all other countries under Arabic domain were still arid. They were not lush, green jungles like the fabled lands of the South. Even an enemy could not be refused water and shelter.

A closed house felt unnatural.

Ibn Yusuf waited with a look of expectation on his face.

"If the Muhtasib is expanding his household, he will finally open up the doors," he mused aloud, eyes widening with hero worship.

She looked at his open face and gave a little sigh for his trust and transparency.

"You make me feel old, Ibn Yusuf," she told him, flattening her voice but reassuring him with a lopsided smile. "Now, get on with you. I will see myself settled. Thank you for your help."

"Salaam Aleikum, Tison." He bowed, and she returned it, nerves welling inside her.

"Wa-aleikum salaam, Hopeful Boy!" she returned, and faced the closed gate while his footsteps took him back to the markets.

She stood and breathed. Thus her life began again. Owned by a man who made her feel all sorts of quivering. His deep voice, his long stride, his broad shoulders. She would bet half of Marrakech was in love with him.

She was taken in by a straight-faced porter almost as dark-skinned as herself—Mandinka or Fulani perhaps. While not in the prime of a warrior, he was not far past it, even if there lingered something of the old man in the way he walked. She ambled through a bare courtyard past an empty fountain to the side of the house where the slave quarters were, and her eyes never rested for long on one thing. This was to be her new home.

She saw no one but this almost-silent doorman. Before they reached the empty dormitory for the female slaves, she had noticed the cool air brushing past her cheeks from vents in the corridors. She had noticed the dead silence within and the distant noise of the city outside. She had noticed dust here and there on bare surfaces and shelves, and also the slight limp to the dour man's gait.

"Bad back, Serious Man?" she asked, reaching out to run her finger over a dusty tabletop, eyes scanning the lines of beds with their bundles of sheets and complete lack of personality or presence. A lectern with a Quran still in its soft leather wrapping waited at the far end of the room.

"Hmm," he muttered.

She blinked. "Do you not speak Arabic, Serious Man?"

She stepped farther into the room and started weighing the options of each bed's position. Perhaps she would sleep in a different bed each night, just because she could, she thought to herself. Her lips twisted in humour. Of course, then she would have to make each bed again.

"I speak it," he replied, his accent strong even to the ears of one new to this city and its environs. "Maybe I don't speak it to you, slave girl. Maybe I don't speak when I have nothing of worth to say."

Tison's lips twitched again. She was weary and dirty, but she appreciated a good joke. A man that pompous was a joke indeed. But perhaps he was just confused. He needed a little time to realise that she was not to be bossed about. Slave or no, she was still herself, and she would not lose that. She refused to lose it. Not again. So she let the little ghost of a smile broaden into a grin and flashed her teeth at him. War had been declared.

"Maybe then, I follow you all the rest of the day and talk to you." She swept off her shawl, baring her head, and deposited it on the nearest bed. "Are there baths here, or do I go to a bathhouse?"

His nostrils had flared. Impressively. Mandinka, she reckoned, by the shape of his nose and brow. He did not answer either her threat or her question. And in all honesty, she was feeling the dirt on her skin more and more. Now that she was in a house, for all the occasional dust, she did not feel right having the filth of the mountains still on her. She had spent years working in the best baths in Tunis. Being dirty felt unnatural. But, if the porter was going to refuse to answer her, she would just irritate him into telling her everything just to shut her up.

"Long way north, are you not, Serious Man?" She tilted her head at him.

"Long way west?" he retorted.

Tison laughed merrily. She was impressed. She liked to be impressed by people. It happened little enough. She had not expected anyone to recognise an Ethiopian this far west.

"Well done, Serious Man!" she commended in recognition. "Maybe 'Watchful Man' from now on, uh?"

"Kanto," he responded, dropping his folded arms, relaxing just enough to stop his nostrils flaring, which she took as a firm victory. "I will bring water to wash the pens away, but you don't go to the bathhouse until the master has confirmed to me that you are part of this household."

"Very sensible, Kanto."

She felt a flicker of something in her chest, a tightness, as the image of the Muhtasib smiling at her over the fence of the slave pen flashed into her head. She tried to shake herself. Clever slaves did not fancy their masters. They were fancied. Like a shiny bauble or a plump piece of fruit. She knew only too well that thinking a master was handsome made a woman easier to control.

She would control him. She sat on the edge of the bed next to her filthy shawl and crossed one leg over the other boldly, determined not to think about those warm, dark eyes and the intelligence behind them.

"I'll get to know all my new friends here!" she announced, looking around at the empty room and gesturing widely at the stark beds. "Oh ... wait ...!"

He grunted again and left at once, swift and purposeful. Tison reckoned he was not happy about being the only man in the house. Only owned one, anyway. If the dust was anything to go by, he had more work than he could handle. She watched him down the corridor, his broad back and thick, muscled body not kindling even the slightest interest in her.

But the Muhtasib was in her head with a faint smile that needed drawing out and muscles that needed revealing, while a handsome man with a brooding manner did not even make her quiver a little. Irritating!

She lowered her foot to the ground and sat more squarely. She missed her friends back in the bathhouse in Tunis. She could have grumbled about the attractive Important

Man with them, daydreamed a little, giggled, and then moved on with the day.

Taking a breath, she let the tension she had been ignoring bleed out through her toes.

She could do this. She could absolutely do this. Even with Important Man and his smooth good looks. Arabic eyes, not so rounded as the shade of his skin would imply, but still such a dark brown she could barely see where iris and pupil separated and with enviable lashes. Strong Ghanaian body—a strong body under the tidy clothes of his office.

She assumed his lineage lay somewhere in the old Ghanaian Empire, slowly falling to the Caliphate on one side and Mali on the other. The strength of the bones and jaw on this side of the continent tended to be so very different to the high cheekbones and fine, perfect oval of the faces that had surrounded her as a child.

Perhaps if she could just think of him as a body and nothing more, it would be easier. She could bet he would strip well, look good oiled and ready to wrestle. That image alone sizzled in her blood and made her work her top lip between her teeth. Her toes curled involuntarily.

Though the fantasy would remain that, she could bet. A man like that did not strip off in public, laughing and ready to grapple. A man like that forced himself apart. But that would make him lonely.

A lonely man could be manipulated, she told herself, breathing deeply. A lonely man could be dependent. She needed someone to need her. That was all. Someone to count her as irreplaceable.

So she was going to be necessary. She would not be sold on again until she was good and ready. If other women could twist men around their fingers, so would she!

She opened eyes she had not consciously closed and looked around the still empty room just as Kanto's dragging gait down the corridor heralded the promise of being clean.

She could do this.

Chapter Three

Sunsets lasted long past hours of business in Marrakech. While mornings started slow, relatively cool, the shadows of the Atlas Mountains shielding the city from the scorching, dusty heat of the Sahara, the nights lingered warm and mellow.

The city had been particularly beautiful tonight, but Sabbah knew that lay in his last few hours. He had spent them amid the cork workers, where the soft scent of the wood soothed, with his friend Abou Saal ibn Musa, the *Sayrafi*. They had been investigating the false lead coins flooding the markets of late.

The company of a friend, good smells, and the rose of the sky deepening to the rich diamonds of starlight. Bliss, despite the trouble at the meeting's root.

Smudging purples were giving way to outright night by the time he returned home. Feet dusty and shins aching, he wished he could honestly claim that the slave woman was gone from his mind. That he had forgotten she had entered his life at all. The flagstones of his city seemed harder than usual as he walked past funduqs full of life and merriment, towards the richest part of town where he had chosen to buy a house.

He had been meaning to get a full complement of staff for his new household every day since he had bought the house two months ago. He had made depositions, caught thieves, and put his name to a hundred or so documents.

And yet, he still lived in a house with only one slave.

Two months since he had finally obeyed his mother's dying wish and sold the small home they had lived in once his brother had married. Two months. Sabbah hesitated before the cedar wood gate as the ache of grief felled him. During the day, he had his work. But nights had always been conversation in the chair by her bed, or games with counters, achi, or qirkat with Kanto while his mother watched, weary but wryly amused.

Alone, though, had been better than thinking about filling the rooms and readying them for a wife. That was a whole other mess of pain and regret and mistakes made. Another thing he had to move past and simply had not. Poor Aisha. A constant, scarred reminder that he had not been good enough fast enough.

It was just all easier with one slave. Well, easier for him, he reminded himself. Kanto, with his bad back, doing all the work of a big house. What sort of friend did that make him?

Until today, he reminded himself, forcing away the melancholy and what he made himself admit was self-pity. Now he lived in a house with two slaves. The guilt in his stomach writhed itself into a new feeling. Excitement. Because that new slave was not just anyone—a lioness of a woman with dancing eyes and a body that moved as though she were choreographed by angels.

He heard a few last, slightly dragging steps, and Kanto opened the gate, banishing any odd curls of desire forming in his chest.

"The bell fallen off?"

The challenge in the low-pitched grumble rang clear. He shook his head, waiting quietly as the locks were once more turned and the bar slid across for the night.

"The woman settled in?" Sabbah broke his silence, opting to face the change head on, and spoke as if her name was not in the centre of his mind. As if he was not tangled into knots by the mere fact of her and her wide grin.

You need Tison in your life ... Shake your foundations ... His breathing hitched.

"More than that." Kanto faced him. "You need to talk to her. She has plans."

Shake his foundations. He had assumed she was offering her body. He had intended to refuse her despite her allure. He had intended to gently tell her he did not take advantage of his slaves. He had intended to pretend he was not fascinated by her, as if his body was not feeling phantom sensation of what she could do to him and him to her.

Perhaps he could have convinced himself that she was too dusty, too flea-bitten. If not, the fact she was under his protection should have sufficed. He had assumed. And ... He was disappointed. It pulled at his stomach and lowered his shoulders. Apparently, she had literally meant the foundations of his house; it was them she had plans for, not him.

A shiver went over his skin, not just because of the cooling night or because he was intrigued by her. Understanding raised goose bumps on his arms.

"Plans," he echoed.

A lick of unease curdled the interest in his belly, dispelling the feeling of a man deprived of a woman. Inexplicable anxiety. He looked to his friend's face, and in the flat lack of expression, Sabbah knew he was caught.

Kanto saw far, far too much. He had known that since the day they'd met and he'd bought him from the hell of the salt flats. And Kanto knew that Sabbah was all on end, or he would not be so silent, so bland, so not judgemental. He also knew that Sabbah was stuck in a nice, tight routine that suited them both very well, and that the mere mention of that changing had fixed his master to the spot in unmanly terror.

A lesser man than Kanto would have smirked.

Sabbah's brother was a warrior—Khalid faced bandits, rebels, and bands of heretics. Sabbah could face down an armed drunk in his markets, a moderately sized mob, and a large one so long as he had his agents backing him up. Apparently, what jellied his knees was the idea of a woman he did not know having *plans*.

"Is she in the slave quarters?" He took a step towards them.

"Hmmmn," Kanto grunted. "For a quarter hour maybe, she was in there. She is now in the pantry. Taking stock. She has been everywhere."

Sabbah looked upwards to the majesty of the night sky, framed by the roof of his house around the courtyard. The purples were now full black, glowing with stars. *You are small*, he reminded himself, just one part of the world. Fears were nothing to the stars, so they would not stop him. Neither would this odd sensation that knowing she had been in his rooms had kindled.

He found Tison in the store room. Every draw had been pulled out, every jar's lid lying on the long table. Amid the chaos stood his new slave, the sleeves of her tunic rolled far above her elbows. His eyes lingered on lithe, supple fore-arms and delicate wrists as she jotted notes and numbers on a wooden board with a piece of charcoal that had smudged her fingers and thumb.

"One moment, Important Man!" she called, her voice ringing in the cool, stone room. "I do not want to forget ... There!"

She set the board down, stilled the roll of charcoal that threatened to slip to the ground, and approached him. All at once, he was warm again, his feet itching through his san-dals. Wryly amused, he realised he was burning through a month's worth of emotions in a few moments. She was like a sandstorm; only he could not bring himself to hunker down and wait it out. He was still wandering blindly in the chaos, and loving every moment.

"So?" Tison folded her arms and jutted her chin up at him with all the belligerent pride of a bush woman at mar-ket, but all the command of an empress. "Where is the fury at my meddling?"

She was scruffy, dry hair still laden with dirt and dust. He could see the line where water had been scrubbed into her neck and face and left a pale smear. But he could feel his body drawn to her, feel surprising, unaccustomed lust deep in his gut. He had not wanted a woman in a long time. Had it always been this strong? Had he always felt a blinding, dazzling heat pulling him by his groin, begging him to taste her?

Somewhere, some corner of his mind recalled the conversation before he started grinning like a fool for no reason. There was a rush to desire he had not felt in a long time, a strange giddiness threatening to overpower his mind. While it was preferable to fear, he did not want her thinking her new master was lusting after her. He wanted her to feel safe. He knew only too well what some masters did to beautiful slaves; he refused to become one of them.

"I bought you to protect you from reprisal," he lied.

The smudges on her neck gave him a sudden, clear image of her in the public baths, naked and slick with olive oil soap.

What was wrong with him?

She laughed at him. A dry, merry cackle instead of the golden chuckle he would have expected.

"Nah! You bought me because you need me. God put me in your path."

"Do not presume to know the ways of Allah, or even of me."

He looked down into her upturned face. Was she closer? Had he stepped towards her? He needed to keep her in her place. He needed to remember that he was a master, not just a man. She could be a thief. She could be anything at all, and he needed to be a figure of authority in his own home. He needed his peace back, his calm house with its nice, controlled emptiness.

Except that her shoulders were angular; they would feel good under his hands. No! He had to hold onto his position. He had to remember who he was, who *she* was. Her lips begged to be stared at, but he fixed his eyes on hers instead. Golden brown, holding light. His voice tripped a little as he continued:

"I am Sabbah ibn Abdella al Muhtasib. Remain in my household, and you must show respect."

A few heartbeats pounded rapidly against his chest. He was nervous, not fearful, but strangely exhilarated. A confounding feeling. His shoulders ached with the desire to put his arms around her slight frame.

Tison unfolded her arms and reached out, patting his bicep gently. The light touch left ethereal bruises.

"Well said, Sabbah."

Her voice dripped reassurance. Shock at having his personal name used for the first time by someone not of his blood ripped through him all the same. It added to his desire somehow, that clear intimacy, but his surprise distracted from the physical contact that otherwise would have felled him by now.

"You may not call me ..." he attempted, still battling against the swelling of emotion in his chest.

"Out there, or when others are here, you shall be—" she lowered her head, hushing her clear voice into a simulacrum of respect, "—al Muhtasib."

Her hand lifted once more and squeezed his forearm, her touch cool and hot and not enough. "In your home, you are Sabbah. Come."

She released him, and he almost staggered from the lack of those fingers.

"Your store will rot. You do not have enough servants or slaves," she said, gesturing. "Your grains are wasting. You will need a cook. He or she will need an assistant."

She marched past him, back towards the courtyard. He turned, blinking unsteadily as he followed her silent but determined steps. He did so blindly, blinking, thrown off his stride and not knowing at all how he had thought he could be master to such a wild creature. His peaceful home whistled away into the past, blown by a sandstorm of a woman. Would it be so bad to appease her? The thought of bending to her every whim sounded oddly attractive.

"You need a housekeeper. That will be me." She waved a hand flourishingly over her head. "And Dour Kanto needs two under him. You will need three serving girls. At least five when you marry."

Sabbah's heart was pounding from the swing of her hips. He was deep in a fantasy of wrapping his hand around them. That was too much, though. His mother had wanted him to marry. So far, all he had done was get a house big enough for a woman to have her own quarters. Guilt shot through the desire, old guilt, the oldest guilt in the world. Before men had found God, they had already been terrified of letting down their mothers.

"This courtyard needs trees, vines, flowers, herbs." She pointed to the cooking spit, and his eyes followed her hand rise. "That should be producing food all day, soaps, too, and everything the house needs. And we need a place to give water to travellers or guests."

She tutted at him, then started towards his quarters, the study, and receiving rooms on the ground floor, and he had a vision of her striding into his bedroom that brought his voice back to his throat.

"Stop!"

Too loud, his words hammered against his own ears, echoing from the bare courtyard's walls. His home was a quiet place. Kanto did what had to be done. They spoke over food, but no voices had been raised in this house.

His hand was on her shoulder. He had reached out to turn her. He could feel her bone, too close to the surface. She turned and was looking up at him with challenge in her eyes and a smile ghosting around her lips. Or did he imagine the challenge? Was it in his head, like the conviction that her lower lip needed to be touched by a gentle thumb?

Snatching his fingers from the threadbare gown she wore, he summoned his professionalism, girding himself in the armour of his title and his position in Marrakech's society.

"You going to scold me, Sabbah?"

Raising a hand, she set it on his chest, warmth from her fingers seeping through his tunic.

She called him by his name, and she touched him.

"You are ..." he paused. Could she stop his heart with the gentle pressure from her palm? Worse, could she feel the way it thumped? "Too much. Too fast. Things should remain ..."

Except they should not. She was right. He had to have a household worthy of his position. He needed to find a wife.

"You are Muhtasib." She was correct. "Your household should reflect that." And again. "You need servants, slaves, and food, always ready to entertain. And you should marry while you still hold the position. You are handsome."

The hand lifted, leaving its warmth behind, and she tilted his chin. His world shifted. He felt it. Felt the moment he went completely mad instead of slightly crazy for this hot-fingered woman with her bold words and slender body. His jaw felt molten. Almost bruised when her fingers left his skin. He could have groaned aloud, and did not know quite how he stopped himself doing so.

"You could have any woman in two days; your house must be ready. One slave in such a house? Tch! What would your mother say?"

The heat from her hand had been flowing downwards, pooling at his groin. Mention of his mother turned all the alluring temptation to ice water. *Sell this place, boy*, she had told him, her once commanding voice reduced to a deep croak. *Sell it and get yourself a nice, big house up on the hill and a nice wife, too.* There was the guilt again.

"How do you know about my mother?"

His voice was cold, clipped, alien on his tongue. His mother would have approved every change. He was sure she would have been angry with him, taken him to task. But after she died, after he had freed the household slaves, only Kanto asking to remain with him, he had not had the heart to make the changes needed. So the new house was empty and gathered dust while he worked in the city, and the women's quarters remained just as vacant.

"Your father was the Arab one, seeing as you're the high and mighty Muhtasib. She's the half of you that's African." Tison shrugged, pursing her lips and jutting her chin, adding to the confused mess of emotion making thinking all too hard. "Amharic or Mande, Songhay, or whatever that blood might be, no black woman would tolerate her son having risen so high to live in a dusty house. You have mice, Sabbah. Mice!"

She spoke accusingly, as though he had deliberately brought vermin into the house.

"But if all this is too much for you to think of, just give me coin and some sign of authority, and I will buy the slaves, order the cooking, sweep the floors, and all you have to do is look pretty."

Her hand came up again, and though his desire had been tamped down, his skin revelled in the touch as she patted his cheek. He could control the thoughts, but not the way his skin burned and tingled under her fingers.

"Which you're doing very well already."

He caught her hand and trapped it, because if he could not control her fixing his world, he could stop her exposing him to hours' worth of sensation in a few moments. Only then, he was holding her hand, and he could feel her whole body through it for some reason. So aware of her, he was barely aware of himself.

"So as of tomorrow, you'll just sort my life into order?"

He wondered if he sounded afraid or hopeful.

"Nah, nah, Important Man." She slid expertly from his grip, retrieving her hand almost before he noticed she was moving. "First, I go to a bathhouse, I get clean. I buy new clothes suitable for the Muhtasib's housekeeper." She raised her hands and delicately fussed her hair. "Then I go buy you a household, Important Man."

For a moment or two, he merely stared at her, at those golden eyes and her questioning, appraising expression. He could almost believe that she did not know how he would react, that she had not planned out this conversation while she totted up his jars of grain.

"I will bring you the necessary note of authority after morning prayer," he told her. "The closest baths do not have a day for women tomorrow, so I will walk you to another. After that, will you be able to find your way about the city?"

"I will learn, Important Man."

She looked curious, wide-eyed, an expression which sent heat slamming once more to his hips. Somehow, that slight opening of those eyes, the tilt of her head, the uncertainty, were all more seductive than lazily drooping eyelids and pouting lips.

He would go upstairs. He would wash. He would pray. He would sleep. Nothing had changed. Nothing except that he wanted a woman in his bed. A temptation he had thought he had grown out of years ago. He should be too old now, past thirty, to be driven mad by a woman.

"Until tomorrow then, Tison." He gave a little bow. To a woman he owned. Then he passed her, dipping his shoulder to stop his arm brushing against her.

Relief and regret warred in his chest. She was the sort of woman that cropped up in poetry, or in Holy Books bringing down kings.

Sabbah would not go mad for a slave, even one with golden eyes and a thin body he longed to wrap himself about.

IT WAS JUST BEFORE midnight when he realised he had no water to wash before prayers. Kanto, disturbed by the addition of Tison to the household, had forgotten to bring it. Or perhaps to instruct Tison to do so.

He picked up his ewer, eyes heavy after a long day. With the handle loosely grasped in his hand, he made his way towards the doorway of his bedchamber and had looped around the wooden screen in front of it when he stopped dead.

There was a woman in his household now.

With just Kanto off in the porter's rooms by the gate, Sabbah would normally walk bare-chested at night. Not any more, he realised, swinging around and fetching the tunic he had worn that day, setting the ewer on his bed so he could pull the garment over his head. His cheeks felt hot. Here he was, blushing, because a slave might have seen him without a shirt. A *woman* might have seen him without a shirt.

And it was not quite embarrassment.

She had cast some sort of enchantment over him. His mind revolted. No, such a suggestion implied it was magic that attracted him. It was not. It was her movement, her eyes, her joking.

Her palm on his chest.

He breathed deep and retrieved the ewer. It was not magic, but something wrapped up in his body. It came from him and not her, and he could not blame her for the attraction. He was just being a man. Just because he had managed to cut himself off from his desires all these years did not mean their emergence was due to machinations or spells.

She was just so ... And she might have seen his body. Would she have liked it? Would she have admired what muscles he had? He was no bathhouse slave, with a honed, oiled abdomen that seemed sculpted rather than human.

Grow up! he told himself. She will be long asleep. Christians do not have to wake and pray in the night.

He walked out of his apartments, through the barren atrium, and across the empty courtyard. He glanced up at the sky. A few clouds attempted to blot out the shining stars. The sun would burn them off in the morning. He was almost into the store room when it finally sank into his awareness that a lamp burned.

He halted on the threshold.

Tison.

Of course.

She looked up at him and got to her feet without needing to push herself up with her hands. That told him she was limber, and tormented his mind with what a woman with such strength could do.

"Sabbah." She bowed slightly. "Did I wake you? I am sorry if I did."

She seemed to see something in his sleepy expression that worried her, and she became solemn. "I am sorry, Muhtasib."

"No, you did not wake me." The use of the title he had insisted upon earlier that very night felt wrong. It disturbed him in a way he could not quite identify. "I came to get more water."

"Is it midnight already?"

He looked around at her feet. Many of the jars were now empty and stacked. The draws were all back where they belonged. She had gone to bed and then got up again.

"You could have left this." He gestured to the room's floor generally. "It will wait until morning. You deserve sleep in a proper bed."

"Pshh." She waved a hand and sat on the floor again, crossing her legs. The dress pulled as she sat on it, tightening around her body. Around her breasts.

He swallowed, but because his eyes had gone shamefully downwards, he saw the way she briskly rubbed her arms with her fingers and gently dragged her nails over her skin.

He marched past her at once, headed for the hatch to the water channels that ran beneath the city. Cold, he thought, cold water. Cold stone tunnels with lots of cold water. All the way from the mountains in those cold, cold tunnels. She was nervous, could not sleep because of the changes in her life, and her master was ogling her.

He could not block out her voice, even if he attempted to control his desire.

"Stupid raised beds," she muttered. "Going to fall off and kill myself is what will happen."

It made him grin as he finally made sense of her words. The grumpy little monologue eased the tightness in his chest, and he was smiling when he returned to where she was rising. With an armful of jars, she once again stood straight up without needing to balance herself.

He wondered if she was a dancer. Her dress remained pressed against her bottom for a moment, and a grip tightened around his heart as heat flooded to his groin. Saints preserve him, would his body not remain calm for long enough to stop himself being shamed before his new slave?

Then she took a step. It loosened, and he forced himself to pour out the water so he could wash.

Just as he would have to if he bedded her.

Cold. Cold water. Cold, cold water.

"Do you mind if I pray here?" he asked, wanting to be near her more than he needed something soft beneath his knees.

"Not at all." She looked at him in confusion, her burden returned to its place, her eyes questioning. "It is your house, Sabbah."

She had hesitated before speaking his name. He was glad she had gone with her familiar irreverence. He was not sure why. His hands and the back of his neck still damp, he took a deep breath and then sank into the comforting ritual of prayer.

If he could pray in the same room as her, he could absolutely maintain his control in the marketplace from now on. He would not think of her as he spoke the ritual words.

Except he was aware of her. He was as aware of her as he was of the hard flagstones on his knees. They were, it happened, very cold. Instead of helping the icing of his want for her, all he could think of was her cold legs and bottom on them. In need of warming. Of rubbing to banish the chill.

Sabbah did not think of women this way! Ever!

When he rose, he was frowning. Was this weakness? Was this venality?

He raised his eyes and met hers. The gold was dulled to brown in the half light of the lamp, but her skin came alive in its glow. She was half cleaned, her hair dusty and paled by sand and grime, and she wore a tattered gown that had once been white and was now the colour of the desert beyond the mountains.

And she was beautiful.

Even still, she was agonisingly, throat-tighteningly attractive. That was the word! Attractive. He was drawn to her. Every inch of him wanted to be close to every inch of her. He wanted to touch what he saw, and he had absolutely no right to do so.

Then she drew in a deep breath that raised her shoulders an inch and looked down at her work.

"If you'll excuse me, Muhtasib," she said, and began stacking empty jars in her arms.

"Let me help." He moved forward, unsure if he had issued a command or a plea. It was instinctive, bred into him by his kind, dutiful father and strident, proud mother. "Consider it my punishment for letting my house get to such a state. Have you caught any mice?"

"I may be elegant and graceful—" she flickered her eyes to his face, almost as if she were nervous, despite the laughter in her voice, "—but I am not actually a cat!"

"What a relief!" Elation at making her laugh gave him a pleasant, tingling feeling. He picked up a load of his own jars and followed her to the racks on which they belonged. "Or you would not enjoy your trip to the bathhouse tomorrow."

Naked. Caressing her own skin with soaps and oils. Wet and slick and ...

She gave a groan, and Sabbah felt it to his toes. A whimper attempted to escape his throat, and he brutally suppressed it.

"Ah, the bathhouse! I will be clean! Clean! No more desert dust, no more mountain dirt!"

She sighed, or hummed, some sort of soft noise that made the hairs on his arms and chest stir to attention. She had not read his mind and liked him thinking of her body. She just wanted to be clean.

What was this woman doing to him? His intention to blame himself had fled. He had to think. He had to think about being her master, not her lover. He had to think about her position as an owned person, depending on him for protection, not as a beautiful woman whose voice and eyes reduced him to raw, heathen want.

"It must have been hell crossing the mountains barefoot." He thanked whatever part of him was still compassionate and not this new lecher he could not control.

"I gave my sandals to someone who needed them more," she remarked offhandedly, as though it were no great sacrifice for her to walk over rock and grit.

The simple tone made him blink. They moved back towards the jars on the ground. Another two trips, and they would all be stacked.

"I see." His lips pulled into a smile. "You are in fact a saint."

She gurgled with laughter, and his heart soared from that second victory.

"Oh no, Important Man," she replied, and she grinned at him, calling his eyes back to hers for a moment. She straightened the lines of jars with her long, slender hands. "Not a saint. Nor even a particularly good person. Though ... when I buy slaves to fill your household ..."

She walked a little less purposefully, and he followed as she sat cross-legged once more, pulling a last draw filled with junk towards her. He sat opposite her, entranced instantly by the way she untangled string and sorted different sets of measures into appropriate stacks.

He looked at her feet. The pale soles were bruised, the toes bloodied. Older scratches were crossed with newer, and though she must have washed them that afternoon, dirt was already darkening the pink soles and lightening the darker whole.

"Come now." He searched her face, staying conversational and walking a thin line between the call of passion and the pain of knowing this woman had suffered. He wanted to make her laugh again. "Don't go cowardly on me now, brave and not-saintly Tison."

She shot him a heavy-lidded glare and then smiled, her face going from predator to temptress in an instant. And he did not think she intended to seduce. She did it just by being.

He had to conquer this. It was one thing to make her happy, another to think about making her moan. He could not afford to think about her naked, her hair about her shoulders, her eyes lazy and demanding as he hovered over her.

"I want to buy the girl I gave them to. She is sickly in the heat, she struggled so much. I do not want her broken or sold cheap to some—" she stopped her tongue, even though the mounting passion and anger had made his heart patter like a small animal's, captured and held close.

"Of course you must buy her," he told her. "My porter is a man whose back frequently leaves the gathering of water or goods to me. My second slave is terribly mouthy and over-familiar."

He grinned at her.

"Oh, sure, Important Man! Like you didn't need someone to shake you up! See—" she gestured towards him, and he felt an urge to capture her hand and bring it close, "—already, you make jokes and tease. Teasing is fun! Cultivate that skill!"

The sigh he felt leave his lips had the hint of a groan, too quiet to be heard, or so he hoped. Oh, how he would tease her! How he would touch her, how he would make her feel every emotion and passion he could think of, all at once.

I want to tease you. And who did that make him? It certainly did not make him serious and dependable Sabbah ibn Abdella. It made him somehow more of a man and less of a gentleman.

"You'll have to teach me, Tison." He rubbed at his still-damp beard and noticed her follow the movement with warm eyes. Her hands slowed in their seemingly chaotic wander through the draw.

"I will," she promised. She let out a long sigh, and it turned into a yawn that dipped her chin to her chest and stretched her face. She moved her head, and for a moment, looked very much like a cat indeed. "I think I am more than ready for my bed."

Sabbah felt an odd, peaceful sense of repletion settle on him.

"You deserve rest," he said, rising quickly to hold out his hand.

She had touched him before, but he had not yet touched her bare skin. She reached up and took his hand, rising without pulling even slightly on his palm. She was warm, her fingers strong, and he would take this touch as a reward for not begging on his knees to follow her to her room.

"Sure, if I don't fall off the bed!" she retorted.

"At least you won't end up with a scorpion for a bedfellow!" he flashed back.

She jerked her hand back and shuddered head to foot, bouncing on her heels and shaking her head back and forth.

"Aaaaargh!" She scrunched her hands into fists over and over. "Why would you say that?"

He could not help but laugh, even when she promised that if she could not sleep, she would bang pots and pans in his bedroom as revenge.

It was a strange moment. In an odd way, it reminded him of the way he and his brother had been as boys. What sort of slave, what sort of woman, could make him feel that way?

Tison, he supposed.

TISON WOKE BEFORE DAWN. The red-bellied flycatchers were yelling at each other in the tree outside the window, and the call to prayer followed soon after from the minarets. She stretched on her pallet. The beds in the slave dormitory were raised from the ground, half a foot of space for shoes and clothes to be kept beneath them.

She hated it.

Scorpions be damned.

She sucked air through her front teeth in a little click, and then she sat up, stretching once more. She had been a slave for almost all of her life. She put her feet down to the floor. Tomorrow, she would take the mattress off the frame and sleep closer to the ground. She would keep the place clean, and there would be no arachnids of any kind. She ignored the tension in her stomach, simply pretending it was not there. If she focused on silly details, she did not have to think about the big, new beginning the morning represented.

"So, Tison ..." Her voice, fresh in the morning, croaked a little. "Who are you now, uh?"

Was she insolent Tison? Seductive Tison? Demure Tison? He had no wife yet, though she intended to get him one, but Sabbah had been the sort of man to expect demure, she was sure of it. Maybe she would be Strong Tison. Controlled Tison. Maybe she would even be Important Tison.

So long as she never became Serious Tison, everything would be fine. She had had enough of serious. She believed she had appeared as Capable Tison the night before. It had been difficult, more difficult than she had imagined, to always be calm and smiling and arch, when she had been nervous and almost sick with guessing at all times if she had gone too far.

Then she remembered Sabbah would be showing her to the bathhouse. She would be Clean Tison. Hot water, scented soaps, maybe oils!

The journey from Tunis through the mountains had been hard and dusty. Not as bad as the journey to Tunis from Cairo, but no doubt her childish mind had exaggerated the sand, the heat, the dust, the lack of salt or water. Her skin rose and crawled in memory, and she shook her shoulders. She would not remember today. Today was a new start. No memories.

A new Tison.

Walking through the silent household, she imagined it noisy with sleepy people dressing and chattering, planning for the day ahead. There would soon be children, too, getting underfoot and running errands. Resisting the urge to hum, she set the fire in the cooking pit. The clacking of flint and steel was crisp in the courtyard, the white sparks determined not to leap to the kindling until she had bashed her thumb twice and was considering letting the men get their own food.

She would have liked one of them to have heard her, to appear and be ordered to the nearest well. Sadly, dawn had risen, and there was neither the Important nor Serious man to be seen. Surely, this was something which could be dismissed with a Tch!

Men! She had been rising before dawn all her life. Even thinking about staying in bed made her stomach tighten with dread. She had been whipped for laziness when she was younger and her growing body had demanded more rest than her mistress of the time had deemed acceptable. Looking back, she thought about how none of the other girls had woken her. What a miserable place that had been! No house she ever run would punish those who simply did not wake.

Gathering an urn left near the cooking pit for whenever a woman came by to organise the men at last, she raised it to her hip and set off to the gate. Before sliding back the bar, she hesitated, head tilting.

Tison.

Housekeeper to the Muhtasib.

She straightened her back, jutted her jaw, lifted her brows to a smoother level, and stepped out into the street.

Other women were going for water, jugs and jars on heads or against hips. In the bleaching light of dawn, Berber and Black alike shone with vitality. Beautiful or not, for a moment, they were all intimidating. Even the young girls moving in pairs seemed to Tison to be somehow insurmountable.

In this part of town, though, they would all be servants or slaves fetching the water. She was the Muhtasib's housekeeper. She outranked them, and rank was important. Even a pack of hyenas understood rank. She picked her way across the immaculate street, thinking of her bare feet and ragged clothes. The flagstones were cool under her soles; they would be burning hot in a few hours. She hoped she had sandals by then.

The women gathered around the well watched her approach and take her place in line. Tison waited for questions or appraisal, her breath short and her fingers pressing against the ceramic of the urn.

A short, Arab woman, with covered hair and arms and veil hanging alongside her throat in case of a sudden man, nodded to her as she stepped forward. When the woman spoke, the pleasant chatter about a sick child and a handsome man halted around her. Tison felt them focus on her like a pack of rabid monkeys. The hair at the back of her neck stood up as if it wanted to flee her head in fear at the cold tone.

"Does your master not give you shoes, my dear girl?" the Arab lioness asked.

Tison could feel her sucking the light from the sleepy sun. She could feel the steel of the woman, hard and glacial. She found her heart quailing in memory of more women like her who had beaten her, mocked her, isolated her.

"He only bought me yesterday." She met eyes so dark, the irises seemed black by the dawn light. Everything about the woman's expression and bearing ordered Tison to feel small.

She was no longer a young girl to be cowed by bitter middle-aged women. Something like steel entered her spine, and she found her snarl deep in her heart, turning it into a pretty little smile. "Today is shoes and gowns and the bath-house."

Turning to the pair of girls who had approached together, she transformed the smile into a grin. *Come on, join me, flout her and be happy!*

"It is long overdue!" she continued, trying to forge an alliance, but as she opened her mouth to talk about something innocuous, the cold woman interrupted once more.

"You should not have come out before you were clean and clothed." Her voice was stridently soft. "You master's reputation can be broken by slovenly slaves."

Tison smiled. A smile so forced, she had to concentrate to keep it in place. Churning resentment for every woman like this one boiled in her stomach. She was reminded of the jealous, steel woman who had forced her to be sold on alone when she was eleven years old, losing her father's support and daily kindnesses. What would this woman say if she knew one of the most powerful men in Marrakech had sat with her on the floor while she sorted nails by size and untangled string?

"My master?" Talking about him was safer than thinking about similarities. They did not know her. They never would. They knew him, though. "My master is al Muhtasib."

She tilted her head and felt her smile turn venomous as the power around the well shifted in her favour.

"He makes his own reputation, and it will stand my desire to complete my tasks as they should be completed, despite my own pride or vanity." She stepped forward and began to pull the rope to lift water from the well.

Silence pressed on her back, and if the cold woman had been able to shove her into the well without reprisal, Tison believed she would have. Some women needed to be in control of their fellows.

When she had filled her urn, she stepped aside, not surprised that the cold woman had turned her back on her. She smiled at the others, but they were too cowed to respond. Shrugging, she lifted her water to her hip and made her way back to her new home. Soon, she would have young girls and strong men to fetch the water, and she would not have to face that woman again. Now, she was a housekeeper. She did not have to put up with women like that.

So long as al Muhtasib did not marry one. He deserved a wonderful woman. And that wonderful woman would be a lucky one, too. What a good, nice man he was. She had had enough of rogues to last her a lifetime. Nice went a lot further than charming.

The water urn pressed against her hip, just uncomfortable enough to be mildly irritating, and she was readjusting it when a man in far too many layers of coloured clothes stepped from behind her and half-trotted, half-skipped to her side. Tschyah! *The well is a busy place at daybreak!*

"You the Muhtasib's new woman?"

Her skin prickled, and she stopped in her tracks. Every instinct she had warned her of him. Her skin crawled, and a shiver passed over her neck.

"You want an introduction?"

He was not imposing. He was smiling. She was still intimidated.

"No, no." He grinned, all easy and relaxed body, but he was between her and the compound now. "But if you want to earn some coin, you could tell me a few things."

Fear intensified around her heart. So she laughed merrily.

"I have only just come into the household." She shifted the urn, both hands on it, in case she had to throw it at him. She tried for a bantering tone, but she could feel the shake in her voice. "It is far too early to betray my new master. He might be kind and sweet."

The smiling face did not falter, but the heavy lids of his eyes lowered. Did he darken those lids with kohl? Or were those just dark lashes? Silly details would help with the fear.

"Of course."

He bowed with flourish, and she released the tight knot of breath she had held unknowingly in her chest. He stood aside, and she took faltering steps past him. She did not like feeling nervous; she hated fear. Fear bled the Tison out of a lonely, thin woman.

She felt him watching her like he was a wasp buzzing past her neck.

"We'll meet again, Tison!"

The urn slid, and she had to shift her grip, hold it against herself. She had said her name in the market. That was all. Someone had been listening. Someone who did not like her master.

But the unsure man who had baulked at change but admitted she was right? How could he be anything but worthy of loyalty?

He needed Tison.

Even with catty old women and dangerous men in the street who knew her name.

Chapter Four

Today, Sabbah was a man who embraced the golden light of morning warming the buildings. It was rare to be able to share his love of the city with anyone. He was no poet to sing of the soaring minarets when Berber chieftains or Arab lords came to Marrakech. He had always considered himself a quiet man, could not recall a single instance of boasting even in childhood. After all, with a brother as mighty and magnificent as his had always been, how could he brag about his skill with letters or numbers?

Still, as they walked down the uncluttered streets towards the trading part of the city, he found himself holding forth like an overly proud parent.

"... and that water then flows down under our feet, supplying the entire city. Al-Hajj, the architect who designed the waterworks, still has family in the city, though he himself returned to ... Cordoba? I think?" His eyes scanned the skyline, drinking in the sight before they would bear down towards the bathhouse where he would be depositing Tison. Flickers of imagination threatened his control. He ignored them.

"Did anyone design the marketplaces?" she asked, cutting his mind off from a mild wish to follow her into the water, hold her towel for her, and stare like a callow youth at her body.

He carefully refocused his mind where it belonged. Architecture was safe.

"Not exactly. I believe some of the smaller souks have been there since before there was a city around them. Al Djemma, though, there used to be a mosque on that site. But it was too ornate. Too Almoravid."

Was he imagining the heat coming from her? How could any human being hold that much warmth without dying of fever?

"Ah, yes." She was smiling when he looked at her, an indulgent, amused smile. "Why have beautiful things when you can have severe things? You are very Almohad yourself, Muhtasib! All business and function and no silliness around the edges. No fuss!"

She deepened her voice in an utterly unconvincing imitation of a man. "Knock down that habit! It serves no purpose! This mannerism is too frivolous! Away with it!"

Sabbah felt those words like a hammer tapped against marble. One servant, because he needed only one. No frills in the house, no luxuries brought in. He blinked, his flow of talk about the city gone as he realised that if she had asked about him, and not the buildings, he could have told her all manner of things up to two years ago. The past two had been nothing but the same. His mother's death and his appointment as Muhtasib: two life-changing moments. Though they had forever altered his life, he had ceased to change once they had happened.

"You have gone very quiet, Important Man."

Tison's voice, beneath his shoulder, sounded concerned. His slave, concerned with him. Worried about him.

"I realised I do not know ... you. Not at all well, Tison."

He led her down a cool, covered street with potted ferns and palms giving a green light that soothed and beckoned. Learning about her might help him as he realised he barely knew himself. Thinking of her more and more as a person might halt the wanting, hungry imaginings hovering in his mind.

"Ah, there is not much else to know."

She kept flickering into his field of vision, her clothes the colour of unbloodied bandages, undyed, and dirtied by the road. But she moved like a queen stepping into court. Not a queen to a Caliph, either, but one of the old pagan kinds that good Muslim boys did not think about. The ones that led armies and mothered kingdoms in blood and glory. She was not large, but she had a mightiness to her.

"Is that a lie, Tison?" He aimed for a joke, and she rewarded him by chuckling with a low, sweet laugh like warm, sun-kissed fruit.

"I am everything you need and want me to be, Important Man!" she declared. "I am Tison. No need for grand descriptions when you know me. You know who I am."

But he did not. And he wanted to, and that desire went all the way down to his toes. Sabbah met people every day; he learned new names and frequently slotted them into families or kin groups he already had stored in his head. The compulsion to know Tison was setting him on edge, the feeling new but not unpleasant. It was as intense as pain without the hurting. He just had to know what manner of woman he had let into his life.

A pair of pillars marked the entrance to the bathhouse courtyard, and he halted.

"I cannot go with you, of course," he apologised, looking within to curious stares.

The thing was that he regretted that he could not go. Even though it was ladies' day and it would cause the mother of all scandals, he still did not want to part ways. It was more than the coursing need to see her naked shaming him every moment. He just sort of wanted to keep prying, to keep finding out little bits about this woman who had deposited herself in his life.

He quickly added, "Do you want me to meet you here later?"

She was looking right back at the women inside, watching them as they did her. He wished he knew if she was nervous, so he could reassure her. He could not imagine Tison even had fear. She was probably relishing the challenge of going in there in rags and daring them all to comment.

"Oh, no, I shall be just fine! When you next see me, I shall be squeaky clean." She stepped slightly away from him and bowed deeply, touching her palms to her face with reverence. She then spoke clearly, almost loudly. "Thank you, Al Muhtasib. For the honour of serving you."

Chins moved as gossips drew closer to relate her words inside the courtyard. She backed away from him like a servant to a mighty lord, but rather than it being a shuffle of nervous worship, it was a casual, loping step. One that drew his eyes to her feet, her bare ankles, and her slender calves. He looked back to her face, and she winked at him.

Only then did she turn and go within, and Sabbah, blushing hot and made more unsettled by the whispering women than she was, quickly strode away back the way he had come.

His cheeks burned, and his collar rubbed tightly against his neck, even before he remembered that in a short while, she would be naked, sinking into water and lathering soap over her body.

He paused at the entrance to the street and rubbed his hand against his jaw. He was a respectable man, and more than that, he was a servant of the city and the Caliph. He would not find himself overcome by daydreams and desires in the street. He would not picture her body and wonder about the shape of her small breasts and long legs. He absolutely would not think about soap lathering on her skin. Or oil smoothing it.

He told himself that through three incidents and two sessions of prayer.

"Assalaam aleikum, Ibn Abdella!"

The Sayrafi's voice was a welcome diversion when it came, his friend's outstretched hand a distraction he needed. Not from the work and petty incidents he had been dealing with, oh no.

Had she finished at the bathhouse? Or was she lingering, luxuriating naked in hot water or plunging into cold, bringing her nipples to peaks and her skin to ...

Sabbah forced a smile.

"Waleikum Salaam, Sayrafi."

They clasped hands. Abou Saal ibn Musa had been Sayrafi of Marrakech long before Sabbah became Muhtasib. He had been friends with Sabbah's father when he had taken the position of overseeing the money and trade of the markets, and his wrinkled, leathery face was more familiar to Sabbah than his own. Surely with his dear, respected friend, he could banish the primal urge to run all the way uphill to his home and bed his slave over and over until he and his imagination were exhausted.

Who would have combed the tangles from her hair so it hung in black tendrils on her shoulders?

"Something troubles you, boy?" Abou Saal folded strong arms across his chest. Short, with a stocky, implacable frame—just because Sabbah was taller did not mean he could move the Sayrafi when he had found focus. "All is well with your brother and his wife?"

Sabbah shifted on his feet, wincing slightly as he realised that he was giving himself away. But mention of his family slid his mind into another realisation. He had never envied his brother, but Jessamine bint Nusair, his sister-in-law, had become the tally by which all other women were measured. She was a breath-taking woman of pure Arab blood.

Sweet and calm and quiet, but with sparkling intelligence in her eyes and a ready smile for her husband whenever he was near, it had seemed an impossible comparison for any mere mortal. Tison, though, eclipsed her. Perfect spice-gold skin could not compare to her deep brown like fertile earth. Jessamine's liquid brown eyes were outmatched by fiery gold.

"Alhamdullillah, all is well with them." Sabbah folded his arms over his chest, pulling his tunic against his shoulders. "I am making changes to my household. I find myself … distracted."

He was consumed and confounded by desire to intimately learn every inch of a woman he barely knew beyond her strength, courage, and interest in his city.

"I'm glad, Ibn Abdella."

The Sayrafi had nodded with slow deliberation. How long, Sabbah wondered, had his friend been silently concerned? A smile tugged at his mouth, and he gave in to it.

"Have you been fretting?"

Abou Saal's cheeks deepened in a rapid flush of embarrassment, and Sabbah's smile became a quick grin.

"So I watch over you, boy," his old friend retorted. "You need someone to help you organise it. You'll go mad trying to fix your home and this city of ours, but leaving your household as second best just left you uncomfortable."

The Sayrafi scratched his beard, flexing his jaw. Pressure built in the moment of silence, until the tiny truth dwarfing the rest of his life forced its way, overly loudly, past his lips.

"I have help. I bought a woman to act as housekeeper."

And he saw amusement in the older man's eyes, and the heat of the day scorched his own cheeks, giving Abou Saal his vengeance.

"Not the way I heard it," Abou Saal told him, jerking his head to set them walking. "I heard she rescued you from a tricky dilemma and trip to our friend the Qadi."

Sabbah cracked his neck to one side almost before he realised that mentioning the judge had set tension from his heels to his head. Easier not to focus on what might have been when he was already thrown so totally off balance by the present.

"She was already ensconced when I reached home. Terrifying."

And elating. Exciting. She was inexorable, unstoppable. All he could do was follow. He had never followed anyone.

"We will be equally terrifying walking the markets together."

The Sayrafi nudged him, empathy in his voice, but also a line drawn beneath the conversation. Work had to be done. Sabbah's diligence had claimed him the Sayrafi's friendship and respect. Lolling about the market daydreaming about a woman and vice would not be in keeping with the post of Muhtasib. They set off shoulder to shoulder, Sabbah a full foot taller, and the Sayrafi humming a tune behind his ready smiles to friends and acquaintances.

Work, Sabbah thought, *and prayer*, as the cutting, keening song of the call to devotion sliced overhead. All around them, men set aside their trade and unwrapped prayer mats to kneel.

After washing his hands, face, and feet in a fountain, Sabbah unfurled his mat and knelt beside his friend. Christian and Jewish slaves and citizens stood aside, heads lowered respectfully. Maybe they, too, took the time to pray to their facet of Allah. Quiet fell over the bustling hive of Marrakech. The ritual words were spoken all around, and Sabbah bowed his head, his own lips moving.

And yet, through the words came a smile, a grin, and the warmth of her hand against his chest.

Tison.

His peace was shattered. Last night, his heart had raced with dread. Now, even at prayer where a man should be safe from temptation, he could not escape her throat, her eyes, that grinning mouth.

He wrestled his thoughts back to piety and dedication, but he was relieved when prayers concluded. Noise started up around him. Helpful, salvaging noise that could drown her out, or at least convince him that the whole city had not heard the thoughts of its Muhtasib, devouring a woman's image instead of dedicating himself to Allah. Still, he felt he could hear her voice, her laugh, on the edge of the crowd around him.

He stood, helping his friend and colleague to his feet as the Sayrafi sighed about his aching knees.

Walking on for the moment in silence, surrounded by the cheerful noise of the market after the calm and peace of prayer, they turned into an artisans' street. The smell of wood being worked scented the air, but the pleasant bustle did nothing to prevent goose bumps rising on his strong forearms. He could definitely hear her.

And then, he could see her.

She was sitting outside a shop, chatting easily to the retired master carpenter Tashfin while his once-apprentice turned back inside with prayer mats under his arm. Sabbah knew him. Ammar. No father but the man he had apprenticed to, with a rough past thrown in for good measure. Ammar was a swarthy Berber-blooded man, with thick hair and a short, black beard. Sabbah was very concerned with the man's looks. He certainly did not know if a brooding man with a dark past would be more attractive than a straight-and-narrow servant of the city.

"A moment, friend."

He strode from the Sayrafi's side. Tison was making the old master, Tashfin, laugh. More irrational jealousy. He wished he did not know that it was envy twisting his gut and tensing his broad shoulders. It would be nice to pretend he was not going mad so fast.

"Tison!"

His voice left his throat harsh and commanding. A moment of embarrassing hush lingered for just a few heartbeats while people turned to be sure the Muhtasib was not angry or conducting any business worth gossip and a crowd. She looked up at him despite his tone. And she smiled, rose like a queen. Not like a slave, his slave, under his protection and thus beyond his reach.

So why did he wish for the first time in his life that he was not al Muhtasib? Why did he want to cause a public disturbance and crush her to him, or throw her over his shoulder and march her back to his house?

Only then, with a rush of blood and sound, did he realise how different she looked. Only a tuft of hair was visible above her face, soft, a little sun-bleached, and fluffy. Definitely fluffy. The rest was mostly covered under a tight wind of cloth, rising up around her head like the dressings of the Mande people. His mother had covered her hair like that when she still left the house. But his mother would never have worn such a bright yellow gown.

Sabbah blinked at her, and she smiled differently. A smile that saw his tongue robbed of speech and his eyes wide in his skull. She knew. She knew he wanted her body, and her eyes were hot with smug approval. But seeing her like this, the ochre dye giving her eyes a brightness that muted any words on his tongue, he felt something more than the lust he had been shaken by since she had demanded a place in his life.

She was beautiful. Not just desirable and alluring, but beautiful. A queen indeed, with perfect, high cheekbones and a long, slender neck. For a moment, or perhaps a year, he stood transfixed, fighting his mind and body to stop them from shaming him in the street.

Then, she took pity on him.

"I am ordering furniture for the women's quarters."

She stepped towards him. Maybe it was not pity. Maybe she was going to shove him down in the dirt and show everyone how low the Muhtasib would fall for an enslaved woman.

What was she doing to him?

Tashfin stood behind her, the old man stiff in his joints but still strong. His movements were sure, sending ripples into the pool of desire that surrounded Muhtasib and slave.

"Your housekeeper has good taste, Muhtasib," the old carpenter said once traditional greetings had been given. "You need have no fear of gaudiness."

"From yourself and Ammar?"

Did his voice sound normal? Was he in control? His tongue felt odd in his mouth, heavy, unwieldy. The yellow gown made her skin glow. There was no dust, no smears, just inches of perfection. Unadorned.

Damn, what had he been saying?

"UH," THE MUHTASIB HESITATED, blinked, and then waved a hand. "What I mean to say is that I do not think anything gaudy has ever left your shop."

Nice recovery, Important Man, Tison admired. Still, though, his composure was unsettling the way rage would not have been. And was that her, or was it still his influence? No. No thoughts of him and that and then. She was not small and insignificant. She was housekeeper to an Important Man. Her past had no command over her anymore.

"Well, I must go, Al Muhtasib." She bowed with respect and caught a glimpse of his toes emerging from sandals and the linen of his trousers, the pinker, paler underbelly of them just visible above the leather.

She rose, somewhat taken aback.

They were just toes. Not a symbol of his gentle spirit. Not an intimate moment at all. Just toes. Better to remind herself that lack of anger or no, feet were for crushing and stomping. He had to need her, not just want her. The wanting was in a new dress and clean skin. The needing was furniture and slaves and order. That, she would give him. All those years of knowing she could do better than her superiors, the little ideas they had rejected, all came to fruition now. It did not matter that he desired her, not when he could still shake it off and continue as if nothing had happened.

She would be indispensable. Her uncertainty would be crushed and forgotten amid the tide of Tison's importance. She would be sold on at the highest price, and then she would become indispensable to someone else! Someone just as helpless, as hapless, and hopefully just as handsome.

Then he bowed to her. The Muhtasib bowed to a slave in the street. It had been strange enough that he had done it the night before, in private. It had been marked and compelling then. Now? In full sight of anyone who might be passing or doing business, it was downright peculiar. In front of his shorter companion with his thoughtful eyes over Sabbah's shoulder.

Instead of discomfort, though, a burning sense of gentle pleasure filled her. She liked being bowed to, apparently. She wanted to run all the way back to Tunis and yell, "The Muhtasib of Marrakech bought me on sight, and he bows to me in respect!" into that certain hated face. That would show him!

"Good luck, and happy haggling."

Sabbah's smile overtook a handsome face and made it godlike, shaking her determination hard. Her heart clenched awkwardly in her chest, and all thoughts of bitterness fled in the face of something that felt like a bubble full of giggles, waiting to erupt.

"Something tells me, Tison, that you are a haggler."

This time, the grin came to her face before being called, but she managed to contain the giggles.

"Oh, yes." She looked up into his face. "I would never get bullied into buying someone without a list of their skills and reason for leaving their last position."

And like that, her grin went into hiding, and the bubble popped, because no amount of imagining a snarled victory in a once-loved face could chase away the sinking feeling of worthlessness her great love affair had left her with when he'd broken her life the second time.

She felt her joy sucked away and watched that reflected in her master's face. His brows lowered, his feet shifted, and he almost asked. So she was gone. A false smile over her shoulder for Tashfin, and she was slipping into the river of bodies in the street. In an hour or so, the slaves would be taken into the shade until the heat passed its peak. She wanted to have placed her orders by then.

Focus on that, and she could cope—she would not fall backwards into the past and disappointment, and pain, and doubt. She was not going to tell her new master what her old one had done and have his view of her change.

How many of the slaves she bought today would have stories like hers?

Tison shoved up her chin. Pride. Strength. Importance.

She jutted her jaw even further.

Yes, there it was! New Tison! Not a Tison that wanted to live in the past, torment herself with the moment she had first felt truly like a slave. She was not property. She was an asset. That moment had never, ever happened. She would not allow it to have happened. This version of Tison would have no painful memories or doubts about herself.

As she swayed elegantly through the streets, she held remembrance at bay. She forced her face to be impassive, to keep the tightness from her eyes. Eight years of doubt and hurt and ill treatment tried to bury her in dust. She was not that young girl anymore. She was not weak and would not remember tears. She was away from Tunis and old, bad memories. If only she could raise her spirits the way she raised her chin.

Arriving in the slave market made it hurt more. She felt insignificant, her bravado used up, dried up. Stepping to the side of the street, she searched for strength to match her stride and manner. A face from her past laughed through her declarations, her intentions, her barriers, looking out from her mind, not as he had been—a lover, a kind master—but as he had become. Or maybe been all along. The dismissal. The irritation. No shame or apology or acknowledgement. And then, he had come back and broken her life all over again, just for the sake of it.

But you still dreamed about him, didn't you! she accused herself. *He was still tender in your nights. He came a hundred times to rescue you in your head when he never did in the real world.* Better to think of the man who would be coming to her bed soon than the one who had bored of having her in his. Sabbah was not just *important*. He was handsome. Strong-backed and broad-shouldered. She imagined his hand on her stomach, her waist; his jaw, lightly bearded, across her shoulder.

Passion. The best way to find peace and a touch of naughtiness. Though she doubted he had a wicked streak even a hairsbreadth wide.

There!

Now she had a smile. And … Tison slowed her breathing, her lips twitching as she realised just how little imagination it took for Sabbah to slicken her palms and heat her to the core. A knot of nerves had tightened from sorrow and doubt into a nugget of desire right behind her belly button.

Next, she thought of the moment he had seen her, focus drawing him from wandering down the street to striding to her side. The power of his dark eyes, the dormant want she had watched him wrestle back to its cave. Two days of Sabbah ibn Abdella were worth far more than the eight years of confused loss after *he*'d sold her.

Tison stepped back into the crowd.

She spoke proudly to three slavers, purchasing a cook—who was leaving the household of an older couple whose children were all married—in search of somewhere busier. She ordered four girls with some experience—two of whom had family near Sabbah's household; she hoped not the jackal-bitch from the well that morning—coaxing an excellent deal from the broker by dropping a hint that there would be need for more when the Muhtasib married. A lick of self-doubt was kicked onwards like a pebble at the toe of a young boy.

Two young men to help Kanto. Big and strong and likely intended for the salt mines. Absolutely no worries about future wives there!

Finally, she returned to the man who had bought her in Tunis. He did not recognise her until she spoke of al Muhtasib, at which point his obsequiousness was matched by his slack-jawed amazement.

"Where is the Slav girl?" she asked as he blinked and goggled at her gown and neatly swathed hair. "The one who was sick from the heat."

She knew for a fact he had never been able to pronounce Yelizaveta's name.

"Inside at the funduq." He gestured to the tavern whose cellar had been Tison's first home in Marrakech for two nights. "The sickness is on her again."

Tison's breath hitched. The girl had almost died as they left the edge of the Sahara and began the long uphill climb into the Atlas Mountains. The heat was too much for her alone, but the slaves had walked through the mountains and with bleeding feet and a head addled by the sun sickness. The blond, red-skinned girl had fainted more than once, throwing up her food and water at mealtimes.

"Consider her bought." She folded her hands to stop herself plucking at her sleeves. She was a housekeeper. Housekeepers did not show their compassion or their nervousness. She was no longer vulnerable, and she might not be an old crone like the woman from the well, but she was no child.

"Of course, of course." He bowed. No, he scraped. He grovelled. A wash, a dress, and a new master. All it took. Once a slave had a master, she had value and not just a price.

"I am sure you will be relieved to sell her." Tison met his eyes. "After all, she is sick. It will save you the cost of a healer. And you made such a profit on me."

Finally, he stopped dipping and bowing, and frowned. Finally, he decided to haggle. She did not mind being desired. Being fawned over, however, turned her stomach. In haggling, she almost forgot this man had once owned her.

Chapter Five

Sabbah's overly eager feet had him almost home before he realised he was promised to his brother for dinner. He looked up at the faint evening stars for a moment, appealing, seeking guidance for his madness. All day, he had struggled to dedicate himself to his work. All day, that damned yellow dress had plagued him. He was so tempted, so very tempted, to return home and change his clothes, as though his brother would expect such a thing.

Stop being a fool! he chastised himself.

Turning his stride towards his brother's compound, he wondered what Tison was doing. He wondered if she still had her hair covered. He wondered if it was frizz or curls or locks.

As the smouldering, scented brazier light of his brother's open gates welcomed him, he breathed the scents of the richer part of town. Incense, jasmine, spices, the aromas welcomed and beckoned. The scent of food made his stomach growl, but his heart wanted him to tiptoe back into shadows and escape home. His brother's house was only a short distance from his own, but he always felt it to be just far enough. Not so close that his brother felt obliged to always include him in dinner invitations, but close enough that he could be on hand to help, if his big brother should ever need it.

Now, however ...

"Sabbah!" His brother emerged from a group of his warrior friends, his arms thrown out. Even in soft linen, Khalid looked like a fighter. He enveloped Sabbah in a hug that would have knocked the wind out of someone unused to such assaults. "Little brother! Have some sherbet! We have fresh ice down from the mountains today."

The only women present were gathered around his sister-in-law, isolated from most of the guests. As he was family, he was able to speak to her, but Jessamine bint Nusair had barely answered his compliments before her husband pulled him away. Khalid had a young soldier in his troop who was struggling with the violence of the profession. Half an hour later, the young man was recruited to the Muhtasib's agents, and Sabbah had had some respite from having to control every thought in his own head.

The spiced lamb was delicious, and Jessamine's people had done something wonderful with nuts and dates and pastry. Sabbah even managed to forget he owned a woman in a yellow dress and with golden eyes. He was quite impressed with himself, hopeful that his infatuation would fade once he was used to her incredibly good looks.

"Heard about you getting rescued by a slave woman." Khalid's arm once more descended across his shoulders. "It's a good little story! How true is it?"

Sabbah sat heavily on a bench, and he and his brother moved in unthinking unison, elbows onto knees, eyes forward.

"She tricked the troublemakers into exposing themselves."

The price of being Muhtasib was being constantly exposed to gossip, but Sabbah had never before done anything to warrant their interest. He pictured her grin and felt his shoulders unknot from the flash of horror that people were spreading a story about him.

"She pretty?"

His brother's voice was laden with a grin, and Sabbah kept his eyes on the servants as they cleared and cleaned the cooking pit.

"She's trouble," he admitted.

Khalid laughed. "That good, huh?"

He shouldered his brother, and Sabbah swayed gently away. All those storage jars that she had spread around her, lids off, while she took inventory. She would be into every aspect of his life soon, taking note of what was lacking.

"I said, 'that good, huh?'" Khalid nudged him again.

"She reminds me of a cat." Sabbah felt the words on his tongue before they even entered his head. "And I do not know if she sees me as a dog or a mouse."

"Or her master? There to rub her belly 'til she purrs?"

A clench of desire fortunately brought blood to his cheeks instead of sending it elsewhere. Khalid laughed at him.

"About time a woman turned your head, untouchable brother!"

Important Man ...

Sabbah forced himself to turn and look at his elder sibling, catching Khalid exchanging a smile with his wife across the courtyard. Khalid had gone to the house of Malik ibn Nusair in search of a dowry. Apparently, his big brother was lucky, as well as wealthy.

"She is not just beautiful." He once again lost his tongue to truth. "She is ... real. Vital."

He dropped his head, touching his chin to his collar. "She is already planning for when I have a wife, and spent the day ordering furniture, food, and slaves."

Khalid laughed again. Sabbah personally thought his brother was far too amused by his plight.

"Kanto must be overjoyed," came the false reassurance. "I am going to go and host, Sabbah. Do not go anywhere until we have spoken more. I want details!"

Khalid strode away, chuckling audibly and full of energy and purpose. Sabbah's jaw weighted, drawing his face and making him feel his years. He had been lacking purpose of late, he realised. He had worked to become Muhtasib, and now he had achieved his life's dream, he was faltering.

The loss of his mother had shaken him, he knew that, rationally. He was a man of sense. There was no logic to leaving the new house unmanned and understocked. No point could be found in remaining unmarried. Plenty of unwed daughters and sisters in the city. Merchant stock with connected families. Nobility wishing to strengthen their roots in Marrakech. Jessamine had two unmarried sisters. Dembo Sosseh, a Ghanaian gold merchant, too, had sisters. The al Hajj family had a daughter.

Yellow dress. Golden eyes. A hot palm.

How did she speak of him marrying when she was driving him to constant distraction? He had become a man who lusted after his slave. The sort of despicable animal he loathed.

But by Allah, he wanted her!

Sabbah drew off his head covering and ran his hand over the slight prickles of stubble on his scalp. She could be the push that made his life move once more.

He wished she was there.

Damn it! He shifted on the bench. He actually missed her!

His interaction with her amounted to buying her, being told how she would change his quiet, ordered life, walking her to the baths, and meeting her in a street.

But he missed her.

Raising his eyes, he watched his brother move to the brightly coloured couch where Jessamine sat with attendants and a couple of wives of other guests.

A yellow dress and a grin flickered in his imagination. He was mad. Proof positive.

His brother trailed two fingers over his wife's covered shoulder.

How long since Sabbah had been with a woman? Years. Long years, which had not seemed empty before her. He had been serving as an example. The Muhtasib: above bodily temptation.

He got to his feet. He needed to get home. He did not want to spend a long night being teased by his brother once the guests were gone. Eye contact, a jerk of his chin, and Khalid's grinning, shaken head, and he was free.

Once he had left the noise and laughter of his brother's home behind, he found that his abstraction was nothing compared to giving Tison all of his focus. Each footstep was taking him closer to her. She would confront him, be smiling, be challenging with those eyes. Excitement flooded his stomach, fluttering nerves and surging blood. It was like hunger without the growling.

Or with a different sort of growl.

He could hear music. Smiling, he listened as he walked, glad of others having joy. Voices and drums, an indistinct but happy clamour. He had not danced since he was a boy. He would dance with her if she told him to. He could imagine obeying her commands all too easily.

His feet stumbled beneath him, and he stood still in the street, heart pounding as he was caught by a wave of crushing lust. He was a rational man, he reminded himself, a logical man. And yet, the Muhtasib, who had spent his entire adult life succeeding under his own merit, commanding a cadre of agents to protect the markets of Marrakech, wanted a certain stare to tease while a beautiful, kissable mouth took responsibility from him and just told him what to do.

The worst or best part was, even though he knew it was dangerous, he was helplessly, hopelessly excited. His entire body was craving her, anticipating her.

It was then he realised the song came from his own home. Alive with noise and rhythm as the light from braziers and torches lit the sky above the courtyard. The difference was astonishing. His neighbours must be horrified to have his silent home transformed into a place of welcome and song and ... Damn the neighbours!

Light and colour greeted him amid a gust of wood smoke. The drums he had heard were revealed to be pots and pans and barrels. He stepped through the open gate, and then, through the smoke, he saw her dancing. She was not alone, but she sucked his attention to her. That yellow gown, her headscarf held in one hand, fluttering and flaring around her as she danced like windblown fire.

His heart pounded. His body shuddered.

Curly. Her hair was curly. A mass of fluffy curls that bounced with her as she moved.

And then, he was wrestling his need down, forcing it back, deep, hissing breaths of food and spice and cedar wood smoke clearing his head. She had stopped dancing. His eyes were on the ground, but he could feel her approach. Kanto appeared at his side just as she reached him.

The singing had stopped, the drumming faltering to nothing. There was a shuffling as his slaves, his servants, rose and straightened clothing and stood at attention or in nervous uncertainty, depending on their experiences of masters in the past.

"I have ruined the fun." Sabbah grimaced, forcing his eyes to Kanto's face, trying for the thousandth time to read his friend's expression. "I was with my brother. Had ..." he raised his voice a little. "Had I known we had such a celebration here, I would have run all the way home."

Nervous laughter, relaxing shoulders, hope in a few faces. They had wanted to trust that their master would be a good man. Apparently, Sabbah wanted to be liked, and he did not know whether to pity himself for his neediness or be glad that he was human enough to have noticed they were uncertain.

Finally, he turned his head and pulled his eyes to Tison's face. She was proud. Every line of her body spoke of her success and demanded acknowledgement. The strength of her, the insistent forcing of notice, was so powerful, he once again wondered if he dared let her boss him around. He felt as nervous as his new slaves. His ribs felt too narrow for his lungs. There was a tug, and he looked down to see her taking his head covering, still loose, from his hands. One of her smallest fingers moved against his thumb for a moment. His eyes dipped to her lips, slightly narrower than he had been imagining them to be.

"Come, Important Man," she murmured, quiet, so only he and Kanto could hear. "Come meet your people."

FOR A MOMENT, SHE HAD felt his hungering stare, and for that moment, she had wanted to dance for him. She had been encouraging the other girls to joy, to exuberance, to dance for the fun of it. But seeing him had made her want to writhe, to caress her own skin until he fell to his knees or slammed her against a wall. Except that their eyes met, and she lost her rhythm somehow. Her knees faltered until they held her up as well as melted cheese might.

She walked towards him with care, determined not to wobble or stumble to his feet, knowing the growing silence had put the focus of all these people on Sabbah. On the Muhtasib, her master and theirs.

Tison bowed from the waist. She glanced at his toes, that oddly impersonal intimacy striking her again, and rose with her eyes scanning up his trousers past ... Did she imagine the slightest tenting there? A bulge against the loose cloth? Or was that just greedy, wishful thinking on her part? She felt tense, with that taut, crinkling feeling behind her belly button.

"Come, Important Man," she said, hushed and quieter than she had intended. "Come meet your people."

Then she turned and lifted a hand to the small crowd of nervous strangers who would be part of the same household, share each other's lives, be his people until he sold them or they worked through their Mukharajah agreement to freedom.

"Al Muhtasib!" Tison then intoned, forcing her voice stark and as official as she could, not breathy and winsome as it wanted to come out.

"Tison."

He lacked her control. She heard desire. She heard lust. But no demand.

It was more like a plea, a call for help, for her aid against his struggle. His dark eyes drew the heat from her jellied legs up to the apex of her thighs at the entreaty.

"Meet the household," she suggested, but his eyes held hers for a moment, and her heart had started to thump in her chest and ears and other embarrassing, stupid places, too, just from that brief look.

The brazier light illuminated eyes she knew were deep brown and warmly soft, and she wished it were day just so she could see their colour again. They were intent on her, and all in that moment, she felt connected to him, alone with him despite the crowd of anxious people. His lips began to lift in a smile.

She raised a hand to lead him towards the gathered slaves she had purchased with no mercy for his rasp-edged voice or her own tense stomach and the odd feeling at the back of her neck that was begging to be touched lightly and with desperate passion. She was utterly lost already, and at present, she could not remember why it was so important to keep her distance, so important not to give him the power over her that sex would bestow if she did not have control of it and him.

"Al Muhtasib. Meet Kasseh and Adan. They will be working with Kanto. Now, I must say this correctly ... Hudayda? Yes. Our cook. A master of his craft. Here!"

Impulse took over. Her hand came from her side without permission from her brain, plucked a sliver of the roast lamb from the platter where Hudayda had shredded it, scooped some of the chopped, spiced dates atop it, and raised it to Sabbah's lips.

Her heart shuddered.

No! Not Flirty Tison. Professional, Indispensable Tison! What a mistake!

His eyes held hers once more, and then he lowered his chin and took the meat from her hand. A slow, soft gasp chased into her chest. His bearded chin grazed her fingers, and his lips burned them. Warm. Soft. He groaned slightly, and she felt the sound down to her toes. Just as a smug heat reached her heart, he looked over her shoulder.

"So good, Hudayda," he enthused. "I beg you not to repeat it, but so much better than my brother's cook could ever make."

There she was, a-quiver from his brief contact. Longing for him to kiss her palm and stare at her with those dark eyes, and he was more interested in the lamb.

She should have chosen a worse cook.

Ignoring an internal mutter of irritation, she introduced the rest of the staff, even pale, sick Veta, who he insisted sit down at once, who he spoke gently to, even though she did not understand a word he said.

Tison stood and watched him awkwardly assure them of his fairness and their opportunities for freedom. He appealed, rather than commanded, and it warmed her differently than the touch of his lips on her skin.

She had had her share of bad masters. His kind welcome and manner of hope rather than scorn softened her face, widened her eyes. She could forgive him wanting the lamb more than her when he chatted lightly to Kanto's new assistants. Tison looked down at her hand. Phantom-like, she felt the dry warmth of his lips, imagined them on her throat, and found her breath to be a little deeper, a little heavier.

Why did he affect her so strongly?

No. Why did she let him? Clearly, he had full control of himself. More interest in lamb than her. So perhaps she had not quite forgiven him. Allowing a master to affect her so strongly was madness, dangerous madness that promised pain and sorrow to come.

That thought turned the knot of desire into a bundle of nerves. It threatened her housekeeper-in-charge air and made her wish she was just another face. A face he would not see and desire. She wanted him, his broad-shouldered body and warm, brown eyes, but she did not want to want him, not with eight years of mourning and grief behind her.

She would not let someone hurt her like that again. Not even a man who kept glancing at Yelizaveta in case she was in need of more water or a chance to slip away. She could use Sabbah; she could use her body with him to solidify her position. She would not let him use her. Moments of passion to cheer herself up were one thing; fantasizing about him wistfully quite another.

She introduced him to the rest of the staff and then stood back, taking a moment to breathe.

Sabbah turned to meet her look of enquiry and hope, and she found she had no need to force or summon her smile once more. After a moment, he approached her, moving his large frame through the modest crowd. He was big. He carried himself small, as though his importance was secondary. As though he were the slave. As though they were equal to him. But he could have been imposing, with his height and the broadness of his shoulders.

"The words every woman wants to hear."

He inclined his head, and her heart shuddered. She knew he was not going to make a declaration, that she did not need or want affection from a master, but for just a moment, her chest thought he might, and that she did.

"Oh?" she prompted. "Important Man knows those words?"

He leaned towards her a little. Over her. Her heart was thumping hard. She felt like a young girl again. His voice was low.

"You. Were. Right."

A grin split her face, and she laughed. The tremor of girl-ish misunderstanding swept itself up into her mirth, and the moment passed.

"Tison is always right," she replied, jutting her chin up at him.

He grinned at her, his teeth very nearly perfect. He closed his lips over his smile, and she thought he looked like a boyish, mischievous man, instead of a responsible, collected one.

"Furniture is ordered," she told him, remembering that she had been a proper housekeeper before he'd walked over and made her feel everything all at once and all over again.

Her hand had risen without her notice, moving to touch his arm. Just the sort of over-familiar contact she was used to giving. For some reason, she turned the gesture into a sweep over her clean hair. Despite the dancing, it seemed to be tidy in its fluffy, frizzy heap. As tidy as her hair was capable of being when not tightly braided or severely covered.

"Ordered, not delivered," he replied, and she took a blink to remember what she had said moments before.

"So your home is still as you remember it." She flared her eyes and waggled a finger. "For now, at least!"

"Ominous!"

He was grinning again. And her heart was doing its best to stop altogether.

His bottom lip was so much fuller than the top. Men's lips were not meant to be soft and kissable. Men's lips crushed; they did not entice. She could feel the gap between them asking to be closed. Could imagine them against her own. Heat flourished from her core, filling her. She could sense her own wetness, responding to him, preparing for him. So much for returning to Professional Tison, Clever Tison who was also careful! No, now she was Craving Tison. Desperate Tison! Needy Tison Who Was Going To Get Hurt Again.

She swallowed hard, then finally looked up from his mouth to his eyes and saw a glimmer in them that made her go from hot to molten. He felt it, too. Despite the way his grin was gone, his eyes were hungry. All at once, she could imagine what it would be like to straddle him, to lean into him, to arch beneath him as he covered her. It came not as pictures but as a real sensation, as though she could remember how his body felt between her legs. She ached; her arms and legs and heart all at the same time!

"Why don't I show you some other changes?" She could hear the need in her voice. Sex, her voice suggested, now, at once, immediately? Anywhere, any way!

"No," he replied, and the satisfied smile that had begun to unfurl over her lips froze, then faded. He swallowed, but she stopped her focus going to the bob of his Adam's Apple. "You have duties to see to, and I, I have responsibilities of my own."

He walked past her, through the nearest door, fast. His eyes were firm on his path, not glancing to her. Tison's cheeks grew hot with blushes. Any woman would know exactly what was wrong. Even if her Ethiopian skin and the gloom of night would conceal the flush, she knew she would look frazzled, all on end with need. Shock began to join the throbbing want. It splintered the heat and added the unpleasant sensation of shame.

Of rejection.

She turned her back on the fire pit, staring the way he had gone. She took one step, and then forced her feet still. She would not ask outright. He knew she wanted him. He could come to her, and would. She would be vital to him. This Tison was strong and proud. She would not chase. She would never beg again.

So instead, she took a few pointed breaths and then went to check on Veta and start ensuring those slaves who had converted knew where to find prayer mats, and that the fire pit was properly tamped down, and the carcass of the lamb stripped of scraps of meat. Little, important things. Duties, as he had said.

And if she occasionally caught herself thinking about him shoving her against a wall and pulling her dress off her shoulders, she pretended not to notice. She controlled herself, and it should not have been as difficult as it was. She should not have felt so unsettled by him. Surely, heartbreak and hard lessons learned should protect her from feeling hurt as well as frustrated.

Slowly, quiet fell. Tison saw the women settled. She had moved herself into a small room intended for a eunuch to guard the female slaves, where she could sleep on the floor. Also, she had assumed, so when Sabbah came for her, they would not disturb the other slaves.

Some hope.

She then went to the threshold of the men's dormitory. They were chatting idly, learning each other bit by bit the way all slaves had to in a new household. The women would be doing the same thing as they undressed and before they prayed. Silence fell almost immediately once she was noticed. She smiled and inclined her head.

"Assalam Aleikum, I will not be here long," she told them. "I just want to say that if you have need of help in any way, ask me or Kanto. You obey him as though he was al Muhtasib himself."

She paused, scanning faces, wondering if there would be trouble. Wondering if she had brought difficulty into the household in any of these men.

"Yes, ma'am," one murmured, and she felt some of the tension lessen as others echoed the acceptance.

"Also, know that if any of you pushes unwanted attentions on any of the women here, you will be sold to the salt flats." She kept her voice even and spoke quickly. She did not want it to sound like an empty threat. "I will not have any woman in this household feeling as though they are in danger in its walls. Am I understood?"

This time, the assent came in a chorus, and she saw nodding respect in Hudayda's eyes as she once more ran her gaze over them.

"Pray and sleep well," she bade them.

She turned and caught Sabbah as he walked away down the corridor towards the courtyard and his own quarters. She wondered if he had intended to give the same warning, and if she just wanted to think he had thought of such things.

When she finally returned to the courtyard, she expected it to be empty, but Kanto was there, kneeling on a colourful prayer mat. His back was to her, his right side presented to the now locked gate. She waited as he prayed. Even if the Muslims did not believe that Christ was God and His Son, she would never interrupt another's solace. Only when he had risen did she scoot forwards and sweep up his mat, rolling it deftly between her hands.

"Save your back, Serious Man," she told him.

"Kanto," he corrected. "But ... Thank you."

She handed him the prayer mat.

"How did you injure it?" she asked.

"Salt mining."

He shifted his grimace to a smile for her as his spine straightened. It was not the first, but every smile from Kanto felt like a small victory, and she would take whatever she could to drive away the ripple in her self-worth Sabbah's rejection had caused.

Kanto continued. "It became worse and worse. I could not rise one morning. Ibn Abdella ... our master was inspecting the salt flats and mines for the Caliph. Before he was al Muhtasib. He bought me and two other injured men. Bought me at three times my worth."

Tison shot out a hand and swiped his shoulder.

"Nonsense, Kanto!" A rush of anger was swiftly pushed down. "Three times your price, perhaps. No man, not any Caliph, could afford a tenth of your worth."

Kanto's faint, friendly smile split into a proper grin. Triumph squashed the last of the anger as she smiled back.

"He knows how to grin!" she crowed, hands shooting up above her head.

"She knows how to be serious!" he retorted. Then he folded his arms, his prayer rug tucked over one forearm. "What you're doing is good."

"Thank you, Serious Kanto. Now—" she chivvied him with her hands, "—To bed! Off your feet! Ensure you make use of those nice, strapping boys I found you. We will speak tomorrow, and you can help me get everyone to a bathhouse and clean and clad. Much to do tomorrow, Serious Kanto!"

His grunt was particularly masculine, making her chuckle in response. He nodded and ambled slowly to his porter's building by the gate. As for her, Tison sat on one of the benches that had been pulled into the courtyard. The household was quiet, the stars a silken, diamond shawl draped over the firmament.

Clasping her hands, she bowed her head. Her lips moved, the occasional whisper of Amharic leaving her. She remembered the singing, but only snatches of the song.

"*La Eyesus Yedelu Kaber wasabahet wa'azaz la alama alam.*" Her voice was crisp in the still night. She opened her eyes.

La Alama alam.

Forever and ever.

Five years was a frightening enough time. Forever was unthinkable.

Slaves did not have forever.

TISON DID NOT SEE MUCH of Sabbah the following morning, since she was directing order from the chaos of working out what duties the new slaves had. She saw his broad back as he left, but she was so terrified someone would realise that she had no idea what she was doing that she barely stopped to admire him or fret over the night before. Fortunately, it was not night when he returned, but the middle of the day.

She was teaching the new slaves how to sweep, having caught Veta half-heartedly pushing a broom in the direction of the cobbles and getting herself hot and bothered with wasted movement. Leaving Kanto in the middle of a discussion—or argument—about whether or not Sabbah wanted the women's quarters prepared, she had taken the broom and gathered all of the other women for a lesson.

Bent almost double, her colour reddened and deepened by exertion, she was attacking the flagstones when Sabbah returned. She looked up from the push-push-tap-tap-tapping with widening eyes and her bottom lip clamped between her teeth to stop herself from laughing. She handed the broom to Yasmin, dismissed them back to their duties, and approached her master, drawing close so she did not have to watch her tongue.

Her master, who was covered from chest to knees in turmeric, his hands and forearms stained by it. She glanced down at those peeking toes, and they, too, were coloured a vibrant yellow. A shiver of a giggle escaped, and she compressed her lips for a moment, before bowing with respectful formality. His eyes met hers without conceit, a self-deprecating bid for pity all she saw there.

"Oh dear, Important Man," she sympathised while she rose, inhaling the scent of the spice as she reacted without intention to his closeness. Even made ridiculous, he was terribly affecting. A bubble of laughter threatened to follow the inevitable half-gasp, and she exerted great control.

"I've had worse, Tison."

Humour on his voice was all it took for her to relax her hold, and she whimpered a squeak of a laugh and then cleared her throat. She leaned closer and lowered her voice.

"I will bring water and soap, Sabbah!" Getting him ready to return to his duties was far more important than howling with laughter and demanding an explanation. "Go! I do not think we will save your clothes, though."

"I doubt it, too," he concurred, pulling off his head covering. She snatched it from his yellow hands before he ruined that, as well. He sighed a last, mournful word. "Turmeric."

"I did notice." The mirth bubbled in her voice again. "Do you want me to fetch Dour Kanto?"

She folded the head-cloth while her eyes sought the porter. The material was warm. She looked back up at Sabbah, bracing herself for the attraction she had still not become entirely used to but was determined not to give in to until he was giving in to his.

It hit her all the same. Perhaps struggling against her amusement had left her defences exposed and unable to fight the whoosh of heat his smiling face gave her. His eyes, impossibly alluring when he was thoughtful and serious, proved knee-weakening when lit with good-humour.

Some vague wondering what the spice would taste like licked from his hands split her into two Tisons. One of them knew only too well that turmeric was not the sort of taste one enjoyed on another's skin. Or on its own. The other Tison was a quivering mess of not caring about that or the silly wish to want him to come to her before she threw herself at him again and begged for his body.

"Water!" she forced out abruptly.

One hand rose and then fell to smooth the cooling cloth in her hands. She cleared her throat again and flared her eyes at him, acknowledging her lapse in control even if he had not noticed it.

"Yes," he replied, a little of the humour replaced with something indefinable which she hoped was interest in her and not confusion that his housekeeper had lost her senses.

Turning smoothly, she made her way to the food store, her breathing harsh and her heart skittering in her chest. *All ridiculous over your master*, she chided herself. Some fool you are! You know how that ends.

Setting aside his head covering, she took a basin and knelt by a wooden hatch in the floor, one she wished she had known about on her first day, so she could have avoided the cold woman by the well and the Wasp Man on her way back.

She lifted it, and a whisper of cold, moist air caressed her face. The determined rush of water beneath her, a noise neither quiet nor loud but utterly impossible to mistake, momentarily arrested her. She still had not quite made herself understand how easily available cold water was here in the house of al Muhtasib. She had worked in a bathhouse, lived there for years, and still, the flow of mountain water through Marrakech was a wonder greater than the pyramids.

Dipping the copper bucket into the liquid took a moment, and years of carrying buckets and sluicing tiled rooms, not to mention the strength required to knead knots from muscles, made lifting the vessel easy despite her thin frame.

Absently, she ladled water from bucket to basin and considered how best to stop her silly crush on Sabbah until he had an even sillier one on her. Her body's reactions were clouding her mind, and his very proper rejections would hurt in time. Already hurt, in fact.

She set the trapdoor in place. At least, she could blame her goose bumps on the cold wind the water carried with it. The heat at her throat? That, she could not explain away; nor the jellied, still not familiar sensation in her knees.

"Hrmmph." She glared at the basin, but then forgave it for existing and lifted it, setting off with it and pausing only for some plain, olive oil soap. She frowned, the rough soap taking the blame away from the basin for a moment. It was basic and unscented. He might own her, he might be Sabbah, but he was also a customer of sorts.

Hips swaying to keep her gait from upsetting the surface of the water, Tison cut across the courtyard to the master's quarters, nodding approvingly at Yasmin's progress sweeping the yard. She wondered if Yasmin could be taught to make proper soap or if she should do it herself anyway, as it was something she had enjoyed in her past life in the bathhouse in Tunis. She started planning ingredients and wondered if rose would be too feminine a scent or if she should invest in sandalwood oil.

And imagined Sabbah washing his hands. Heat rocked her stride, but she was able to stop the water sloshing and get herself under control. Not even her plans for the household could protect her from her attraction for long. Sabbah made her tingle and burn, and that would get her nothing but heartbreak and possibly impregnated. However beautiful a child of his would be, growing up a slave beside wealthy and prominent half-siblings would be hard on anyone.

Besides, she was nervous enough about being a house-keeper. She would lose her mind if she had to be a mother. An incoherent grumble left her lips as she stepped into the master's quarters. Thinking of being a mother? Not even the most perfect specimens, flexing their muscles before she massaged them, had made her consider motherhood. Not even the great love of her life, who had ruined said life twice over, had made her think of children.

Must be the big, empty house, she told herself as she entered his chamber.

Sabbah's back was to her, and he had stripped off his tunic. Broad and imposing when his warm eyes were not visible, his height only adding to the sense of massive perfection, her master made her throat dry and then her mouth water. He was powerful, hard flesh contoured to the waist of a rider, only slightly thickened, making him all the more tempting to a woman who had never felt like this when faced with warriors made of nothing but muscle and bone.

He turned.

Tison had a brief moment of tingling shock and rushing heat before the basin dropped from her slack fingers.

Blood rushed to her cheeks, but the flaming heat was matched by the one between her thighs. Dropping down so fast that she bashed her knees on the flagstones, she caught the bowl's edges to stop even more water spilling out as it rocked on the floor. The soap skittered over the now slick surface to Sabbah's feet. Shaking, she stared at the turmeric-yellowed toes.

"I ..."

Her voice shook with trembling uncertainty. She blinked at it. For a moment, she had been transported back to childhood, to slaps and canings for mistakes. *You are not a child*, she reminded herself. Now with the basin half empty but no longer sloshing and steady, she could unclench her fingers from the shining copper.

"You realise I'll have to sell you on for this, of course." His voice, brimming with mirth, brought her eyes up. Then his laughing face stilled, and he held out a hand. "It was a joke."

A shudder rumbled in her chest.

"Are you all right?" He chuckled, but the sound was tentative. "I thought you would laugh. People make mistakes, Tison. It would be ridiculous to sell on a housekeeper for dropped water. So ... it ... was a joke?"

Tison looked at her shaking hands and felt a bubble of laughter rise up. She took his offered hand and rose. The wet cloth of her ivory-coloured work dress slapped against her knees. Once standing, she let herself laugh, at herself but also at his nervously amused face.

"You are too good to be true, Important Man." She smiled, relaxing despite a pounding heart. "There are plenty of masters who would be furious. I have a couple of scars to prove it."

"Not me." His response was a little crooked, his eyes narrowed a little, affected by her words. "Forgive me? Are you all right?"

"Pride's a little sore, Sabbah," she teased softly, seeking a sense of the superior Tison she was meant to be but struggling. Flickering her eyes to his face once more, she dipped them down to avoid the searching concern in his. She took a deep breath, stretching her ribs. "The water is cold. I figured you were in a hurry."

"You know me well already."

The creased worry retreated from his eyes, and she moved to set the basin on the desk, the only suitable table for it.

Atop a pair of ledgers lay her bill of sale.

As ever, her skin prickled, and her stomach clenched. Seeing it had never bid well for her security. She hated it. Sabbah should wear it around his neck to ward her off; it was so effective at quenching the desire from her body.

She stepped back to give him room, dragging her eyes from the loathed parchment. Even as he stood close, sluicing his hands, water on his fine forearms and crystalline drops on his stomach, she felt sunk in cold dread. She stared somewhat bleakly as he lathered his hands, picking a bit of dirt from the soap he had retrieved.

She was a fool. Why did she do this to herself?

"I will leave you, al Muhtasib," she managed, bowing.

"Tison, you can stay and talk if you wish." He shook off his hands. "I am not the sort of master who has distance from his slaves. You are a member of my household, which makes you family of sorts."

"Thank you, Muhtasib," she replied. Her chest was tight, her body confused by the tumult of emotions she had felt on the heels of each other. "But I ... I should ... I ..."

She swallowed, bowed again, and made her escape, feeling small and wretched and stupid. She hoped whoever had spilled spices on him had a terrible day.

Returning to the courtyard, she took a moment to wait in the cool shade of the atrium, simply breathing and trying to steady her quivering breath. No matter how often she reminded herself of her still-healing heart, of the eight years of missing a man who had wrecked her life once he was done with her, she could not stop herself reacting to Sabbah. He was just unfairly handsome. Those beautiful eyes. That solid, strong body. His hands. Even his toes. His toes!

She slapped her hand against the white-painted stone, and then for good measure, she stomped her foot on the mosaic floor.

How was she supposed to resist a man like him? How did anyone? Her eyes narrowed to slits. Was that why he had been covered in turmeric? Had some woman thought that if she covered him in bright spices, he would go back to her home to change? Had it been a tactic? Jealousy roared in her, loud as a lion and just as vicious.

Striding forwards, she moved to Hudayda and his assistants.

"Is there anything you need, Hudayda?"

She held herself as primly as she could, hands clasped in front of her and chin high, pretending she was not a lusting, jealous creature who wanted to bite Sabbah's neck so all other women would know he was hers. She wondered if this was what men felt, that made them close their women away in harems or simply in the screened quarters of their homes where no man could go unless he was castrated.

Tison would happily shut Sabbah away and snarl at any woman who came close. It was stupid, ridiculous, but she could not deny it. She only wished she could.

"A great deal, I am afraid." Hudayda straightened from his fire. "Tools and pans. I will send Aziz with you. He can carry the heavy items back."

"Thank you." Tison gave Aziz a medium smile, so as not to encourage him to think she was flirting or that she considered herself above him. She had been thinking seriously about smiles as she went to bed the night before. She never had to force one with Sabbah.

"Madame." Aziz bowed his head.

"Allow me to wrap my hair and gather my purse, and I will be with you."

Aziz was Arab, so she did not feel the need to warn him to drink water before they left. She wrapped her hair quickly in her head covering and went to her master's part of the house to recover her purse of money. Mostly, she set accounts to be delivered to the Muhtasib's house so she did not have to carry actual money, but she felt as though she may need to buy little things, and these were easier to purchase at once.

Sensible thoughts.

Then Sabbah emerged, clothed once more as befit his station. Her heart turned over. Seeing the purse in her hand, he smiled.

"Are you going to the markets? Shall we walk together?"

"If you wish, Important Man." Excitement swelled in her, and she tried to frown it down. She would have managed if she had not seen him without a shirt. Now, he just seemed to be naked under his clothes, a patently obvious statement and yet potent, too. She could imagine the contours of muscle, not obvious, not the sort that looked like one could grind meat on it, but just so much more appealing. "Aziz will be with us."

"Aziz?" Sabbah looked over her shoulder where the lad in question was covering his head and straightening himself for the foray into public. His eyes flattened, the humour draining out of them.

"Is there a problem?" she murmured, concerned.

He inhaled, straightening.

"No." Sabbah shook his head firmly. "Forgive me. I ... It's nothing. He has not done anything."

A little confused, Tison fought the urge to think he had been hoping they would have more time alone. In all honesty, she should be glad. She did not want to be reduced to the stumbling mess which his shirtless body had rendered her. She needed to be professional.

But he was so handsome. So beautiful, in truth. Every inch of him. His bearded chin, his large hands, his fascinating eyes, and his pink-bellied toes. Why did she keep thinking about his toes?

Hudayda met her eyes across the courtyard, and she went over to receive his list. She had to ask for explanations of some of the local implements, but luckily, Aziz had experience in kitchens and grinningly assured her.

"I will rescue you, infidel northerner!"

It was cheeky, but she could not stop herself grinning a little. She wagged a finger at him.

"I am a Child of the Book," she chided. "Not an infidel. But yes, do rescue me! I shall stand back and look too proud to haggle!"

Aziz laughed.

"I heard you haggling for us," he reminded her.

"But the cook shop owners do not."

She gave a little sniff and brushed down her dress, turning down the corners of her mouth, which made Aziz laugh and Hudayda grin from ear to ear. They had all, it seemed, known housekeepers like that. Her back warmed, and she turned to see Sabbah standing behind her. His face looked somewhat grim.

Was he jealous? She should be glad; it was how she would control him. And yet, she felt the urge to reassure him, to put her hand on his arm, show him that she was only interested in him. Stupid, dangerous, but undeniable.

"I will walk into town ahead of you." His hands were still faintly yellowed at the nails. She stared at them. Then frowned and raised her eyes to his face.

"If you wish, al Muhtasib." She let her frowning eyes ask and apologise, but he seemed more distant than he had been since he had walked into her life and rescued her.

"You may talk amongst yourselves without worrying about me listening that way." He nodded and turned.

"Look out for errant spices!" she advised, her heart hurting.

He paused and peered back at her, gave her a little curve of his lips. Then some of the stiffness left his shoulders, and he nodded at her.

"I will, Tison." He released a breath. "Forgive my ill temper. It would be best if I walk back alone and gather myself." He nodded over her shoulder. "Keep her safe, Aziz, for as long as you are with her."

"Yes, al Muhtasib!" came the instant response.

Relief relaxed all but her heart, which still pattered and quivered as if it had forgotten how to beat evenly. She was barely even troubled by it as she watched him walk away. His shoulders reminded her of when she had seen them bared, and the urge to rub oils all over him and then herself proved overwhelming.

Today, it seemed she could not control herself. No matter how hard she tried, he was affecting her. Her intentions meant nothing. All she wanted was to walk beside him and joke at him and let her heart go mad with flutterings.

Chapter Six

Staring at the steel grey as it bleached his room, Sabbah told himself to rise and pray before the dawn broke over the Atlas Mountains. Told himself he would sleep again after the traditional washing and incantation had soothed his mind.

Hauling himself off his bed, he tried unsuccessfully to ignore what would give him most relief, to ignore the morning insistence of his body. He had almost kissed her. More than once. Every time he saw her, he wanted to reach for her. Drenching his hands and neck could not drive back the heat of that burning, though the sun was still soft and cool over the Atlas Mountains.

Nothing could cool her; nothing could extinguish her might and beauty.

No! He roared inwardly at the smile that had started to creep across his face.

She was his slave, under his protection. His mother would have slapped him hard for even dreaming of such a moment, for staring at her, let alone standing before an entire household and being a breath away from taking her in his arms and kissing her until she was stammering and moulded to his body. Or when she had brought him water and been in his chambers, unguarded and unprotected by anything but his own control.

He washed once more and then knelt towards Mecca to pray, water still trickling down the contours of his bare back as he forced the muscles there to be smooth and relaxed. In prayer, his mind focused, but his skin prickled the instant he rose, as though she were standing behind him. Getting up from the prayer mat, he stood and stared at his bed.

If I don't sleep, this afternoon will be hell, he reminded himself. He could step into a funduq over the full heat of the afternoon. Rent a space. Sleep. Maybe even one of the funduqs he turned a blind eye to, too. He could slip into a room with some willing woman. Release the need.

Sabbah wished very hard for a moment that he could. That he felt no obligation to his position as Muhtasib to avoid vice. That he would not feel shamed and wrong. That any woman but Tison would do. He groaned into his palms and then rubbed them over his scalp. He needed to shave his head. Have it shaved. Would Kanto be awake yet?

Dropping his jaw to his chest, he sighed at himself and went to his coffer for clean clothes. The cool cotton of his undershirt flowed over his naked chest, and then he paused and rolled up the hem. He pinched the flesh above his hip. He was still strong. Still muscled.

But …

Was he perhaps a little meatier than he had been? His stomach a little less defined? His back's breadth would aid him, but was he attractive to a woman? Did she like his body? She had been breathless, but she made his heart pound and his body crave hers.

A crunch of irritation hit him. He absolutely hated this.

It was ridiculous. He was not yet forty. She had dropped the water. She wanted him. She was attracted to him. Maybe he should buy a mirror. Just to be certain. His movements were a lot crisper, a lot rougher, as he finished dressing. Apparently, not sleeping made him feel his age.

And as though someone had poured sand in through his ears until it clogged his brain. He was making a fool of himself! A sleepless night over a woman under his protection?

Dressed with his usual smartness, even though his linen trousers and over-tunic would crease by the time he was home again, his head covering in his hand, he walked down a cool, quiet corridor. Weariness stagnated his mind, but his body, at least, was somewhat rested.

He stepped through the atrium and out into the courtyard and found the cook, Hudayda, lighting the fire in the cooking pit. Beside him sat Tison, and the sight of her kindled flame far quicker than the cook could hope to manage. She had one leg crossed over the other, her yellow dress tucked up, allowing her lithe, brown skin to emerge.

His stomach jolted.

Every time he saw her, he felt his knees brace. She was silken and incandescent, and that leg could have made him crawl across the courtyard to her side.

She saw him.

She smiled.

A smile that welcomed, instant and unthinking. His feet responded while his tired mind reeled. As he drew close, she rose, and the cook bowed before setting himself back to work.

"Do you ever sleep?" Sabbah asked, hoping his increasingly smitten mind had just missed the signs of a restless night in her flawless, golden eyes and smooth, dark skin. Perhaps she had dreamed of him. Perhaps she had thought of him as she lay on her pallet.

"I do not need much." She shrugged. "I am like a cat. Given half a chance, I would laze around all day."

She had folded her hands neatly before her. It creased the front of her dress, tantalising, begging him to be base and try for a glimpse of her breasts. He was so busy holding his eyes on her face, he barely had time to resist the image of her stretched out on pillows, lounging in feline apathy. His own imagination was manning an assault on his control and using his sleep-deprived distraction to its advantage.

"So you make yourself get up and work?"

He admired that. He had his calling. She made her own. It was safe to admire her work ethic.

"I must lead by example."

She turned, swivelling around to exchange a grin with Hudayda. For a moment, he almost felt unwelcome, outside of something. Left out. Then she twirled back and set her fingers on his arm. The light touch made his throat dry instantly.

"You need a shave," she told him, stretching up, with her body almost touching his, her dress pushing ever so slightly against his trousers. Her hand caressed his scalp, stirring the stubble there and sending tingles down his body to his belly button. He had to fight himself all at once, a sudden battle to stop himself becoming visibly aroused. She chuckled, going back on her heels and looking up at him, pointing vaguely to a bench far enough away that he would not have to worry about interrupting Hudayda's lesson. "Sit. I will get a razor and such."

In a haze of sleepy warmth, he obeyed. She walked out of his sight. She smelled of something wonderful. Earthy and suggestive and apparently exactly the scent required to drive him utterly insane.

The cook was joined by his assistants, and grains and fruit were added to the cauldron over the fire. Half listening to Hudayda teaching his new underlings, Sabbah tried to force his body not to keep on betraying him.

He could not lust after a slave. It was a betrayal. It would be forcing her, even if she seemed willing.

And she was willing. He was certain of it, and it made resisting that much harder. It made being a good man almost impossible.

He felt her approach and looked up to see her walking the length of the courtyard. She was a desert mirage. Far too good to be true. Far too much what he longed for to be real. *Concentrate*, he ordered himself, *do not become aroused*. Not here, not with witnesses.

As she came alongside, she once more ran her hand over his scalp. The odd sensation of hardening and melting at the same time shuddered through him. Carefully, he released a trapped breath from his chest.

"So fuzzy!"

She sounded like she was tickling a puppy. His pride twinged, but the ache of weary, helpless arousal chased the feeling away. Her hands were on him. She was so gentle that every touch felt like the caress he wanted it to be. He was so very tired; she was so very close.

He heard sloshing, and a bowl was set beside him. Once again, her hands caressed his head, agonisingly intimate. He did not think he would ever be able to have Kanto shave his head again. Her fingers shifted from ghosting caress to deft, massaging movements.

"So tense, Important Man," she chided, her hands sliding to his neck and shoulders.

The cook and his assistants did not halt their lesson. The world did not stop or shake. No mighty wind or storm bent the sky to match the tumult in his heart, mind, and body.

She wrought magic there. Sabbah felt a groan escape him as she worked her fingers into a hard knot of ignored tension. One of the cook's assistants laughed a little across the court-yard, and he flushed deeply, glad the blood was above his waistline, at least, relieved when he realised that they were joking among themselves and completely unaware of him and his struggle.

Deciding to brazen it out, he leaned back and tilted his head to look at her. Her gold eyes were warm with self-satisfaction that soothed away the last of his embarrassment. He might be a fool, but how could he mind when she smiled like that?

"You are very good at that," he told her, though she knew. His voice was oddly deeper than usual, crackling to his ears.

Kiss me, he heard his heart hope.

His heart. Not his body. Dangerous. And yet undeniable. She called him important. With her, he felt it. And it was a good thing to be. Not a weight of obligation and appearance. With her, he was a man, as well as Muhtasib. She had told him he was lonely, and now, he craved connection. He craved her.

"I worked in …" She took hold of his head and faced him forward, and he wanted to nuzzle her hand like a needy cat. "At least, I was owned by a baths for a while. I learned the art then."

Her voice was indecipherable, and he wanted to meet her eyes. She sank her hands into the water beside him. Her fingers, he had noticed, were quite long, her palms rather narrow.

"What were we saying, Hudayda?"

Was her voice breathy as she called across the now quiet courtyard? Was she as aware as he was? Was she as affected as she had been kneeling in his chamber, steadying another bowl of water?

She made him face forward again.

"Ah, yes!" The cook smacked his hands together, the sound leaving a sharp, immediate echo on the courtyard walls. "Fast days!"

"I and Veta will not eat meat on Fridays, though she can have fish. I do not eat any flesh on Wednesdays now until Easter," Tison said with calm practicality in every intonation of her voice.

Sabbah blinked. He knew she was a Christian. He just assumed as a woman of sense, she would convert. Though how a woman of sense was talking calmly about religious obligation when he wanted to kiss her and have her narrow hands on him, he did not know.

"And Easter is?" the cook asked.

Tison's fingers slid over a sore knot in his neck that had been vaguely troubling him for weeks. For a moment, he winced, and then, she smoothed the pain away and once more wrought bliss as the muscles released their tension. The oil was not scented, but it mingled with his skin and her hands and that hot, basic aroma filled his being with peace.

"Not until part way through next year."

The cook exclaimed, and she laughed, and Sabbah blinked. She was working his other shoulder, and he felt distant from the conversation. His entire world was just wondering about what those hands could do to the rest of his body. He could not stop his mind wandering south, imagining her palms smoothing down his stomach and her fingers pulling down his waistband the way she had gone beneath his collar.

"Any Jewish slaves who join us must only have animals slaughtered by a rabbi. Can we get that easily?"

Sabbah blinked again, not quite indignant but somewhat wistful. Her hands were smoothing oil soap into his skin and reducing him to a boneless heap of man flesh, and now, she was chatting about killing animals! He was reluctantly headed towards bliss at her hands, and she was talking salt and vinegar.

She rinsed her hands, flicking the water away, and picked up the razor. He barely felt the blade glide over his skin, found his head lolling back as she talked and moved his chin with one finger.

Those hands on his chest, he teased himself again, the path in his head resuming, would glide down to his hips and take command of him. If only he was of eastern African blood, or so extreme in his faith that he had to shave the fuzz of black hair that started around his navel. He could have been stripped of his shirt again, with her smoothing soap into his stomach, and the fantasy could have been complete.

She tapped his shoulder insistently, and he jerked his daydreams back, only wishing he could believe he would keep them at bay. He shifted, uncomfortable even if he was still gentleman enough to be hazily imagining rather than letting the blood stiffen at his groin.

"Hey! Wake up, Important Man!" She tapped out a rhythm on his skin. "Do you wicked heathen heretics not need to shave your top lip? Hmm?"

He wanted to kiss her top lip. He wanted to see it parted from the bottom with crazed pleasure.

"Only when there's a nosy imam in town, or the Caliph is under pressure." He absently rubbed his jaw. He was tingling from his toes to his brow and felt rather dreamlike and distracted. "Being half true Black helps. If I was pure Arab, people would notice more."

"Well, your beard and moustache suit you, Handsome Important Man."

Had she said it loudly, including the cook in the banter, he could have remained relaxed and hazy. Instead, she had leaned down and purred it against his ear. A low murmuring sound; breath against his earlobe. It was not a joke said aloud for everyone's understanding and amusement. It was for him, and that did something to him he could not quite understand.

Jolted by a lightning strike of sensation, he realised he was instantly hardening despite all his intentions. His breathing required focus, and he wanted to collapse backwards off the bench into her arms. He could not have stopped the quiet, awkward groan from leaving his throat with a giant cork and a hammer. She chuckled, still close, seductive. Whether or not she intended it that way, he was utterly seduced.

"Now, don't move!" she recommended, and then froze him to the spot by leaning forward against him to concentrate on the area around his ears. So while she wielded a sharp knife, all he could think of was her small, round breasts against his back. Her hands were deft and sure—a faint, hissing scrape, and she was shifting to address the other ear.

"Tison."

He had no idea why he whispered her name. He just did. Not a plea, or a question, just a statement.

Because she seemed to be all that existed. Sense pushed itself forward—the people nearby, the situation, and their particular paradigm.

"We must discuss your Mukharajah."

If she was not a slave. If she was free, he could have her. He could beg her to have him. No control and no denial. Mutual possession. If she wanted him. He could have her body beneath him, or over him. She could have him at her feet, kissing his way from her ankles to her belly.

She had stopped moving. Did she think he was lying? All at once, the heady warmth at his back was gone, and he swayed on the bench from the loss of it. He frowned, trying to shake the lust-filled haze in his head.

"With all you are doing for the household, your earning it is not in question."

She picked up a cloth from somewhere and rubbed it briskly over his head. Brusquely, even.

"Have I—" He turned as he heard the cloth hit the ground, and rose to his feet, thankfully with no evidence of his previous arousal. "No, no, no!"

She made it barely four steps before he caught her. He was baffled, but he took her shoulders under his hands and turned her to him. He was in shock, he realised. If he had been burned, he would not have felt so dazed or shaken. The look on her face would stay with him in his nightmares. The horror and pain he had seen made no sense to him, but he had seen them clearly. She had felt rejected and hurt, and it made him insane to think he had done that to her.

"Tison?"

She avoided his stare for the first time since she had approached him in a slave pen.

"Tison." His voice was tight, apparently unable to convey the dismay that twisted his stomach.

"We agreed," she said, her lower lip pouting a little as soon as the words were spoken before being bitten hard by her own white teeth.

SHE COULD SEE HE DID not understand, and she had no intention of baring her soul before she had even had breakfast. Just because he was beautiful and responsible. Especially not because he was strong and handsome and made her want to stop walking away, to turn and lean on his chest.

That was not the Tison she was being now. She was independent and brave and did not lean on anyone. She would not trust again, because it had turned out she was a terrible judge of character.

"You deserve your freedom." His face was intense, his voice or the words themselves tingling through her, raising her flesh.

"I deserve ..."

She closed her lips, pursing them tight, waved a hand, and walked out of his grip. Her mind was blank, and there was not a future in the world she could see. She could barely see today. The fear of being cut loose tangled her mind, and not one wish or threat showed itself so that she could explain what she was feeling.

He did not restrain her.

"Tison, please?"

And yet, she could not walk away.

After all, though he had offered her love and freedom in sweet, lying murmurs, never had he mentioned a mukharajah. No official contract the way Sabbah did now. But a free woman? What would she do? All a free woman could be was a wife. As a slave, she was a housekeeper, with prospects and a future and a chance to get rid of a bad master.

How to explain that to a man as good and open as the Muhtasib?

Stupid Important Man!

She had been touching him. All had been going to plan. He had been enjoying her caresses; he wanted her, and now? Now, he was talking about her having a future, a career that would extend beyond their knowing each other.

Still, he stood, watching her. The gates opened as the girls returned with water urns on their shoulders. Tison looked up at him and then jerked her head towards the main house. She set off briskly, knowing he would follow. Her stomach was twisting. Once inside the cool atrium, she fixed her eyes on the mosaic tiles beneath her feet and hesitated. Answers might be the only thing to silence him.

"Important Man," she began, her voice echoing slightly. Anxious fear flooded her stomach. She needed to talk. She needed to explain, even if he rejected her again, even if he was angry. "You need plants in here, Muhtasib. Wall coverings. Padded couches for guests."

Stop! Tison, focus! Why do you do this? Inane and stupid!

"Tison." He stood close, looming over her.

No. Looming suggested a marauding male elephant. A bully. Sabbah was more like a rock face in a sandstorm. With her empty stomach churning and her chest aching, a void around her heart, she once more wanted to put her head on his shoulder and just lean. Perhaps even more than she wanted him to take his pleasure with her, she wanted to be able to take comfort with him.

She felt so sad. So suddenly and completely unhappy.

"We had an agreement." Her eyes skittered around him, seeing nothing. The world was blurred, fogged, anywhere that was not him. His broad chest. His sun-darkened skin and kissable, tempting lips, every feature an ideal she had never held before seeing him. Feel his power and position in the way he stood. "I make your house great. You marry. You sell me on at a high price. You agreed."

Silence thumped between them. There were sounds outside, elsewhere, but here, the gap between them sucked all noise away, at least until he spoke.

"Honesty, Tison?" He spoke her name the way she invoked angels, as though the word was precious and fragile on his tongue. "I cannot have you if you are my slave. And I want you. I want your ... I want to be intimate with you."

He huffed a noise of embarrassment and growled at himself, his eyes not meeting hers.

Where was her triumph? Where was a flood of lust and laughter? Why did her heart hurt and she still want to lean against his broad chest? Wanted was good. Love was a lie, but better while it lasted. Needed, though, was best of all.

"I don't have to be free for you to have me." She inhaled a puff of air through her nostrils, looked up into his yes, and gave him her best, heavy-lidded, curving-lipped smile. "You can have me any time you want me, Important Man."

She lifted her arms, moving forward, only to be caught off balance as he stepped back. Disappointment startled her. Her body keened with it. She was a beautiful woman. She knew he wanted her, so why was this not working? She needed proof. She needed him to be all hers.

"I don't want that, Tison." He rubbed a hand against his own cheek.

She was instantly jealous of both his skin and his fingers, feeling things she wanted to feel.

"You want me to let you reach for me?" she asked, forcing a chuckle that sounded tinny in the bare hallway. She must have misjudged him, after all. Maybe he wanted a chase. That must be it! It was not that she was unable to attract him ...

"I want—" he broke off and closed his eyes, hiding their warmth and part of him from her. "I should have just stayed in bed."

Blinking, thinking she understood, she tried to reach for him again. She lowered her voice to a gentle, teasing murmur. It had never failed her.

"You want me to go wait for you there?"

This time, as she raised her hands, he knocked them aside. Nerves sent sparks of familiar fear through her, and she braced herself. Except no shouting or violence followed. He merely stood. In his eyes, there was no anger, but pity. Disappointment. Longing.

"I want ... I want to be sure it's Tison who kisses me."

His shout dropped to a puzzling tone she did not know. His words were slowly and carefully chosen. She frowned, tilting her head in confusion, hands coming against her chest, feeling small.

"I want the woman who laughs and teases, not the one who forces herself to speak like a concubine because it's what she thinks ... what you think I want."

"You do want me!" She lost control of her voice. She burned with mortification at the word 'concubine.' But if she did not even have his want anymore, she had played and lost. The word had lost all meaning, anyway.

"I want *you*, Tison!"

His words hit her square in the chest. Her heart shuddered, and she felt him there beneath her ribs.

"Not some …" He waved a hand and turned his back to her.

Panic began to seize her aching heart.

"Sabbah?"

Where had the shouting defiance gone? She was pleading, her voice more a cracked whisper than seductive murmur. *I lost him. I lost him. No, please.* She did not realise that he had felt the same when she walked away from him; she just knew that she had to stop him walking away from her.

Chapter Seven

Sabbah took a deep, steadying breath.

"You said you would shake my world." His voice was calmer than he was. "Do you always turn a man's life upside down?"

The answer was desperately important. For some reason, this woman he barely knew had to find him different. He could not be just one of many. He did not know why. Then he realised that while he did not understand her, he still knew her better than any other woman he had ever known. It was the way of his people, the way of his religion, and he had never questioned it.

He had no sisters, and his sister-in-law, Jessamine, was sweet and devoted to his brother, Khalid, and usually let the brothers talk without interruption. He knew she had a large family, but beyond that, his knowledge of her ran to what she looked like. Even that was rare among the elite of Marrakech. Most women took the admonishment to conceal their adornments very strictly, covering their faces as well as their hair. They would never be in a room with him, even in official capacity.

Even the girl he had hoped to marry had only once spoken to him and ever after had been silent behind her veil. He had not even seen her since she had married.

The only women he spoke to were black women in the market from the Akan and similar tribes who would not let trading in an Islamic city prevent them speaking their minds about other traders trying to edge them out or blame them for altercations. Seeing as they reminded him of his mother, he was hardly going to feel an attraction, and having to remain wholly aloof as a man of the law and the city, he could not even attempt friendship.

His mother had never tired of reminding him and his brother that women should be allowed male friends, that it was Arab insecurity to not trust a woman to choose her friends wisely. She had even given Jessamine that particular talk more than once in the short months between Khalid's marriage and her death.

And he was certain that she and Tison would have agreed and argued and shouted and embraced. What thought was more dangerous right now than how well Tison and his mother would have bonded? He knew it deep in his heart and soul. He could almost imagine them playing qirkat and teasing each other and probably him. He could only wish that Tison had come to Marrakech sooner.

He had questioned very little about the way of life in Morocco, but in this moment, he wished he had more chances with Tison. Earlier chances. Before he had become so rigidly devoted to being Muhtasib. Perhaps before he had become— But no. He never would have met her then, would he? And that would be, he knew, a tragedy. Looking down at her, feeling so utterly connected to her and yet not knowing what she was thinking, he hovered between certainty and a total lack of it.

Her delicate jaw lowered as she ground her teeth and then forced them apart. Her eyes were darker than usual, her pupils blown wide, obscuring the gold until it was just a thin, glowing ring. And they were sad. She looked sad.

And it hurt him, deep in his chest.

"No." She swallowed down her dry, crackled voice. "I ... You need someone to shake you, Important Man. That's what you need. That is why it is what I will do."

The way she called him that still tickled his skin. But the hurt gave him the only response possible.

"What about what you need, Tison?"

Her lips parted. Strong, witty Tison was struck dumb. Simply being asked what she needed robbed her of all answers. It was horribly, bitterly sad to see a woman as vibrant as her silent and unsure at such a simple question. He moved without thinking or noticing. It was not giving up; it was too good and right to be that.

Drawing her gently against his heart where she absolutely belonged caused the hurt in his chest to fade, at least. Peace descended. He had to resist the urge to kiss her hair, to smell it, breathe her deep into his lungs like he had a right to own her body and soul, and not just her freedom. It tickled his bearded chin. Soft. Like Spanish wool rather than silk. Never in his life had he held a woman like this, close to his body, her own trusted in his embrace. She relaxed slowly, and her form fit perfectly to him.

"What about what you want?"

He repeated it quietly, against that fluff of hair, and it had all the power and meaning of a prayer. But despite the reverence he could hear in his voice, his body only responded to the feel of a woman's form. Despite how intense and serious he wanted to be, there was excitement in having her there. Despite how intent he was on discovering her wants, his own were making themselves unmistakeably known. Moreover, deep in his gut, something was humming away and filling him with a word:

Mine.

She shifted in his arms, and he loosened his grip in case she needed to be away from him. But she just curled her fingers into his linen tunic.

"I am a slave." Her words were muffled. "I have no need. No want."

He raised his head reluctantly and sought eye contact, touching her beautiful face so he could gently tilt it up. As gently as he could with hands that felt big and awkward.

"A woman like you?" He smiled, wry and humorous, needing to drive back the deadened hurt in her eyes. No, worse than hurt—a blankness. A resigned, sad nothing.

She took half a step back, and his hands slid to her shoulders. On a deep breath, her chest rose, the air wobbling as it left her lips. Her arms fell to her sides, no gestures or broad caresses anymore.

"I want to be necessary." Her voice came out awkwardly, as clumsy as his hands had felt. "I want to be so vital that I cannot be overlooked." Her voice strengthened, and finally, the sadness was pushed away by a flash of anger. The exhausted tilt of her body rose into strength. "Cannot be cast aside."

She raised her hands and put them on his chest. His heart doubled its pace, unaware of the emotion, noticing only the touch despite his disapproval of his own attraction.

"So don't talk about setting me free until I can prove you need me, Important Man." She shrugged up her shoulders. They were thin under his hands. Bony. "Tison needs to be needed."

He lifted one hand from that worryingly fragile shoulder and set his palm over both of her hands, pressing them against his chest.

"I need you, Tison." His heart shuddered in its gallop while his head stared into a void, an abyss of emotion. He had no idea what words he would speak until they curled off his tongue. They were dangerous words, he knew that much, for all he had barely spoken to any woman outside his position as Muhtasib or boyish forays to the funduqs outside the city walls. But the truth of them settled on his heart as they left his lips. "I do not know what I need more: Tison who sets my body beyond my control, or Tison who has pulled me out of solitude."

He hesitated for a moment before continuing.

"Kanto does not want to be free. He believes that with his injuries, he could not earn his keep. Even though nothing would change." He increased the pressure of his hand on hers. "It is your decision, Tison. Just know that I would be ... more than inconvenienced if I set you free and you left me. You need to be needed? I need to be sure you are choosing me, and not merely submitting to your master. I need to be wanted."

And she laughed, quickly, before pursing her lips over her teeth and amusement. He was not sure how she could be amused when he had just done the most frightening thing in his life. He might as well have dressed in garish costume and danced in al Djemma, for how exposed he felt. Her eyes, meanwhile, roamed around the atrium and then fixed once more on his.

"You don't know?" she asked, her murmur replaced with challenge.

His heart kicked into a gallop again. There was something glorious in her eyes, stroking his skin to heat without the slightest touch. She had returned. Tison was back in her eyes.

She turned her wrists, taking one of his hands and drawing it to her chest, guiding his palm over her left breast. A lightning blast of sensation shot down to his groin. He was shamefully staring down at the passage of her hand, but he caught a jerk of her head as she pulled in a harsh breath. His own breathing echoed hers. He slowly raised his eyes, as though his stare was as sweet and sticky as honey, and devoured her face.

She was smiling, but her brow looked furrowed, her eyes closed. Her lashes seemed to touch her cheeks, and the beauty of them cut through the mad desire and the cracked mess of his emotions. Unconsciously, he flexed his hand against her soft flesh. Almost soft. Her nipple was hard, rising against his touch through two layers of linen. His breathing proved hard to maintain, hard to keep even.

And then, she moved his palm down over her flat stomach with the one hand while the other reached down to gather up her skirts. Now his breathing was as hard and harsh as a stallion scenting a mare. His eyes stayed on hers, too afraid to look down, worried that his lust would chase her away. This was happening. It was actually happening. She was letting him, making him, touch her so she could breathe unsteadily and he could almost pant for her here in his atrium.

She twisted, pulling his hand until he was stooping a little, pushing his fingers up between her warm thighs to a slick heat that beckoned and pleaded, wet, hot, and ready. The slightest ghost of the scent of her desire reached him, and he actually felt the blood drain from his body to stiffen his already gathering erection.

"I want you, Important Man."

Her words were against his ear. Was she leaning on him or him on her? He curled his fingers, searching, exploring, and she gasped.

Sliding forward, between the soft folds of flesh, he finally pushed a finger inside her. Her breathing was hot against his ear. One hand had released his and was gripping his wrist as it moved. The other folded into his tunic, pulling it tight against the back of his neck. She gave a harsh little cry, twisting, pulling them off balance, and they moved together, awkward and stumbling, until she was pressed against a wall and he was standing over her.

"What are you …? Sabbah!" She arched, but immediately put her hand around his wrist. "You don't have to … I was just … oh …"

She was right. What was he doing? This was not like him. This was the action of a man who gave in to the temptation of flesh. But touching Tison did not feel like vice. It felt real, vital, and so good. She would be worth a thousand days of fasting, but that was not the point. He just wanted to see her lose herself. Was that so very bad?

His thumb, fumbling from lack of practice, rubbed over the budlike centre of pleasure, and he flexed his hand, never more glad of the size of them than now. In an open atrium, Tison clung to him, her breathing filling the space. Though she was quiet, it was the loudest sound in the world. It *was* the world. No woman had ever gasped his name. The women he paid for had never used his ism.

His eyes met hers, his hand worked, and her grip left his wrist. With both hands, she held onto his arms. The scent of her, the sound of her, the slick, hot touch. She breathed hard, whimpered in her throat, dug her fingers into his forearm, and came. Her head bobbed forward, her eyes went wild, her mouth opening wide, and her hips bucked once.

She mouthed his name, but only the middle consonants made any sound.

He had never seen anything more beautiful.

So he kissed her, while her eyes were still unfocused and her lips parted. His arms wrapped themselves around her waist, taking her slight weight as she held tight to him. She breathed softer, and shudders passed through her. There was something primitive in the way he felt himself responding. Pride, smug and strong. Want, primal and deeper than the soles of his feet, filled his being. He had never felt this way. Never in his life had he felt so much a man, or so much himself.

He wanted to thank her, even though she was the one who had taken pleasure at his hands. Had his mind been clearer, he would also have worried that she would have given him a stern look had he dared do so.

"Sabbah," she murmured into his shoulder, finally getting all the sounds together.

Important Man made him tingle. But when she said his name, sated and shocked, he knew he would love her. Or did. Maybe he already did. He rubbed one hand over her back, looking down into her dazed face and flickering his eyes from her brow to her chin, loving every single piece of the beautiful whole.

He certainly needed her. Soon. Or he might as well split into pieces for aching.

"You should take my offer of a Mukharajah." As he spoke, she stiffened. "Or I might never let you leave me."

She relaxed again, chuckled, and pushed against his chest, freeing herself and barely tottering at all.

"Your wife will see you sell me quick."

She did not shrink or diminish. There was no bitterness or spite, and she still smiled with hot contentment, but she was already drawing away.

"I don't want another woman, Tison." He hurt even thinking of it, and feeling anything with a length as hard as his was somewhat impressive, even with the soft tenderness that wrapped him about.

"Well, no, not now, but you need a wife."

She fussed with her gown and then her hair. She might be amusedly resigned to that fact. He was aching, an uncomfortable feeling tensing his shoulders and twisting his stomach, drawing attention from his bodily need. Was she amused? She was not looking at him.

"I need you," he reminded her, his brain sluggish and under assault from lust and confusion and want. So much want.

"Careful, Sabbah." She smiled, but it was not mischievous. She almost seemed solemn. "You are close to breakable promises. I've had those before."

She turned to go, and then swayed over a stride and returned, pressing her lips to his, stopping his heart and his head once more. His hands dropped to her back.

"Thank you, Sabbah," she murmured against his mouth. "That was ... good."

Then she was stepping out of his hands and walking slowly away, leaving him hard with a reeling heart. He stood for a moment and then lifted his hand to breathe the scent of her left on his skin.

What was wrong with him? What was different about her? His sense of propriety meant that he needed to wash, even if his religion did not demand it. A wild, primal part of him wanted to have her scent all day. Perhaps for the rest of his life. Reluctantly, unsteadily, Sabbah walked through to his chambers, lips closing over her kiss as though he could keep it imprinted there.

Each step was slow and unsteady, and he stumbled when his mind wandered back to her body.

He washed, cooling his skin and easing his tension with a massive effort of will and focus, and then turned his head to his desk.

Ignoring the ledger where he recorded incidents pertaining to his job, he lifted his ink well off a stack of carefully transcribed records. Proof of purchase for each of his new acquisitions, with histories, whole lives, in small and often scruffy annotations. All lives. Belonging to him and under his protection.

Anxiety jangled his nerves, the sight of the papers easing the last sexual tension of his body, even if his mind could not quite keep from the knowledge that she had come for him.

He stowed them one by one in the lockbox, looking for family details. His weariness banished by unslaked lust, and his lust banished by cold water, his eyes moved swiftly, his hand reaching for a stylus when he found one of Kanto's assistants had a sister, born like him in the south and sold in Marrakech to cancel debts.

When he reached Tison's, his throat dried, and he swallowed. For all she belonged to him legally, reading her life felt like an invasion. He held out his hand for a moment and was surprised that it did not shake.

She had first been sold at five. By and with her father. Listed as Ethiopian, not by tribe. Was she Amharic? Oromo?

At eleven, she had been sold because her father had died. There was no reason given for the next sale at fifteen, but her price was high. Skills were listed: singing, dancing, cooking, sewing, bead craft, and caring for children. She had been bought in Tunis.

Then, scrawled in stark ink.

Sold. 3 fals. Outlived use.

No age or detail, just sold for three of the lowest denomination of coins. Three copper coins.

She'd had five sales in quick succession. One bothered to list her age as being about twenty. Then the bathhouse. Skills had been noted at different times as she was trained. Then for some reason, the same, stark, cruel hand as before.

Sold on request of valued customer.

The same hand. Sabbah was certain. No wonder she was so desperate to be necessary. Insha'Allah, if he ever found the man who had held her so cheap he had her sold twice over ...

Now his hands were shaking. The curling script blurred with the shivering motion. Three coppers. For a woman worth her weight in Indian rubies. He placed her life in the coffer with the others. He needed to see her. He needed to hold her close.

He should not have let her walk away. Never mind that they could have been caught or that she was still under his protection. He should have brought her to bed and rubbed passion across her skin. She must have such fears of rejection and being used and cast aside! He was not a stupid man, merely one who had been dazzled by the heated curve of a woman's lips as she breathed his name.

Pushing away from his desk, Sabbah went in search of the woman whose body drove him past all his control, all his duties, and whose life had just broken his heart for her sake.

The courtyard was an anthill of activity. Benches had been delivered, and braziers were being filled with cedar charcoal. Tison stood overseeing the filling of the fountain and the arrangement of the furniture, dipping between conversations like a grebe on water. Pride filled him. No, no bird was she. A queen in her kingdom.

And he had made her whisper and pant with pleasure. He grinned despite himself, and despite it all. She had had pleasure at his hand, and that made him feel like he was a mountain of strength and virility.

She turned. Her words seemed to falter on her tongue for a moment as she smiled, conscious, rueful, but welcoming. Then, her eyes flared in amused irritation, and she swept herself into directing order out of chaos. Had she washed? Was she still hot and sticky from his touch?

He could walk into a street brawl and find the man who had thrown the first punch. She was an instigator of mess and the only one who could sort it out, all at the same time. They were both people who found order in chaos, not that he could discern that in the pandemonium that now filled his courtyard. And even though his home was in uproar and he liked calm before he left for the markets, he was still smiling as he retrieved his head cloth and readied himself to leave.

"What on Earth?"

He looked up sharply, his smug, sexual pride pinched away as his brother strode into the courtyard, past men carrying a cedar planting trug. Khalid was in his light armour and looked every inch a warrior—if he ignored the mischievous expression on his brother's face.

"Khalid." Sabbah approached, trying to keep his head free of Tison. "Is all well?"

"Oh, yes." His brother's eyes devoured the noise and bustle. "Just showing my presence at the Qasbah so here I am dressed up in my best. Been some unrest so they want more military in the city rather than out fighting bandits. But you know all that!" He gestured to Tison's chaos. "Are you really putting this place to order at last? Planting boxes and benches, brother mine?"

"Uh." Sabbah gestured, talking over Khalid's last few words. "If you can call this order! Tison!"

He did not know why. Perhaps it was because Khalid had heard the story from the market. Because he knew that his brother would recognise the power of her that was driving him mad. Perhaps it was just because he wanted to show her off. She was a member of his household, so of course he was presenting her. It was nothing to do with her being a woman, let alone a woman he was so wrapped up in, he felt her walk across the courtyard.

Khalid's face was amused. Sabbah searched it for interest, feeling a twist of guilt for his sister-in-law. Jessamine was beautiful, but she was a whisper in a sandstorm next to Tison.

And yet, Khalid seemed unaffected.

"You managed to make changes in my brother's life, Tison?" Khalid offered her a slight bow. "My thanks. He was turning into nothing but his position."

Sabbah caught his breath, finally distracted from Tison's interested but wary face. His brother had seen his own crisis, putting it into words even he had not been able to realise. Words he had been afraid of recognising.

"I have barely begun." Tison jutted her chin. He loved the way she did that. Challenging all around her to put her down. "I am only on the house. Next, I start on him!"

Khalid laughed, a deep belly rumble, his hands on his mailed torso.

"Good luck, brother!" He wiped away what Sabbah was sure was an imaginary tear of mirth. "My lady wife has barely begun to change me after six years!"

Tison snorted.

"Time wasted!" she exclaimed, reaching out and giving him an unslave-like poke on his armoured shoulder. "Tell her if she needs cavalry support to send for me!"

Khalid laughed again. Sabbah was not watching for desire this time. He was staring at Tison, and his stomach ached with it.

What a wife she would make.

Not sitting in her quarters, meek and docile. Not adorned with gold to show off his wealth. At his side. In his life. Sharing every moment and challenging him daily. She would be the worst sort of wife for the Muhtasib, but possibly the best sort for him.

Even if she distracted him so he did not listen to what was being said.

"That would be so generous of you!" Tison's wariness was all gone now. She turned to him, eyes alight. "Your brother is going to gift us some vines and jasmine."

Us.

He liked that far too much. For the first time in his life, he was tumbling under the thumb of a woman. Perhaps he could blame his long celibacy or the fact that he worked all day creating order and liked having someone who bossed him about and made him change. Still, it was foolish and too quick and should be humiliating.

"Some fruit trees, too, I think." Khalid waved a hand. "Our courtyard is by far too cluttered. And if I gift you some of the old, my wife can buy new."

Tison clapped her hands together and dipped her woven fingers towards his brother.

"You are as generous as your brother, Ibn Abdella."

And Sabbah noticed that she gave Khalid no nickname. No 'Soldier Man' or even 'Generous Man,' and she bowed, too respectful, despite that earlier poke. Her wariness might have faded, but she was still fulfilling her promise not to disrespect him. At least in public. He wouldn't mind some more disrespect in private. Her hand, her boldness, her gasping pleasure.

"And you are just as much in control as my own housekeeper." Khalid grinned. "Bully him well, Tison. He needs it." Turning to Sabbah, his brother flashed him a toothy grin. "I must go. I may see you about town today."

Sabbah embraced his brother in silence and watched him go just as tacitly.

"Do you think I passed muster?"

She flared her eyes at him, but he almost imagined she was genuinely concerned.

He looked down at her. He wanted to kiss her, taste her, and marry her. He was not letting this woman slip from his reach. He just had to work out how to get her to act like a Muhtasib's wife but never change. To convince her to take the true faith, which she had not yet done in all her life.

"You look serious, Sabbah." Tison tilted her head at him. "Kanto will feel usurped and get jealous."

"I am headed into town."

He could not ignore her, but neither could he answer. She clouded a future that had always looked clear and certain and organised. Now, maybe he did not want to know what would happen each and every day from here until he was relieved of his post or died, bored out of his skull and too afraid to admit it in case it made him a bad Muhtasib. But he could not tell that to a woman who still doubted that he needed her. She might think it empty words, and they were too close to his heart to be laughed away.

And those three coppers made him concerned that she would take protestations of mad adoration as lies meant to get him his pleasure, now that she had had hers.

"Ah." She flared her golden eyes at him. Eyes that had been filled with blazing pleasure joked at him now. "Reason to be serious indeed, Important Man!"

He almost turned craven, then he deliberately mimicked that little chin jut she did.

"Not what I want to be doing, Tison!" He leaned over her, catching her scent, earthy, making him hunger the way the aroma of fine foods might, but for a different sustenance entirely.

"Oh?" she challenged, wild and brave and irresistible.

"I want to take you to my room and waste the whole day." A quiver of boyish rebellion raised its head. Ridiculous, since as a boy, he had never rebelled, not against tutors or parents. He was a grown man, past thirty, and he was acting like a fool and loving every moment of that peculiar freedom.

"Waste?" Both eyebrows arched up.

He wanted to touch the line that it put on her brow.

"I have to tell myself it is a waste, or I'll throw caution to the wind. Throw my responsibilities to the wind." He closed his eyes. The heat in hers, the promise in her lifting smile—it was too much.

"I have to help you then," she murmured. "Because if you stay here, we would not spend the day ..." she hesitated, forcing him to open his eyes. Triumph flared when he did. Then she finished on a whisper. "... wasting time."

He groaned, only half-exaggerated. His heart might be pounding, his body might be yearning, but his head was ... amused. Engaged. This was fun! Silly and dangerous to a man's heart. He found himself grinning.

"What would we be doing?" He tried to sound overly seductive, dropping his tone to a rumble, and was rewarded by a short, simple bark of laughter.

"Organising, Important Man!" She smiled, her lips wobbling and her eyes creasing at the edges. "Oiling the locks so that they turn smoothly. Making sure everyone knows what to do, when to rest. Kanto cannot answer every question. I have not told him the answers yet!"

"So ..." He folded his arms, one wrist brushing the cloth of her dress. "You take your duties just as seriously as I do. Dutiful Woman."

He was rewarded. She laughed again. Triumph! Success! Sweet and satisfying. Knowing what he did of her life, getting to make her day better was an honour.

"Dutiful Tison is meeker," she told him, glancing around and then running a single finger up his sleeve. The contact still scalded him. "Flirty Man!"

He was going to have to see a physician about how much his heart was skipping and leaping. But to make her laugh again, he bowed with flourish.

"Get on with you, Important Man," she commanded. "Before the city falls apart. If I do not see you in town, I will see you tonight."

And for some reason, that made the length of the day manageable.

"Until tonight, Tison."

Chapter Eight

Spending a day obsessing over a word was not something Tison liked to do. It was too much like what Young Tison had done when she'd thought she was Grown Up Tison and was proved to be Trusting Idiot.

Sometime about half way through the afternoon, she ran out of details to arrange in the household and thus ways to keep her from focusing on how he had made her body feel, how her master had made her skin sing with joy and her mind shatter with mad exultation.

So she left with a list in her head of things to organise in the city. They needed a source of olive oil for making soap, cooking, and cleaning. She wanted herbs for a garden on the roof. Tools. Better knives for the kitchen. A dozen little things which would make the household run better.

And while back at the house, Veta was likely cowering in shadows thanks to the potency of the blazing sun, Tison was pleasantly warm. She had nothing but good feelings for Marrakech today. Even once the Important Man was done with her, this city would likely be her home.

Having demanded directions from Kanto, she could go with confidence from market to market. Always looking for Sabbah, and unashamed of that much, at least. She slipped into a narrowed road, almost covered thanks to the brightly coloured awnings over each stall. Incense burners, prayer mats, spices, fruits, ironwork, beads, books—a sample of all the crafts from the markets. She was called to, complimented, sure those offers would be even more generous if they knew who her master was.

Still, she pressed on towards the leather workers' district. She needed ledgers, records of food and goods used so she could predict what would be needed. Somehow. While she knew it was necessary, she had never done it before. Frowning, she had to admit to herself that she had no idea where to begin such predictions. She supposed she would just have to guess for a few weeks.

Puzzling over that gave her a moment's respite, protection from 'tonight.' Unfortunately, it also distracted her from her surroundings.

"Assalaam Aleikum, Tison."

It was the brightly coloured wasp who had approached her while she was fetching water. Fear, inexplicable in the crowded street, ran a damp finger up her spine. It sliced through the wondering about Sabbah, sparking a distinct resentment in her, but it was not quite strong enough to overwhelm the cringing fear of someone who had been broken before and was used to bowing her head.

But she was brave, not meek. She was the Muhtasib's housekeeper, and with any luck, soon his mistress.

"We have nothing to say to one another." She kept her eyes forward. Even if her Important Man were not so attractive, with his big, broad shoulders, and warm eyes, she could not have betrayed a man like him. He was too good, too kind, and too unsure.

He needed her. She ducked around a vendor. The warmth of her memories warred against the skin-prickling chill of her current, unwanted companion.

"Inspires loyalty, does he, Tison?"

Even more than the first time, his use of her name grated on her, banishing the physical pleasure and replacing it with crawling repulsion. She should have kept walking, ignored him, but anger flooded her, and wisdom was shoved aside by pride. So she stopped and looked at the brightly dressed pest with her fists bunching at her sides.

"The Muhtasib is an honourable man." Her nails pressed into her palms as she controlled her anger at this petty man and his annoying attempts to subvert her from Sabbah. He had weaselled into her nice, intimate wonderings, and she resented it.

"The Muhtasib is an official." The bright colour of the wasp's sleeve flashed at the edge of her vision while he spoke, but she kept her eyes on his face. He was not much taller than her, and he was smiling. And yet, the dread would not go away. "He has his weaknesses. We just want to know what they are. They are fair game while he is Muhtasib."

"And who is 'we'?" She eased backwards a little. Somehow, he had become very close to her. She could smell stale soap and a whiff of tanned leather. A familiar smell here in Marrakech.

Then the wasp laughed, and she found herself flinching from the sound.

"You're a clever woman, Tison. Come now, you are a slave, you have been for a long time, no? You know he will betray you eventually."

"No." She felt her nostrils flare as the word escaped her. This man did not know Sabbah, not like she did. She knew him. She was sure of him.

Wasn't she?

She had been sure before, after all.

The wasp had not answered. He was smiling differently now. She forced her legs to turn and walk down the alley. What had she given away? The vibrant colours around her drained to grey as she struggled with panic. It only increased when the wasp did not follow her. Tension gripped every inch of her. Her eyes narrowed until her lashes darkened the uneven flagstones before her. Why had he given up? What had she revealed?

Or was he playing her anxieties?

Tison strode on, head snapping back up. Strong. Brave. He was trying to make her feel unbalanced. She should give him no satisfaction, she decided. She would not consider him a moment more.

Needing something else to think about, she willingly pushed her mind back to pondering the meaning of 'tonight.' She drew some deep, soft breaths as she walked, overly aware of each step she took. She would not think of a sneaking, false-eyed wasp! Thinking about kind, delicious-to-kiss Sabbah with his surprisingly wicked fingers was far, far better.

In all honesty, his touch had shocked her. She had lost all control of him the second his fingers had slid inside her. His eyes had entreated pleasure from her and for her. He had held her against the wall rather than slamming her into it, had given rather than taking.

Would 'tonight' be more of that, or a return for her delight taken in her hand, her mouth, or her body? Her breath shuddered in anticipation for a moment.

She hoped for all. She felt greedy where he was concerned, excited and curious. It banished the unease just to think of resting against his chest, feeling his arms around her.

And yes, feeling his fingers inside her.

She had not had a man give without taking since her love affair began ten years ago. She just had to believe that she would not love again. The thought of Sabbah breaking her heart made her feel small. Like a sliver of glass pressed against the organ, ready to push inside.

No! She would not think of the end at the beginning. She would just wonder instead if he would come to her or she should go to him. How long should she wait before she switched rooms, just in case? He had always come to her, but Sabbah ... Her Important Man was unsure. She would go to him in darkness, perhaps ...

There! Just enough imagining gave her a secretive smile and armour against the man in the street and the lover in her past. Not so much that she was seeking fountains to douse her skin and cool her ardour.

The alley opened out onto one of the city's larger souks, as promised when she'd asked Kanto that morning. Sweeping flickering eyes across the nearest avenues, she saw a few of the Muhtasib's agents, pale green head coverings acting as a livery of sorts, their ledgers clutched, ready to make note of any problem. Their arrival at the slave pens had signalled her chance to escape and find her place. But it had been Sabbah who had shown her what that place could be. That he would need her as much as she needed that position of security. But he clearly had enemies for his own standing. Rivals or merely criminals. She did not know.

No! No more seriousness! Tonight! Tonight was her talisman, and no one would approach her with so many Muhtasib agents walking about the market. Now, things to do! She had ledgers to buy and orders to place. She was Housekeeper first, even if she still hoped against hope that Mistress would be her next title.

She smirked to herself, amused by how easily sex could be used to stave off worry. Though, oddly, she felt more worried about Sabbah's political enemies at present than her own heart, or for that matter, her safety in being approached by an obviously villainous man. More worried about the master than the self? What a good slave she was! Tison's brows twitched down, and she hovered by a pottery stall, chastising herself.

He was handsome. She would get him addicted to her touch. She lightly touched her own fingers, tip to tip, gentle, absent caresses while she plotted. Get him naked, that glorious body she wanted to indulge in, and never mind that as Muhtasib, he obviously had enemies. Never mind that they might have more success with the other slaves she had brought into his household. Nakedness, she could control. Her eyes narrowed to hazy slits. *Tonight, remember tonight!*

"Madame?" The stall-owner showed her a concerned face. "Are you quite all right?"

Tison instantly smoothed her face.

"God's greetings, sir, forgive my abstraction." Her cheeks grew hot, and she attempted to give the impression she had intended to come to his stall and not just slid out of the way so she could daydream about her master.

All smiles, she ordered several basic dishes and one ornate vase painted in a beautiful blue that stood to her waist for the entranceway to the master's quarters. Pleasant as it was to pick any wall to frolic against, it was too stark for a Muhtasib. He needed some luxury, some display of wealth. Though she was learning that the city was a focal point of the starker Almohad movement of austerity and devotion, she could not imagine any other city official with bare halls. It would certainly be too plain once the women's quarters were occupied.

Jealousy bit the thought, asp-like.

She sulked at it, turning her feet towards the towering minaret that beckoned all to the leather workers' and book-makers' district. They were not fun purchases, but she could shop for perfumes and fabrics once he had chosen a bride. She ignored the adder bite at her heart. She would not get jealous over him. There were plenty of heart-throbbingly handsome men in the city. She would not get wound up over inevitability. She would eventually lose him.

That was simply how it would be.

THE CHAOTIC BUSTLE of the city was a peaceful haven compared to the upset Tison had brought into Sabbah's home. He had always stepped from a quiet broken only by opportunistic birds searching for crumbs into the beloved craziness of his city. He had striven to take that calm and serenity with him, to ensure that he was bringing it to every incident, every road blockage, every incensed stall-keeper or drunken fool. Now, his home was also mad and loud and chaotic.

Though he had slept deeply, he had woken to his new cook teaching his assistants. Female slaves fetching water. He felt wrong. Only then, she had touched him, shaved his head, making a simple matter intimate and oddly precious, and the chaos had taken up residence inside his pounding heart and an uncontrollable body.

He could not have been more upended if the ground had become the sky.

And he liked it.

As he made his way through the familiar bustling but oddly lonely streets, he could only find solace in one thing. Tison had been happy. He might be the master, but she was running things. His departure would have changed nothing, except that he could not accidentally devastate her again. When he thought of what might have become of her if he had not bought her, the depths she could have been reduced to, a cold seized his spine despite the rising sun.

She was like a hot, summer breeze, whipping up dry leaves and fronds and dust and making them dance. And for some reason, her being happy was vital in a visceral way that almost made up for the lack of calm in his heart.

"Muhtasib!"

He stopped, turned, exchanged greetings with the harassed-looking agent who had hailed him, and began his day as usual.

"Also," the nervous agent added, once the night's activities and morning's crises had been addressed. "The Sayrafi has had more lead coins brought to him already."

Falling in beside his agent, his brows lowering and his mood instantly dropping, Sabbah turned his mind to the ongoing lead coin issue. They were bad fakes, but they were turning up in officially sealed purses. His brows lowered, and his jaw set. That reflected on Marrakech as a whole and on his friend Abou Saal in particular. Ibn Yusuf, his agent, was shorter than him, but walked with brisk strides to keep up.

"Where is the Sayrafi?"

Ibn Yusuf pointed up ahead.

"In his office by now, al Muhtasib. He was in the funduq with the sign of three suns speaking with the men who found lead in," the young man hesitated, looking around furtively.

"In the purses with the Sayrafi's seal?" Sabbah rubbed the side of his nose, willing alertness to his mind. He would need it to help his friend. Beside him, Ibn Yusuf nodded grimly.

The coins being passed in purchases were daily blights, but that seal should have been unquestionable, above and beyond reproach. These forged purses were more dangerous than forged coins, to his mind. They blemished Marrakech, an unforgivable sin to Sabbah. Worse still, if the Sayrafi's seal was not trusted, neither was the Sayrafi himself. That fear and doubt could then spread to the Caliph, even in his absence.

Abou Saal had been Sabbah's friend since he was little more than a boy. He had worked for him before he caught the Caliph's eye, operating out of this very office. While he knew he had to be thinking of the office of Sayrafi, and its connection to himself as Muhtasib, he found his heart worrying over his friend instead.

He knew without a doubt that the man had not sealed lead coins in a pouch meant for the markets. He knew it as well as that he would not walk drunk in the street. The people of Marrakech, however, he forced himself to think, would not know that. They did not know Abou Saal, only the Sayrafi. They had not been lectured on responsibility and duty while still raw and green to government work, and bailed out of problems when they were out of their depth.

For once, Sabbah cursed himself for not being more attuned to the jockeying for positions that characterised Marrakech's politics. Sayrafi, Muhtasib, and the Qadi—the highest judge in the city—only answered to the Caliph and the Vizier in his name. Anyone in this who might have any hopes or ambitions on Abou Saal's position was suspect. Sabbah considered with bitterness born of years of resentment that it would be too much to expect the Qadi behind the movement. Pleasant as it would be to catch him in wrongdoing and have some vengeance for past wrong, the Qadi had no reason to target Abou Saal.

Arriving at the Sayrafi's counting house, he made his way past the guards, sending Ibn Yusuf on his way to the new stall owner they had discussed.

He found his old mentor pacing, head uncovered and sleeves rolled up. He met Sabbah's questioning, sympathetic look with a grim face.

"Not good, old friend?" Sabbah held out his hand. "Salaam aleikum."

"Waleikum salaam." The older man's hand was slick with sweat despite the cooled room, and he scratched his beard as soon as that hand was free. "Bad indeed, Ibn Abdella."

Sabbah joined him at a table. Two opened purses lay on it. They were empty, the seals broken away from the leather, very nearly whole. He picked one up, inspected it, and then did the same to the other.

"Which is the fake?"

Abou Saal collapsed into a chair so fast, Sabbah had to hold himself back from rushing to his side, managing to restrict the instinctive movement to a jolt of his body. The Sayrafi leaned back. Sabbah saw such grief in his friend's eyes, he felt his own face crease into a grimace.

"I do not know," the Sayrafi replied. He rubbed his hands against his linen trousers. "There is no difference. I thought if I mixed them, I would find some flaw. The bag is the same from leather to stitches. The seal is the same. But the coins ... I would have noticed, Ibn Abdella. They are ..."

His old mentor closed his eyes and covered them with rubbing hands. Then he repeated, his voice a weary groan.

"I would have noticed." Abou Saal's eyes were haunted when he lowered his hands, striking Sabbah with a sense of the world being off kilter.

Sabbah hefted himself onto the table, hands gripping the edge and his focus on his friend's face.

"Where do you get the bags?"

"An old friend." Abou Saal's heavy voice warned. "I have been using the same workshop since I was appointed."

The defensive notes in the Sayrafi's voice broke over him. Nothing more than the hurt his old friend struggled with troubled him. He knew the hint of aggression was just the snarl of a wounded beast. Even wise men had instincts. He considered, pushing up on his hands so he could swing a little, like he had as a lad in this spot.

"Could be someone buys his excess? Gone through his books with him? Interviewed his people?"

Abou Saal gave him a look he knew of old, putting him in his place.

"Of course you have." He bowed his head. "Apologies. Just thinking out loud." He pushed himself to his feet. "I'd suggest talking to your man about using coloured leather, for a while at least."

He put a hand on his friend's shoulder. "I'll pass the word to my men to keep track of any spoiled monies."

The Sayrafi sighed heavily. He shook his head from side to side and then rose. He went to a draw and drew out a sheet of paper, passing it to Sabbah and immediately returning to rubbing his face. He was starting to look like he had not slept in too long.

Sabbah inspected the neatly drawn map of the city. Markets and main streets and minarets were all carefully inked in blue, the walls in black, and yellow circles were obviously meant to be cases of the money found with lead coins. Looking at the pattern, a recollection stirred.

He frowned, fighting through his memories. Tison would have remembered. She would have worked this out, somehow, with her gift for finding order in chaos. He touched a fingertip to one of the circles.

"Do you have the reports?" He shot his eyes to his friend's weary face as the Sayrafi swallowed a yawn and turned to his paperwork.

Within half an hour, he had a list of names and a copy of the map with the homes of those strange burglaries drawn in red. They formed an uneven ring around the streets just out of the tannery quarter. Folding the map, he put it into his satchel. "I'll talk to my agents. We'll get to the bottom of this."

"It's not just my neck on the line." Abou Saal sat back at his desk, staring at the two purses.

"I know."

Sabbah hoped his voice was soothing. His brows ached from frowning. No wonder Abou Saal's hands constantly rubbed at his leathery, wrinkled face. Sabbah's own hand came up to smooth the lines on his forehead. The city's economy was in coin, not barter. If the Sayrafi's word and seal was compromised, so were the markets, and thus, so was he. So was Marrakech.

"I need to get out there." He held his hand out. "Send for me if I am needed. Salaam, Sayrafi."

Troubled and without true answers, he went out into the scented and aromatic streets. Calming as the myriad scents usually were, he found little solace as he walked. The Sayrafi's fear and anger had not hurt him; he was not so childish or churlish to think his friend was directing his stress deliberately. Still, he felt unsettled. He could not shake that feeling. He wanted to go home and talk to Kanto and Tison. One of them might shed light where he could not.

At least, he knew for sure that no matter how hard this day got, he would be returning to Tison. She had said 'tonight' as though she had plans. For some reason, a very obvious one no doubt, Sabbah realised that her plans no longer terrified him.

Chapter Nine

Tison watched him walk into his own room with his head slightly bowed and his eyes on the tiles. Was there anywhere in Sabbah's home that he felt truly comfortable? She did not move, but still, a jerk of shock raced across his body when he finally saw her.

She instantly wished she had waited for him, stripped bare, as she had been taught to once before. Though that might well have killed Sabbah, given the arrested look on his face. Awareness of him curled her toes, and she was conscious of relaxing so fast, she felt giddy.

"You all right there, Important Man?"

Her voice quivered a little. She would not want him to feel laughed at, but he looked so startled, so unsure, and it was so unexpected. His eyes shot to hers. His skin darkened with embarrassment, and she flushed a little herself. Sabbah's self-conscious colouring at being caught was worth a thousand wolf-whistles and cat calls in the street.

She was certain, too, that he knew she was not there to speak of the household. He knew she was there to be bedded. She felt as though he was tying her into tangles with his eyes. As silence stretched between them, she could feel their tension tighten. She knew it in a tingling sensation behind her belly button and a crushing feeling in her chest.

Her lungs were trying to convince her that only by kissing him would she be able to breathe again.

It was his eyes that did it. He revealed so much in them. His honesty blazed from him, and whether he was exerting his authority in the marketplace, curbing the ambitions of a new housekeeper with plans, or staring at a woman in his bed chamber, everything was on display. There lay something reassuring in that, but also something utterly raw that scraped and gnawed at her, driving her to admit that she not only admired, she was fascinated. He might stare at her, but she was staring back. She only hoped he could read her as easily as she read him.

She watched now as he took a deep breath, and felt it down to her toes.

"Your hair is beautiful." His voice came out strained, dust-bitten and harshened by a day at work in the city.

She felt the smile split her face almost before she understood what he had said. Raising her hand, she patted the mass of uncovered curls.

"It's rather wild," she tempered.

He chuckled, the sound clearly unbidden since he swallowed it back quickly.

"That's why it suits you."

He finally moved closer, and Tison found herself gasping with delight as he came chest to chest with her, bent his head, hesitated for a moment until an embarrassing whimper escaped her throat, and then kissed her.

His lips were slightly dry, and the kiss chaste, but it was slow and impossibly sweet. She slid her hands up around his neck. Her knees wobbled, and the skin on her back burned as his wrists knocked the cloth of her gown against it. His hands missed her buttocks and waist, passed her back, and she felt his fingers slide into the mad mass of curling tresses that clouded around her head in determined fluffiness.

He chuckled against her lips, and she felt a tugging as he tried to run his hands through it and got stuck.

Tison smiled, and the kiss broke. Wincing, she leaned back so he could retrieve his fingers without hurting her. They both laughed breathlessly. She met his eyes. Instantly, her lungs and ribs were once more gripped with needy shock.

The familiar delicate lids and deep darkness were even more flawlessly beautiful this close. She had seen him doubting, annoyed, curious, and concerned. She had seen him want her.

Seeing him with intimate affection in them cut her knees from beneath her. His shoulders took most of her weight as she swayed on the spot.

They kissed again, both moving on instinct alone. There was no hesitation, no careful pecks to test the water, just a connection so deep, she felt no worry about how to kiss him. It just happened. When he drew back, it came just as naturally as the beginning, but she still wanted more.

"You shouldn't be here." His voice thrummed with humour, a world from the controlled, distanced one she had expected. "You should go. I mustn't do this."

He took a deep breath and raised a hapless eyebrow. "Are you convinced?"

Still wobbly-kneed, she found herself laughing a little again.

"Very convincing," she promised.

His hot, hazy eyes lowered to her mouth, and his brows dropped with a groan humming from his lips.

Then, his mouth pressed onto hers again. She swallowed, parted her lips invitingly, and awaited the invasion of his tongue with anticipation focusing every single nerve behind those tingling lips. Instead, she found herself tormented as he whispered tiny, rubbing kisses on first her bottom lip and then the top. Her entire body became enflamed. Needy lust swept desire aside.

A ridiculous, growling groan left her mouth and buzzed against his. She would have moved her hands to urge him on, but she was certain she would end up on the floor.

Giving in to her need, she lapped against his tongue with her own, coaxing and pleading. Sweat beaded and tickled the back of her leg. The gentle swirling, arhythmic and tender, wiped her mind of all other thoughts—locked against him, the sounds of cloth against cloth and lips against lips the only other sense than sensation.

Tison found herself rocked to the core. Every moment was another more than she had ever been kissed. He stroked her hair and touched her cheek with one hand while the other supported her unsteadiness by moving to her hip.

Her half-formed intentions of solidifying her security within the household and wrapping him around her finger had vanished. She did not regret them. This was good and real and honest and made her feel even better than manipulated security could have done.

"Knees!" she told him, amused by how obvious her own voice sounded.

"Knees?" He moved back from her, and she felt herself frowning at the momentary lack of kissing. She also stumbled as her support was removed. He hummed in understanding. "Oh! Knees!"

Instead of coming closer again or pushing her onto the bed, he bent, leaving her shaky for just a moment before he swept her into his arms. A low sound escaped him. A satisfied, needy, promising noise.

Once again, she was torn between amusement and embarrassment at the pathetic whimper that escaped from her own throat. He set her on his bed slowly and leaned over her, making the straw mattress flatten.

Her entire world had shrunk to him and her.

Maybe just him.

As he kissed her, her brow wrinkled. It was intense in a way she had never experienced. She nibbled at his lip to see if he liked it. She began to move her hands over his shoulders, and though he hummed with gratification deep in his throat, she was not satisfied.

"Tunic off!" she demanded, pulling away so she could kneel on the bed and pull off her own dresses. The tangle of cloth came over her head, and when she unbent her long neck, she saw his skin. A clench of desire tensed between her legs and gasped from her lungs.

In her mind's eye, she had given him bulging, meaty muscles. But she cast off the fantasy without regret. She released a long, shuddering breath.

Sabbah was strong, with only a little spare flesh that was not muscle at his middle, and even better, he was real. The muscle itself was corded and taut, and he had more small but perfect examples on him than she had ever seen on a man, despite having worked in a bathhouse. He had not worked for them—he had earned them.

He reached for her, but she knocked his hands aside and sat back on her heels.

"Oh, Sabbah!" she breathed.

Without volition, her hands rose and set themselves on his chest. The heat from him had been gently burning her, but it felt as though it scorched her palms. She ran her fingers up and down his ribs, and he shuddered at her tickling caress. She smiled wickedly and then deliberately held eye contact while she lightly ran her fingertips around his navel, just above the stripe of fuzz that descended beneath his waistband. He twitched.

Shaking her head, she narrowed her eyes, ready to quip about how gorgeous he was. The gleam in his eyes intensified, and an inelegant grunt was shocked from her. The look on his face took her breath away. Sabbah gazed at her with a raw hunger. His lips had parted, his brows lowered. Like a lion in a cage watching fresh meat go by, he stared at her. Desire crackled from him, coming off like the heat that she could still feel against her skin.

It was for her. Men had looked at her with interest as long as she could remember. One had even taken her repeatedly to sate that desire. No one had ever looked at her quite like this. Not a man she was used to seeing controlled and in command.

"Tison," he pleaded, his voice hoarse, begging but still not demanding.

They moved together. Something broke in the air, and she was touching that muscled chest again while his large, warm hands swept from her waist, up her flanks, and drew her tight against him as he moved her backwards. She kicked her legs from beneath her and wrapped them around his middle without shame, exploding with want and needing him to be closer.

The scent of sex surrounded them, and she moaned, soft but long, against his ear as he first kissed and then lightly licked the skin of her neck.

Tison threw back her head. It was so simple, and yet so good. His lips rubbed, his short beard rasped, and her body sang and soared in response. It had never occurred to her that she would have to fight to stay quiet, but when she looked down, met those hot eyes, and watched him slide down and kiss the small bulb of her breast, she let out a cry that hurt her throat.

He groaned in response, his voice muffled against her body.

"Hmmm, Muhtasib!" she teased, but he lifted his head from her skin, and instantly, she regretted it despite the soft tone in his reply.

"Don't call me Muhtasib." His voice shook. "Not here. Not now."

HEAT AND HOPE WERE filling Sabbah's consciousness. Her beauty was undeniable, but seeing her with her hair uncovered had given him a small preparation for how he would feel with her body bared to his hungry eyes. Tison had been attractive and hypnotic when he first saw her. Right then, she had him completely under her control, but from the urgent, fervent sounds that kept erupting from her throat, she did not know it.

But now that she was beneath him, his arms propping him up and her legs around his waist, other details began to intrude, to threaten his maddening desire's control over his mind. She was thin. Bone and a little muscle. Nothing more. Her ribs could be counted even in the beginnings of dusk, and his caressing fingers had traced them as he carried her. Even as his cock strained because of her movements and the soft sound of her breathing, splinters of steel pressed against his heart at how little flesh she had on her body.

"What shall I call you, then?" she asked on an amused murmur. "Important Man? Handsome Man?"

He needed to kiss her again, but he was afraid of stopping her lips and that gorgeous, teasing, throaty voice. It might well stop his heart entirely. He lowered his mouth to her skin once more. The heat of her was everything. Her soft, encouraging breathing filled the room. Quiet, and yet still the loudest thing in the world.

She arched with a jolt in his grip, her head falling backwards. But it was the moan that stripped away the last remnant of his control and sent his hands roaming and let his weight lower onto her slight frame. And not even the prominent fragility of her bones could stop him answering her groan with his own and burrowing his beard between her breasts just to feel her quiver and hear her giggle breathlessly.

Thrills and roaring lust surged in his blood.

"Ah! It's tonight!" She groaned. "Come on, Important Man! I've done my time!"

His cock twitched, and he paused while he roped some semblance of control around his body. She had been waiting, too. Thinking about him, daydreaming, imagining his touch while he was tormented by the memory of her heat. He wanted to see the expression on her face as he brought her pleasure almost as much as he wanted to bury himself inside her. He had never felt so totally, painfully hard from kissing alone. Come to think of it, he had never felt this turned on even while spending his seed inside paid women in his curious youth.

Tison was something else.

"What do you like, Tison?"

He breathed the words over her nipple and then lowered his mouth to the dark brown bud, keeping his eyes up, watching her. She brought her head back down, golden eyes blown and hazy in their pleasure, mouth slightly open, utterly beautiful. And then, gaping at him, she moaned long and with need.

He lipped at the swelling flesh, an involuntary groan vibrating through his throat to her skin. Now the expensive, smooth linen of his trousers felt coarse, almost painful, against the agonisingly sensitive skin of the head of his penis and the throbbing length beneath it. Especially as every arcing movement she made brushed against his rapidly detested trousers. He wanted her slick heat wrapping around him, clenching around his cock the way she had spasmed around his fingers. She would be smooth, molten, and strong. He might want to tenderly explore her flesh, but his body wanted to take her. Now.

And perhaps for the rest of his life.

She broke her lips from where they had been rubbing kisses across his head, and her voice was shaking and slow.

"No ... it ... not ..." She put her hands on his chest. His heart leapt to beat against them. "Not what I like, Important Man!"

She began to slide her palms around to his back and smoothed them against him deliciously.

"I bet I know what you like," she crooned, and his head recoiled, snapping upwards at the change in her tone.

"Tison!" He pushed up onto his forearms, using the sight of her thin shoulders as an anchor of strength helping him enough to resist the need for her.

"Damn what I like!" His voice was hoarse, cracking against the uncharacteristic volume and superhuman effort of not letting her explain and explore what she was thinking of doing to him. "Tison, I ... I told you it had to be you and me. Not ... not master and slave. And I want ..."

A shiver went down his spine, and nervousness fought the painful ache of his manhood. He needed her more than breathing, which was becoming a struggle in itself.

"Sabbah?"

Her eyes had dawned understanding and were sweetly solemn, even if her cheeks were hot with blood and her lips slightly swollen from kisses. She lifted her hands once again and set warm fingers along his cheeks, lifting his face. Then she rose up, pulling him into an awkward kiss until his arms ached. It broke him in a way her sultry promises could not have done.

Pulling her close, he tasted her kiss as her tongue slid fervently against his, breathed her scent, and best of all, felt her naked body as she let him hold her tight to his heart.

"Please be real," she spoke on a warm whisper, barely audible, muffled against his greedy mouth before he kissed her again. She raised her voice after a series of enticing little busses down her chest to her stomach.

And that, he loved. Her confidence. Her demand.

So he surrendered and let his body have its head. No tricks or techniques: just the two of them exploring pleasure and release together. His head over her shoulder so his mouth was brushing her ear, he thrust inside her, slow. His body knew what to do, and his mind was lost in feeling her heat around him. She bucked against him, and one of her legs jerked up. He felt her cool foot against his buttocks for a moment, and then just how she urged him to move.

She curled herself around his body the way she had curled around his heart, and he thrust again. She gripped him, and when he hesitated once again at the peak, she turned his head with both hands and kissed him.

And then, she bit his lip.

"Stop. Making me. Wait," she commanded.

A quiver of delight went through him. Tison. Demanding of him. It was a triumph, and it was right. He shifted so he could slide one of his hands beneath her head and still support himself, because he wanted the other free. He wanted to touch her still, and set his hand to her breast.

"Sabbah!" she warned growlingly.

He had never teased anyone in his life, certainly not like this. She looked at him, sweat on her lip and her throat moving as she swallowed.

He pushed again, and this time, he did not stop. One hand teasing her breast, he surged inside her, holding himself rigid as he settled into a rhythm, anything to stop him just taking her rough and hard and fast. She felt incredible, hot and strong and so slick, the thrusts were smooth despite the way she felt like he only just fit. Like she had been crafted solely to be his, and he hers.

"This good?" But he was still himself. Still unsure at heart, perhaps. The insecurity was worth it when she was merely able to nod and whimper.

"Yah!"

She pulled at his head, wrapping her arms around it, pulling him against her.

She moaned, and his ears roared with blood, his throat aching with a sound he made but could barely hear. He knew nothing but the heat of her and the way they were moving together now, with her curling her hips in little slams against him just as he moved deep inside her.

He found his lips near her throat, and he kissed and nuzzled, every part of his body wanting to echo the rhythm they had between them until it all became too much. All at once, his lust and release were a clamour, and he came. Before he could think enough to worry about her pleasure, he felt her body go into a madness of pulsing and gripping, and her head shot back onto the straw-filled mattress. A high cry came from her, and she writhed and bucked, and then fell limp beneath him.

And then, they were still, breathing in and out of sync.

TISON SETTLED AGAINST his chest like a particularly happy lizard on a sun-bleached rock, totally at peace despite the heat. She breathed steadier and steadier, her ear pressed over his heart, listening to it pound.

Because of her.

Smug, sated satisfaction emanated from her heart and her still very slick thighs. She rubbed her cheek against his chest. Broad, muscular, and solid. A word that should not be as arousing as the reality was. She trailed a hand to the fuzz of hair below his belly button, and she realised something.

Neither of them had power in that moment. They had each other, and pleasure, but no balance of ownership or authority. That and the gentle, largely unconcerned wondering if she had been loud, slowly drifted through her mind. She should probably care. She did not. She just cared about how incredibly happy she felt lying against Sabbah's chest.

A twitch of latent pleasure shook her, and she chuckled.

"You want me to work for you. We cannot do that often! I am melted!"

She lifted her head and looked at him. A shiver of further satisfied bliss stroked her skin, followed by the tips of his fingers. He was quite insanely, maddeningly handsome. He had a smile in his eyes, but he had compressed his lips. The pink tip of his tongue slid out to lick his lips, and she once again shuddered.

She groaned softly and wriggled up to kiss him, her breasts awkwardly pressing against his hard chest. His lips were hungry against hers.

"Hmmm, Tison!"

He pressed his arm against her back and trailed his hand over her bottom, but it was the way he said her name that made her shiver all the more. She chuckled again, the sound descending into an odd cackle that she hoped he would mistake for a girlish giggle.

"What?" He shifted, and she draped herself over him so he could not move as she laughed. But then, he began to sound a little concerned. "Tison?"

"Oh!" She turned her head again, holding her eyes steady despite an odd lick of sudden shyness following her blissful amusement. "Nothing! Not you! I ..."

She shook her head. The moment he knew she had never felt so free and happy was the moment she had to go back to weighing power.

"But it is a good laugh?"

His beautiful, dark eyes were laden with confused worry. She kissed his chest.

"A very, very good laugh." A moment of hesitation, but she could not let him fret when she felt as though Heaven had erupted inside her moments before. "I feel happy, Sabbah, as well as very, very smug."

She grinned, flaring her eyes for effect, and the worry melted from his face as he responded. He did have such fine teeth! And those lips! The top was still just a little fuller than the bottom in a way that tantalised her. If she had sense, she would be using his humour for her own gain, but instead, Tison found she could only stare happily, thinking about how lucky she was that he not only wanted her, but wanted to pleasure her.

The way he was looking at her may well ignite her all over again.

"What?" she asked.

His eyelids drooped lazily, and the smile across his delicious lips was slightly crooked. He rubbed his hands against her back, pulling her closer still.

"Nothing." And there was teasing there. "Not you!"

This time, the cackle was unstoppable and unmistakeable. She shook with mirth on his chest and poked him for his mimicry, jarring her finger against his hard, muscled chest. His hands caressed and stroked.

"I like to see you laugh," he told her. "I don't make people laugh often."

"Of course not." She tilted her head at him, holding him captive with her body as his hands touched her thick, black hair, dreading the moment he wanted to move.

The smell of spiced lamb and wood smoke was starting to merge with the succouring scent of sex and him. Her stomach would start rumbling soon. She should light more lamps, too. She did not. She stayed draped against him, warm and content, reliving the passion they had shared.

He was gentle, but there was something about his touch that made her demand what he did not. And she wanted to demand more. She collected herself, remembering that she had been speaking, and blinked, trying to break the growing sandstorm of desire beneath her stomach.

"You live with Serious Man," she clarified. "Does he know how to laugh?"

"I meant it," his voice chided, but his gently stroking hand did not.

"Ah, so!" She rolled onto her back beside him. "Tison can be nice! How was your day, Important Man?"

She had wanted to put a little bit of distance between him and the lustful wanting of her body, but she instantly missed the closeness of lying over him.

"Too long," he rumbled. She should feel proud of that deep, hoarse grown. Instead, she felt giddy, girlish. "How was yours?"

Too long, she echoed, silently. Then, unwelcome, the face of the brightly dressed wasp who had offered for her loyalty sidled into her head. She flinched, a shudder shooting from her neck to her ankles. Blinking in the warm evening gloom, she banished him. She would not speak of such a thing in Sabbah's bed.

"I got the ledgers I wanted." Her head slipped ahead of her tongue, ready to explain the system she planned to use so he could stay apprised of household goings on without being held down by every detail. "I got a wonderful bargain once I moved my 'the Muhtasib's housekeeper' piece into play."

Her voice was all performance, because she wanted him to chuckle. As she walked her fingers over his stomach, she took a breath, ready to launch into her plans, but halted as he put a heavy hand over hers and shifted away, rising up on his elbow.

"You used my position?"

Her stomach twisted. Instantly, her comfort and joy dropped out through the floor, and cold raised bumps on her flesh. Gone. It was shocking how quickly she lost her confidence, lost the lazy, hazy heat and comfort. Something in his voice sliced through her warmth and sapped her strength. She focused her eyes on the white ceiling. Afraid to look into the face that had fixed all of her attention moments before, she felt his stare all the same. Discomfort swirled in her stomach and froze her legs.

"Tison?"

The question there stroked panic under her ribs, squashing her lungs. There was demand. Control. Insistence. Authority.

Power.

She could lie. The instinct was there. It would preserve her for a little while. She did not want to be in trouble. Trouble meant staring at a floor while other masters poked and prodded and asked questions about her skills while she had to remain mute and selfless. Trouble meant a cold shoulder and icy eyes.

"I only mentioned ... he would have known when he delivered them ..."

He moved, and Tison's feet were on the ground, her arms scrambling for balance, before she realised he was just sitting up to look at her. Suspicion of a different sort pulled his brows down, and she forced herself to stand proud, unashamed of her naked, recently ravished body, even if she was being pulled by guilt and embarrassment at her mistake. The joy and elation sank out of the soles of her feet, bleeding out of her and leaving her feeling weak. Words twitched across her mind.

He'll betray you. Sooner or later.

"Tison." He sounded like a judge, despite his naked body. "Did he lower his price afterwards? After you told him who you ... who I am?"

A trembling fear shook her knees, no matter how high her chin was, no matter how insouciant her mouth. What if he sold her on for this? She was not ready! And she could not lose him. Her traitorous heart trembled at even the thought of not seeing him again. Panic flooded her, and she barely knew what she was thinking or saying. Her breathing kept trying to jolt and catch.

"He ... he just passed on his best wishes."

All her pride, her plans, gone because sex did not protect a woman. A child gave status. Loyalty did not. Pleasure did not. All that was left was her attempts to be calm, to present a version of herself who was not struggling with her own lungs and knees.

"It was a bribe, Tison." He dropped his forehead to his hands and rubbed his scalp with impatient movements.

She swept her eyes over his body. His long, muscled legs; his strong, broad torso. She had no ghostly, caressing memories of the sweet, fiery touches he had given her. She had only the last strand of her belief in herself. He needed her. She could not let him banish her. Not just because it was her life, but it was his. She had not lied in the market. She had used the truth to get a good position, but he had needed her. He still did. If he spurned her for this, she would need to remain until her task was complete and his household ready.

No matter how much it hurt.

"Don't do it again." He edged forward on the bed, closer to her, and her heart shuddered. "You can't do that. What you do reflects on me."

He lifted his head, and his frown was thoughtful. Worse. His eyes pitied.

"I will send the money to him," she told him, the shivery fear replaced by a recoiling refusal to be condescended to, not by Sabbah who made her feel so wonderful. She wanted to curl into a ball and pretend the world did not exist. All too soon, she had gone from Tison to a tiny, pathetic creature who was little more than a pet. She had shamed him.

"Tison," his voice entreated, and he lifted a hand out to her.

Pity. Concern. She did not trust that. She did not know or like it in the eyes of a master, or even a man. Pity was felt by other women. Not a man who had bedded her and held her so sweetly. Was it a trick? Or had he merely realised he had to be nice for her to lie back down and let him take her?

"I will say I mistook the price."

She bowed her head and looked at her gown, the yellow catching her eye where she had left it. She took a step to it. She could sense a chasm swallowing her thoughts, her words, and her mistake. Either that of using his position to get the ledgers she wanted, or for waiting for him so her body could have the pleasure she craved.

Going from an ecstasy of pleasure to that self-satisfied joy had been unlike anything she had ever known. The pain, though, that was familiar. That, she knew. Part of her reached for a way to hide it, but she was so weary. If he could pity her, she could show that she was hurt.

He rose from the bed, her Important Man, wearing nothing but a crooked frown on his brow and a twisting grimace on the lips she now knew intimately.

"Tison, don't go." And it was a plea, an entreaty. He even raised his hand out to her. No command. No order. No blow. Her decision.

What man was he that he could insist but leave the weight of the decision on her? Her heart ached. Physically. Little slivers of pain in her shoulders and chest.

She had loved before. She had loved a master who had promised her freedom and affection and a whole, beautiful future. Then, tired of her, he'd found a new slave to screw and had sold Tison on when she begged for him to love her again. And then, when she had finally healed her heart, back he had come into her life.

She looked down at the fine yellow cloth in her hands. Had she picked it up? Had she moved? Was this happening? Please, please let it be a dream. Dyed with ochre, only a little creased, the finest thing she had ever owned. The symbol of all she could be now. So she could not love Sabbah, even if he sighed miserably as his hand dropped. This was a boon, really. She had seen how easy it was to be comfortably, domestically happy, and how easily that contentment would be ripped away. She had been ready to give over her heart, and she was a fool for it. Work and sex would suffice.

"Tison, please. I should not have reacted so strongly."

"Yes." She drew on her dress, pulling it over her head, tugging the cleverly sewn garment until it fell flatteringly over her thin body. "You should have. I was wrong. Thank you, for not ... for teaching me ... I will not make the same ... mistake. Are you finished with me?"

She forced her eyes to his face to see the jolt of hurt and confusion that tightened around his eyes. She deserved the answering tightness in her chest and stomach. This was her fault.

"I don't think I could ever be." Sabbah's quiet words settled on her. "But if you wish to go, go! I will not make you stay."

His voice was sad, and she could have gone to him and settled on his chest. Could have wept, told him about her past and her fears and doubts. How much she wanted him to fall for her, need her. How much she wanted to love him, with his dedication to the city, and care for his people; his tender, tentative love-making and his ridiculously handsome face.

But she could not have heartbreak again. She could not be reduced to weeping and begging and on the brink of madness because of her aching heart. Tison would not be broken again.

Chapter Ten

An evening for firsts, then!

Sabbah sat heavily on his bed, shock rooting him in his room for the present. The heady scent of sex still permeated his senses. Her warmth was still imprinted on his skin, blissfully and tantalisingly comforting. Her words, though, were salt in a wound in his conscience.

He had bedded a woman under his protection. One clearly so hurt by masters in her past that she feared her own freedom. And then, he had rebuked her as a servant, a slave, when she was soft and tender and bare beside him. He should be thinking of making amends.

But all he was thinking about was how to get her into his arms again. It made him the worst kind of scum, but he would do anything to atone enough to get her back beside him. Even though it was not the right thing to do, it was all he wanted. He was no virgin, but he had not paid for pleasure since he had been awarded his position as Muhtasib. Two years should not have dulled his memory, but he was sure sex had never been that good. That all-consuming! He could never have given that up.

He could not give *her* up. How had it happened? How had it gone so quickly from tenderness to her fleeing from him?

Shock had numbed his limbs, and he turned his mind over and over the collapse of comfortable affection to her walking out, like a scholar reinterpreting the writings of the Prophet, peace be upon him. Had he overreacted, or had she?

Rising clumsily, he moved to wash, reluctantly wiping her from his skin with cool water from the ewer and basin in his room. It was what he had to do. He longed not to, to keep her there as long as possible, since she had walked away.

He dressed just as numbly, a dust cloud of irritation swirling up in his stomach. He would not be angry that his slave had walked away from him, but surely, he could be angry that she had accepted a bribe. He could be angry that she had not accepted criticism. He had scarcely raised his voice!

But the reprimand ... or rather, the moment he had given it ...

He had reminded her that she was a slave while she was still in his bed. That was it. If they were husband and wife, a rebuke would be bad enough, but he had taken a slave to bed, and then when he was done ...

Guilt swamped him, weighting his stomach and brow. He considered himself a practical man, but the feeling her hurt eyes and brisk, blank manner had ripped up in him would not go away. He could wash her scent from his body, but not the sated pleasure of sex with her, or the pain of upsetting her bliss. Knowing that she had been happy, finally herself, and he had pinched that contentment away.

Had she been as shuttered, as stiff with control, when that written hand had put her worth at three coppers?

Should he leave her to herself? Should he give her space to recover?

Moot questions, since he had to see her. He could feel the distance between them like a crevice beneath his feet, and he had to mend it. It was pushing pressure onto his lungs. He felt crushed.

Sabbah stood.

His reputation might have taken his lifetime to craft and protect, but Tison had brought life into his world in just a few days, and in those days, she had become more important than he was to himself. He was most certainly not done with her.

He strode from his quarters, hoping he had not lost too much in his shock and hesitation. Shame snapped at his heels. He had hurt Tison. That fact ruled his mind as he passed by his slaves in the courtyard and entered their domain. He knew which room she had taken, and his mind began to focus on words of apology, when he came face to face with an empty space.

Small. Little more than a cubby. She had dragged the pallet to the floor, with a blanket and sheets folded neatly. The rope and wooden frame of the bed was mostly bare. A damp towel thrown onto it showed that she, too, had washed while he stared blankly at a room that no longer contained her. Her yellow gown, tossed haphazardly onto the very edge, showed she had stripped angrily out of the dress she had worn with such pride. The colour that brought her golden eyes aglow seemed dull when not adorning her body, the cut that made his hands itch to touch her nothing more than woven thread.

He picked it up and folded it, before laying it reverently on the bed frame. He turned, and flinched as the pale form of Slavic Veta blocked his path. She looked suspicious, her blue eyes narrowed in judgement. He could not explain this to himself, let alone a woman who spoke no Arabic.

"Tison?" he asked, one hand flailing backwards in helpless explanation.

Veta bowed her head and pointed out towards the courtyard.

"Kanto," she told him, her accent twisting the name somewhat.

"Thank you." He passed her, and she squeezed herself against the walls to be out of his way.

The scent of smoke and food in the courtyard made his mouth water, but his stomach was still tight with worry and refused to let pangs of anything but guilt be felt. The courtyard Tison and her people—his people—had laboured over was greener now. Flowers and fruit and curtains across thresholds gave colour beyond the pale stone. It was her. All of it. She had changed his life as surely as she had this cool, now welcoming space. He was wrong, so very wrong, to question her intentions.

Striding to Kanto's door, he knocked on the door jamb as he entered, lifting the heavy, woven cloth that Tison had not yet replaced with something newer. With his next step, he walked into Kanto's bare back. His loyal porter and friend turned, revealing a chest that Sabbah had never even considered before. When it had just been the two of them in this household, his friend's skin could have been exposed, and he would not have blinked.

But this time, a cold, clammy sensation went all over him, like ants in his blood. Because Tison was in the room, Kanto tunic-less in front of her.

She's mine.

"What?" He caught his breath. As if he had to ask. She was not naked. But the gown she wore was just a half dress. Her legs were exposed below the knee. As much as he wanted there to be another explanation, none existed.

She had gone from his chambers to that of one of his only friends. Ugly vengeance for a slight he had needed to apologise for, wanted to wipe clean.

This time, it was Sabbah who turned on weak knees to leave. Shock still muted his mind. Blood rushed by his ears.

Warm, delicate fingers touched his shoulder.

"Sabbah?" Her voice was soft, contained, and so unlike her. "I can go. You came to see Serious Kanto?"

"Ah!" There was anger! There was the blazing disappointment that she had revealed herself. "Because your purpose in coming is done? Now I have seen you, there is no need to continue!"

He shrugged off her hand. His own tongue felt sharp and bitter behind his lips. Tison slowly, painfully slowly, backed away from him. Towards Kanto, who was frowning him down with grim lips and heavy brows.

"Did you—" she started, and she picked her words from her throat with obvious care. He cut across her.

"Do not try to lie to me." He could not bear the sense of betrayal keening inside him. "I came to apologise. I thought the bribe was a mistake on your part."

"It was!" Her voice was a cry, desperate, pleading, and confused. "Sabbah!"

"Ibn Abdella." Kanto's voice followed hers quickly in harshly spoken defence. His porter's eyes warned, even demanded silence.

"But you—" Sabbah tore his own eyes to Tison's hurt face. Her nostrils were wide, her mouth pinched, her brows low over her golden eyes. "You just manipulate by nature, don't you? Into your master's bed and then into another to match a slight?"

He was shouting. He did not notice until his voice cracked with the force of it.

How could she betray him like this? How could she pull Kanto into her game? Sabbah breathed hard, waiting for her next argument or play for control.

The silence began to press. Her eyes held his. And the anger in his heart removed its mask. Jealousy. Not righteous fury that she had attempted to sow discord. No, it was just jealousy that she had intended to touch another man when she was his. And it hurt that she could go to another room after they had shared something that had made his stars brighter. Still, she did not speak. Her face relaxed from anger into a sorrow that narrowed her eyes and contorted her face.

His heart jolted with pain as he realised with sick horror that he was wrong.

No. No. *No!* This was not the man he was. He was better than this. What had he done?

She parted her lips, took a pair of shuddering gasps, and then she bowed her head.

"Excuse me, Master."

Invisible ice poured down his spine, wet and chilling. She moved past him. And this time, he had no right to try and stop her. In truth—

Kanto's fist connected with his jaw, knocking him sideways into the wall as Tison left the room. Sabbah staggered and then found a small jar put into his hand.

"She was going to help my back." His old friend stood rigid with fury, the whites of his eyes stark against his dark skin. "She said she did not want to be alone. Your doing, Ibn Abdella?"

Sabbah drove the heel of his hand against his forehead.

"You don't trust her, fine. You only known her a few days. But me?" Kanto folded his arms. "You don't trust I wouldn't bed your woman?"

She was not his now. He had irrevocably spurned the only woman who had ever made him feel more a man than a civil servant. More Sabbah than Ibn Abdella.

"She—"

"Shut your mouth," Kanto ordered. "You don't know how you look at her? Hungry. Starving."

It was a long, long time since Kanto's grasp of Arabic had so much as faltered.

"She asks about you." Sabbah's friend sneered at him. "You stare at her. She goes to your room, and you don't come to eat. You think I don't know what's happening? And then you accuse her like that?"

Sabbah read the list of oils on the jar's label, Kanto's words crashing over him.

"She ... I've never ..." He tried to breathe deeply, evenly. Crawling horror covered his skin. He felt suffocated by his own despicable actions and words. "Why did I do that? I feel … mad …"

"You've no right to beg forgiveness, but you don't and I'll beat you down, bad back or no!" Kanto snatched the jar from Sabbah's hands. "Go. Go now. Ass!"

Sabbah once again strode across the courtyard, and this time, he knew every eye was on him. Veta and another of the women scrambled in front of him as he entered the slave quarters.

"No pass!" Veta ordered. She was shaking, but adamant.

"Please, Master," the other girl begged. "Don't hurt Tison!"

As Muhtasib, he knew how brave they must be to defend a fellow slave against a master. They did not know him. At the moment, he barely knew himself. So he hesitated for their sake, even though for his own, he had to see Tison. These women deserved to know their master would not force his way into their chambers.

"Please," he called out, staring imploringly between their heads. "Tison?"

Nosy silence surrounded him. Eyes watched his back, bearing down on him. Then, she slid from her tiny room.

"Tison," he breathed, relief and guilt sweet and sour on his tongue. She had come to see him, though he did not deserve it. Tears were on her cheeks, and they twisted her voice, drying and cracking it. Her glowing eyes were reddening. All of it combined to twist and scratch at his heart.

"I will speak of my Mukharajah tomorrow, al Muhtasib."

"Tison." Her name was a chant, a word of power spoken by unworthy lips. "I am sorry. I was wrong."

"You were right." Her expression was numbed, the sweet laughter and cunning teasing gone. "I need my freedom."

Freedom. Not from ownership itself, but from the treachery of masters; she needed freedom from men like him.

"I am not him, Tison." He had all but forgotten the audience they had. He needed this put right, but the truth was that he had proven himself as low as any man he had ever judged.

"No." She lowered her eyes, staring owlishly at the ground. "He made my value three coppers. You ..."

Sabbah felt sick.

"You make me worthless."

The world fell silent, waiting for him to say something to make it right. But he was silent, too, staring at a face beautiful even in sorrow. Her eyes tightened, her lips rising in the faintest grimace.

"I thought you were different." She cracked his heart. "I should not have tried for more. I should have been satisfied."

He reeled inside while his body set in stone, enduring the pain of seeing her hurt. He wanted to tell her he was different, was better, but he was now sure it would not be the truth. In all honesty, now, his anger iced, he did not recognise himself in the furious accuser of moments before. What was the more she had been trying for? He would never know now.

"I do not know why I—"

She sighed, her shoulders drooping a little further.

"Tison." He felt himself failing, but he had to turn this around.

"Goodnight, Master." She tucked one bare foot behind the other, and bowed.

"Tison." Her name was the only word he had left.

It was not enough to stop her backing away, turning, and going back to her tiny room when she should still be in his. So much wrong, and entirely his fault.

Sabbah stared at the linen curtain that fell closed behind her. And then, the two women who had tried to stop him stepped once more in front of him. Nervously militant, they faced him down, silent but determined.

Only then did it finally strike how completely he had humiliated himself. Still, all he wanted to do was sit outside her chamber like a faithful dog. No. What he wanted was to be back in his chamber, having stopped her leaving, holding her close, and listening to her breathe until they slept. It had gone wrong, and he was to blame. First, he had overreacted to a mistake, and then in jealousy, he had accused her of manipulation and worse. He was not a man he recognised. He was the worst of them. What kind of man acted like that?

He turned and walked away, because he did not have the right to stay.

TISON ROSE A LITTLE before dawn, so she could watch the simmering grains while Hudayda and his assistants prayed towards Mecca. As she sat and stared unhappily and wearily into the deep cauldron, watching the foamy bubbles rise, she wondered if it would take her eight years to recover from this man, too. She glanced up as Hudayda returned and waved her away from his domain.

She did not know if he looked conscious of the night's drama. She could not lift her eyes to his face. He sounded concerned but respectful as he spoke of a few spices he had not yet acquired and where she might get them, giving her detailed directions of the city that had been his home all of his life.

Here was not her home.

Tison had one memory of a home before she was owned. Not of the house where she had been born, but of a church in a cave, hewn out of rock, painted and decorated and full of singing people who smiled at a child who tried to sing as deep as the men and as high as the women in turn. That little girl would worry over the sad woman standing in a place she had changed with no idea of how to stop it changing her.

Looking about the courtyard at the green plants and the coloured pots, the running fountain and the bright colours of sheets drying and wall hangings, she searched for the Queen-in-her-kingdom feeling she had known the day before, when she had waited for her man to come to her and touch her body.

Conversation was awkward and quiet, and she made promises to take the other women to the baths that afternoon with no enthusiasm or anticipation, even though the bathhouse had been her domain in Tunis, even though she had always thought she would never tire of hot water and sweet smells. The pressure of worry squeezed her, making her want to be small and unnoticed. It was all too close to a day when she had arrived at the baths from the slave quarters, ready for a hard but rewarding day of work and seen eyes turn to her.

And then him. Cool, despite the steamy warmth, tidy and unruffled and smiling over his immaculate, waxed beard. The man she had loved. The man who had cast her aside and had come to her new place to have her thrown from a position she was good at, and ultimately from Tunis, the city that had been her home for almost a decade.

Perhaps she had forgotten some of the shame of it, the pain, but it felt even worse than the day she had risen and the household she lived in had been uncomfortable and awkward and ignored her worried enquiries until someone had finally taken pity on a young, happy woman and told her she had been replaced and was to be sold on again.

She had known he was wicked. She had known she was seduced, that he was not to be trusted by any woman, but she had thought she had changed him. That love was enough. Only afterwards had she learned what a common story that was, how foolish she had been.

But Sabbah was worse, because she had seduced him; she had wanted him and not been pursued. So she had no cause to think he loved any more than the man she had adored with the abandon of youth. How could he trust her not to betray him? He had only known her a week. Less. She had dreamed the affection in his eyes because she wanted it to be there.

"Until midday, then," she said blankly into the itchy silence, rising, smoothing her yellow dress, checking her hair was wrapped and up in its simple scarf. She was still his housekeeper. Even if he did not trust her enough to be his lover or his mistress, he would not take her position from her. She just could not face seeing him when he came out from his morning prayers.

All the way into town, she felt exhausted. The colours did not entrance; the smells did not tempt. She had business and amends to make. At least then, she could work towards him respecting her again. Sabbah. With his smiling eyes and his unreachable heart and his beautiful face. And his strong chest and broad shoulders. And hands that made her feel needed and cherished. And eyes that made her feel like an earthly goddess and not a good Christian girl or a useless, discarded slave. She had been angry for a moment last night, but strength had sapped from her.

His good opinion meant too much to her for such a short time. She should not care. If only she had learned to hate masters as other slaves did. She had been so sure that he was a good, dependable man.

And he is, she told herself. *He will be a wonderful husband someday.*

The thought drove her, for all her determination and tightly held jaw, to the side of the alley where she was crossing through to the book seller's shop. She leaned against a wall, head bowed, chest heaving with harsh, tear-calling breaths. Her face contorted with the onset of the tears she thought she had already drained herself of, but she was saved from weeping in the street.

Saved by pain cracking across the back of her head, the ground rushing to meet her, and white unconsciousness bleaching the world into nothingness.

HIS BELOVED CITY WAS dry and oddly bare. Sabbah could not feel the chatter around him, or even smell the intoxicating scents of the spices or the stench of the tanneries. He felt battered, and he knew it showed. He knew he saw people and spoke with them. He spent an hour with the Sayrafi being no help at all while his old friend discussed with people whose houses had been broken into over the past weeks, looking for links between them and the purses of false coins.

"Muhtasib?" His agent's voice was puzzled, and slightly offended.

Sabbah blinked. He had gone inside his own head again.

"Forgive me." He rubbed his thumbs into his eye sockets, hiding behind dancing silver light. "You were saying."

"There's a woman causing trouble at the north edge of al Djemma. She's laid her wares all over the floor, and when we tried to clear them, she ... bit Ibn Yasher. Twice."

Sabbah nodded, waved a hand, and fell into step beside his agent. This was what he was. A man who dealt with problems as they arose. Order and calm. Not a man who savaged a woman's esteem and then humiliated her in front of the staff she commanded. He despised those sorts of men. He quietly reminded them of what was right, with the inference that the Muhtasib would not allow such behaviour.

He should be flogged.

He would deserve it. It would achieve little, but it would make him feel a hell of a lot better to receive some sort of punishment for what he had done to Tison.

The crowd grew thicker, and the agent raised his voice.

"Make way for the Muhtasib!"

Shame licked across his skin, clammy and vile, and he wondered how they did not all turn on him then. He felt mad. He felt as though every face around him knew what he had done.

Instead, they parted for him, and let him through to where Ibn Yasher met him with a damp cloth pressed to his arm. On the floor was Ibn Yusuf, one of the youngest of his agents, and sitting on him was an Arab woman, modestly dressed apart from the veil which hung beneath her chin.

Sabbah took a long, deep breath and tried to suppress the hate he felt for himself. He would deal with this, and then, he would find Tison and make amends. Somehow. He could not continue as Muhtasib this distracted. So he made calming eye contact with Ibn Yusuf and then stepped forward.

"Salaam Aleikum, Madame."

Chapter Eleven

Tison woke the second time with the overpowering stench of tanneries filling her nose and throat and pain blistering the back of her head. Consciousness came alive with crushing panic as she simultaneously realised that her arms were bound, not asleep, and that she had been taken captive.

With the second blink, the smell hit her harder. Acrid. Filling the air. It made her gag weakly, and she struggled to free her hands so she could cover her mouth. The binds cut and pulled, but did not break or ease.

Pain. Her head. Sharp at the back. Aching at the front.

Slaves were easily stolen and resold. She was new to the city. She was pretty. A brothel was most likely. Men went to mines, women to dank, caging bedchambers. Usually outside the city walls to avoid prosecution by the religious or lawful, and thus out of reach of Sabbah or Kanto.

She started to shake.

Where most souls might cry out desperately for their mother, where she had always cried to God and his Saints, Tison felt her heart keen for a man who had turned on her in jealousy and control, a man she barely knew. She wanted Sabbah. She wanted his arms to close around her as he made all right and rescued her.

She pulled against her bound arms. Behind the pain and the stink lay an unholy, animal terror trying to take over. Her eyes adjusting to the light took in close walls with no windows and a dirty, dusty floor. She had to think, like a person, not let the beast backed into a corner take over.

How did I get here?

The ache on her head told her she had been knocked down. She could not remember anyone following her. She had not seen the brightly coloured wasp. But then, she had been walking with her head down and misery clouding her vision.

Crawling on sore knees to the side of the doorway, she castigated herself. *You were too busy wallowing. This is where love brings you, Tison, remember? To pain and dirt. Every time. No matter how different the man, you're still you.*

Her heart rivalling the pain in her head, she twisted her wrists until her fingers could just intertwine, and she prayed. Because Sabbah would not hear her, but someone in Heaven might. She prayed to God and his Mother, and then to Abba Moses, who had been a robber before he was a Saint, hoping his intercession might stop the men who had taken her from too much violence.

And she prayed that Sabbah might find her, and if not, that he would not blame himself for this somehow.

She would not let the fear take her mind, not when she was travelling with no worth across mountains, lashed by wind and dust, and not when she was put in a stinking hole. Listening carefully, she took her breathing from panicked harshness to an even susurrus with occasional gasps as the terror threatened to overcome her once more. She might be small, but she was fierce.

Fierce Tison.

For the first time in her life, she realised, head rising despite a new, gathering pain in her shoulders, she had an ally. An Important Man. She was sure that despite their quarrel, even if he despised her, he would come for her. He would find her. She could promise rewards to customers who bought her body for a time. Sabbah would save her, despite his anger, his ... his ...

Jealousy.

She paused in her tumbling thoughts. For the first time since he had turned cold and disapproving on her, she let herself remember the sex. Remember the look of wonder in his eyes as it changed to daring hunger. The way he had met her gaze as he kissed her breasts and licked with heavenly wickedness at her nipples.

Sex had never been like that. It was more than coupling. More than pleasure. It had been a sharing, challenging thing. It had been solemn and fun and blissful. So different.

Then she had stormed off and gone back to her duties. And one of those duties had been touching another man. As stupid and selfish as she could possibly have been. But despite all this, she knew he would help her. He was a good man; a far better man than a woman like her deserved.

Thinking was not helping anymore, but she could not stop. Her eyes flickered around her, seeing things the gloom had obscured. Dust. Dirt. A large sack thrown to one side. Marks on a wall where someone else had counted hours or days in careful little marks. Anything to focus on, anything to look at, rather than let the word 'love' materialise in her head. She had promised herself she would not be fooled again, would not make excuses for a man's whims and tempers. She was in charge of her life, her heart.

She had chosen him because he had seemed so controlled, so safe, so much in need. She had wanted him to love her. She would not, could not, dare not love him.

Except she thought she might, or that she would. How else could she explain why even though he had failed to trust her after she had given herself to him, she was trying to excuse him, and missing him, and wishing he would walk through the door? She was convincing herself that his actions were excusable, that her own were wrong. She had done that before. Only it was different than it had been before, with him. Tison drew a breath.

With Rafiq.

There was no pain that came with his name. No swamping, crushing despair rolled in its wake. *So I am free of one master at last.* Only to love another. Maybe she should stay in the stinking hole forever, marking days on a wall. At least then, she would be free of love, if not actually free.

Love was making excuses while she was hurt. Love was needing a person with all her being when he did not need her.

Footsteps.

Her head jerked. She listened with a frown to the uneven sound. They stopped as she realised there were stairs outside. That she was in a cellar. A bolt was drawn, and the door opened away from her. She waited, poised.

"Move where I can see you." It was the Wasp's voice. "Or I'll leave you in this stink with no water for another day."

Her jaw set, her lips pursing.

"Ever been beaten, Tison?" His voice was light and conversational. "Ever been starved or parched? Ever been denied sleep for days on end? We have more time than you, Tison. Move. Where I can see you."

Dread and bravery battled, and then she walked on her knees with as much cool dignity as she could find to a corner of the airless cellar and forced her chin up to stare at him. Hate and fear set her thoughts of love safely behind them, and she waited for his bargaining. She refused to look at the jug in his hand. He would not know how much his words had made her realise a craving thirst, or how much his threats had made her dread pain.

He closed the door with one foot and sat cross-legged on the floor, setting down the jug and two cups. He poured crystalline water into one of them. Then he beckoned. As she edged into his reach, he rose on his knees and pushed her head down. Panic swelled, then she felt the release of her muscles as he untied her bonds with one swift tug at the rope. She grunted and slowly moved her arms, massaging blood along them as soon as she could.

"You will never shift your loyalty," he remarked, removing an incense burner, a small brick of charcoal, and beginning to light it.

"I will not."

"You see," he continued, hands jerking deftly to coax sparks. "This Muhtasib is somewhat incorruptible."

She thought of the ledgers. Of a man consumed with passion one moment, coldly immovable the next.

"When you see him again ..." He edged her cup closer to her and then turned the jug's handle towards her pointedly.

She drank, draining the almost sweet water at once, before filling the other cup for him. She had heard of Berbers before, even seen a few of them at the bathhouse in Tunis. Was that his complexion? Were those Berber features?

"I want you to tell him that we took you. That we could take anyone. Tell him to relax a little. Take a few days at home now and then. Turn away from a few places." He downed his water. "Ah, the incense does help. Since you did not attack, I will leave it here. It may make you a trifle dizzy if you inhale it too deeply, but far better than the stench, eh?"

She watched his face curiously. She wanted more water, but she did not want to act desperately. She was too hopeful that if all went well, they would let her go back to Sabbah. To his household, at least. The Wasp stood smoothly.

"Salaam, Tison." He bowed and then left her.

The door had barely closed before she was gulping the water straight from the jug. Garnished with mint and other leaves she did not recognise, it was fragrant and pure and cool enough to provide relief in the tiny box of a room. She was grateful, too, for the glistening black incense that banished the smells of the tannery with a sweet, heady musk. She had hope. She just had to wait, and they would let her go home.

Time passed in an uneven flow. She had finished the water, her belly full but her tongue still craving before she noticed she could not feel her nose. She poked it with a finger. It was completely numb. She giggled and lay down in the dirt, imagining Sabbah beside her all of a sudden. Kissing her. Touching her. Here she was, captured, used to blackmail him, and all she could think of was the way his weight had come over her.

She kissed him, and he brushed her hair back from her face, mouth eager and hands tender. And she still giggled. She almost questioned why they were making love on a giant rose. And why she was lying so still and not touching him in return. And why she was finding it all so hysterically funny.

SABBAH FOUND HIS HOME imposing, the pale stone walls intimidating. It was more than the lack of the music he had become used to—it was the weight of his own heart. As he had throughout the day, he ground his teeth hard against twisting pain. If he were older, he might have gone to a physician, believed that his heart was giving out. Instead, he had to face the truth. Love hurt.

Love.

He had loved his parents; he loved his brother. This, though, this aching, decaying hurt in his chest, was unlike anything he had ever felt. Apparently, it took her hating him for him to realise she'd had him from the moment she'd sauntered to the front of the slave pens. Sabbah looked down at the ground he was rooted to and planned his apology. It would have to be public, as he had embarrassed her. First, though, he had to find and apologise to Kanto. The man was his friend.

All in all, he had had a day of well-deserved misery and shame so great, he had felt like a spanked hound, tail truly between his legs.

Finally, he forced himself through the gate to his own home. Like birds sighting a hawk, the people gathered in the courtyard scattered in a sucking silence. Even the fire pit was abandoned. Only Kanto slowly turned to face him.

"I was a fool last night," Sabbah began.

"A total donkey's arse." Kanto hobbled towards him, and the Muhtasib frowned at the pain in his friend's face. "Glad you are back early. Tison's gone."

A hole opened up in his chest where his aching heart had been, and his mouth dried. Denial stopped his reeling, and he straightened from an instinctive slump he had not even noticed in the first slap of shock.

"She isn't back, you mean?"

Apology was forgotten. He was suddenly afraid, very afraid, that he might not see her again. If she had fled, he had no right to follow her. He had legal rights, but he would never force her to stay. It would kill him to do that.

He needed her to stay free, and willingly. He needed her to give him her forgiveness even if he had not earned it.

"She told the other women they would go to the bathhouse today." Kanto moved to the side of his building by the gate and leaned heavily against the wall. "And I could not find her."

The limp. His friend had been into town despite his pain.

"I saw you from a distance, as you entered the Qasbah." Kanto rubbed a hand against his forehead and then gestured helplessly. "I was not fast enough to catch you. I looked, Ibn Abdella. I asked every merchant she might have gone to. She intended to visit the bookseller. Make amends. She told me last night before …"

Sabbah burned under his friend's reproach.

"It's early …" He looked back the way he had come, back to a city glowing faintly from lantern and torch-lit funduqs and households.

"She did not meet with the bookseller, Sabbah!" Kanto's patience and voice cracked together. "She does not know this city. She knows certain streets, certain routes. The bathhouse would have been allowing women from noon. She would have come back. I started looking two hours later, and now, we are on the cusp of evening prayers and she has not returned."

She was gone.

He had driven her away with his pride and his jealousy. He had never been in love with a woman in his life. The marriage he would have had had been cleanly arranged with her father. Had the Qadi not rejected his suit, believed his mixed blood would prevent him from achieving enough to be worthy, he would have had a nice, proper, political marriage.

Instead, he had earned his position as Muhtasib on merit alone in a furious, ambitious frenzy, and Aisha bint Wasim al Qadi had died losing a child, months after her marriage.

Eventually, he would have tried again. It was not heart-break, merely a deep guilt that kept him from entering the fray. No one would refuse the Muhtasib. Except less than a week ago, he had bought a woman of dreams he had not even had the imagination to have. A teasing, brave woman he had reduced to hiding from him. But it was almost night and the markets were closed, and he could not use his agents to track the woman he loved. If only today had not been a day to report the incidents of the past fortnight to the Vizier. He could have helped find her already; he could have apologised already.

If she had let him.

"She's left me," he grated, his throat dry and his heart sunk in quicksand.

"With no money." Kanto straightened and shook his head. "Listen and stop wallowing. No money. No other clothes. No papers. Sabbah! She has been taken!"

It was for a moment a hope to cling to, and for that moment, his heart lifted, but then horror split his head. Blood drained from his face, and he, too, had to lean heavily against the wall. Tison in a brothel, used by other men, that sweet body paid for, her soft gasps and moans turned to pain and fear. Her golden eyes losing their strength and humour. Even one night in such a place would hurt her, and he would do anything to spare her that. If only he knew what that anything might be.

"I'll get Khalid," he heard himself whisper, before the idea had even crystallised. "Those of my men I can ask a favour of man to man ..."

"You are Muhtasib!" Kanto stared at him, eyes wide and white, nostrils flaring with anger.

"I cannot use it." Sabbah's stomach twisted. He breathed heavily as he left the courtyard for the street, Kanto's swearing in the language of both their mothers following him as his parched tongue whispered, "Not even for her."

Khalid came to his atrium half-dressed, having been stripping his armour when Sabbah arrived, but the easy irritation of a brother vanished when he saw the expression that greeted him.

"What is it?" Khalid faced him, his eyes intense. "You look like you did when Mother died."

Sabbah gasped on an oddly hysterical laugh stuck in his chest.

"She'd kill me," he muttered, looking around the entranceway rather than meet his brother's eyes. It was true. Their mother would have slapped him silly for hurting a woman. "I need your help. Tison's missing. She's missing, and I need my big brother's help, because—"

"You have it," Khalid cut him off before the whole lot could come flooding out. "Come on, tell me while I arm myself. I'll send word to the barracks."

The interruption was enough to stop him recounting every thought in his head to his brother. Khalid armed quickly and efficiently. There was no time for Sabbah declaring his love for a skinny woman he barely knew, even if she was a golden-eyed temptress who held onto him like he was mighty and unshakeable. He could not admit that he would give up his position as Muhtasib, his grand house, his full coffers, if it meant Tison was safe.

"She left the household early." He tried to remember all that Kanto had said. "She promised she would be back to take the women to the baths all together. She did not return."

"Her state of mind?" Khalid belted on his scimitar, his back to his brother. "Would she have been distracted? Weary?"

"Both perhaps." Sabbah sat on a bench, so heavily, it jarred him to his shoulders. "We argued. I hurt her, Khalid."

Khalid sat beside him, sword knocking Sabbah's hip.

"Sabbah?" His brother sighed a little. "I know you would rather not talk. I know this ... this is not just about a slave, however competent. We need to get moving, but if you need to get something off your chest, then talk, or we're just wasting time."

"I ..." Sabbah felt like he was swallowing his own tongue. When had he last confided in his brother? When had he allowed himself to lean on Khalid or asked for support?

"You're in love with her," Khalid stated simply. "You looked pretty smitten when I came down the other day."

Sabbah spread his hands.

"We lay together." What a simple way to explain away the magic and soaring heights her affectionate body had taken him to, what exquisite pleasure her hands and kisses had given him even before he was inside her, feeling what he had never felt in his life. "And I ruined it all. I berated her for a housekeeping mistake. She was still in my arms, and I was more worried about being Muhtasib than about her, and I hurt her. So then I dressed and found her in Kanto's rooms. She was going to apply salve to his back. I ... I accused her ..."

His soldier brother swore in ways Sabbah's tongue could not have imagined and then hit him across the back of his head, knocking his head covering off into his shaking hands. An instant later, the pain of being buffeted by a cavalryman's heavy, plate-inlaid gloves shocked across his skull.

"This is what comes of controlling yourself and your life for twenty years." Khalid stood. "Come on, we'll search the funduqs, ask if she is simply laying low. We'll keep someone at yours to courier if she goes back. Send my men into the brothels. Let's go find the woman who rattled your cage."

His cage.

Apparently, his brother knew him better than he had known himself. He had thought himself content. Before Tison.

Chapter Twelve

They had brought her more oddly sweet water and more incense to blanket her in warm smoke. As the stranger lit more charcoal, she took his hand insistently. He flinched, and some of the ash from the last batch collapsed in a pretty little cloud.

"Why?" she asked him, the words slow and viscous on her tongue. "Am I not loveable?"

He looked embarrassed, not at all like a captor, and snatched his hand away. But then, he also had not commented on the vibrant green water running down the walls or the bright pink mice scurrying across the floor until it became a rosy, furry, shifting surface. She had tried to catch one before, but they were not there. Were they there? Was she?

Still, though, she would have liked an answer. She would have liked to know if it was her, if she was just not someone a man of stature could love. She would have liked to just be told. Maybe she should have fallen in love with Dour Kanto. Maybe she should have fallen in love with one of her colleagues at the bathhouse. Though then being sold on would have been yet another heartbreak.

She rolled onto her back, hoping the mice got out of the way in time.

How could she imagine loving anyone but Sabbah? So noble. Maybe that was why. Maybe she only loved men too high for her. Either good or bad, they were still masters. She was still a slave. She wiped tears from her face. They were hot on her cheeks but cold on her fingers.

Stupid girl. Not a woman, after all. Still a stupid girl. Stupid ledgers.

She blinked. The man had gone. But there was a woman there. Tison heard the clacking of beads and reached up to touch the swaying braids above her. They were too far away. She blinked.

"Tell me." The woman had part of her face covered, but her eyes were sharp in a world of fuzzy edges. The colours had faded from the room. All was dull and brown and indistinct. Except for those eyes. "Tell me about the Muhtasib."

Tison's face crumpled into a frown.

"No." She reached for the beads again, somehow not connecting the questions with their dangling, clacking temptation.

"Tison," the woman's voice warmed. "He has abandoned you. That is why you are here."

She remembered the argument. The rejection. His pained eyes when he realised just how low she was.

"No." She sighed and turned her head sideways, looking at the woman's bare, cracked feet. "He would not. I am here because of me."

The woman swore in a language Tison did not know, a growl coming into her throat.

"Slaves like you are why children are still sold into slavery!" she snapped. "What food does he eat? What women does he choose? You? Is that why you are loyal? You have been a slave too long to think masters ever love their slaves, Tison. What are his weaknesses, Tison? Tell me!"

Tison stretched her arms over her head and closed her eyes. The ground was dirt. It was soft on her skin. It clung. Where had the mice gone? Why was Sabbah not here with her? Why did he not love her?

"He is a good man," she replied. *That is his weakness. He is good and honourable and this city does not deserve him. So how could I?* She started to cry again, and missed him, and knew she was pathetic and did not care. Not now. Not when she was so worried about Sabbah.

The woman cursed her, told her everything she knew about being a fool. About being dirt to him. She merely lay there, arms stretched out and heart so battered and broken, she barely felt it beating.

The woman left, and Tison sank into the smoke. She had no idea how much time had passed, and her stomach's growling was oddly distant, oddly indistinct.

When they took her, hungry and wide-eyed, into a stinking street, no one seemed aware of the way the road was lurching around and around as though all of Marrakech was in a barrel, tumbling from the mountains to the sea.

She was pushed forward and fell. Her hands hurt, and when she looked at her palms, they pulsed with cracked blood. She stared at them and then struggled to rise. No one lifted her. Her captors were gone. The bright—overly bright, painfully bright—world was still spinning. The ground refused to stay beneath her feet, and she tumbled sideways. She shoved her fist against the rising ground and reached with her other for support. The street warped around her, as though Marrakech had been left out in the sun too long and was melting from the inside out.

As she fought to rise, the surroundings tipped once more sideways and the flagstones came up to meet her. She was drugged. She knew that, but it did not make walking any easier. Fear began to surface through the suffocating haze.

"Sabbah." Her voice was slow to her ears. It sounded desperate. She just wanted him to hear her somehow, to find her, to save her from the dirt and the gathering terror of her own lack of control and shifted reality. Just because she was not worthy of him did not mean she did not need him.

The first shout of disgust and abuse came the second time she struggled to rise.

"Go on with you, slattern! We don't need your like near honest citizens."

She managed to get herself mostly upright. Her ears felt blocked, her face numb, the hysterical laughter long gone. Bruises throbbed on her hands, her knees, her elbows. She felt like a young Egyptian horse, unsteady and likely to break a leg in a gundi hole.

"Help."

Still, her voice sounded odd and distant. She stared down at a pair of saffron-dyed yellow shoes in front of her. Then she raised them to the face of a man bristling with anger. His fury crackled from him. She could see it. Hairy waves of anger.

"Move on! We need no prostitutes here!"

He grabbed her arm, but she pulled back against him. They would not stone her, surely? Not with her Important

Man in charge. He would not allow women to be stoned to death in the street without trial. She was certain of that.

"Sabbah!" she pleaded. He sneered at her. A wave of nausea flooded her, and she swayed on the balls of her feet. "Important Man!"

Terror began to claw at her, and her eyes started to flash grey lightning across her vision. Water seemed to pour down her left cheek, a sudden torrent of unwelcome sensation.

"Al Muhtasib!" she shouted.

"Not on your life!" Her chief opponent started to pull her along a row of stalls, and others swarmed around her, shoving and pushing. They were walking her out of their district. To a gate. To gardens.

Out of Sabbah's jurisdiction.

Shaking her head so hard the world began to fall and spin again, harder than before, Tison tried to dig in her heels. Her bare feet slid on the flagstones, hurting and bruising.

"No! Muhtasib!"

"Relax," a female voice soothed through the angry mutterings. "We're not giving you up. We'll get you some shade, and you can sleep this off. The Muhtasib will never know."

"And we won't get fined because of some drug-hungry prostitute!" the cruel man added.

The terror that had been rising in her finally took over, wiping her mind of rationality. They were taking her away from Sabbah. The gateway ahead of her seemed to loom and close in on her at the same time, sucking her forwards to doom, dread. Danger. Trap.

Berserk with fear, she lurched sideways and swiped at a stall near the edge of that ominous gateway. She hooked an arm around the support for the awning, pulling herself to it with all her might. Shouts rang around her, someone yanking at her arm.

"No!" She curled her body, tucking her feet around the stall-owner's table. Angry yells pounded at her, and they pulled her bodily, and the awning came down.

Uproar.

Noise.

Tison sat on the floor and wrapped all of her limbs around the table leg, putting her head down and closing her eyes tightly. Hot linen swathed one of her shoulders. Splinters prickled her skin. Her ears felt swollen on the inside, and her world remained unsteady if she opened her eyes. But she would not be taken away.

"Fetch the Muhtasib!" yelled the stall-owner.

Relief flooded her, and she held tight to the support until her arms and head and neck ached. She heard the friendly woman pity her, and a few other stall-owners revile her. She listened while the world twisted on the other side of her eyelids. She resisted the urge to lie down on the dirty street and sleep.

Then she felt the atmosphere change.

She heard the press of voices all explaining at once. She felt his quiet, absolute authority settle the world back into order. The world still spun, but now, it had an axis.

She unwrapped her limbs and crawled from the table, setting her palms on packed earth and cobbles and doing her best to rise. Arms closed around her, and she looked up into Sabbah's eyes.

"Thank God!" she murmured.

Then the harsh, painful world fell away as he lifted her into his arms, and she found herself safe and enclosed. He was warm and strong. And he had her now.

SABBAH WALKED THROUGH the streets of his home city with an opiate-riddled slave in his arms. Khalid's man had already gone to spread word. She had been found. He left his agents taking reports and damage statements, feeling his integrity wash away with each step. His reputation. That certainty he had built from the day he decided he wanted to serve Marrakech both like and unlike his brother did.

But he would sooner cut his own throat in a mosque than have Tison flogged for public drunkenness. He would not question her and the others while she was so desperate, so very much in need of fresh clothes, water, shelter, and his arms. Holding her to his chest, deep relief relaxed his bones despite his exhaustion.

She had been found.

She was safe.

Her thin frame made him feel utterly certain. There was neither doubt nor hesitation. Seeing her small and clinging and half-covered in awning, his heart had keened for her. Only when he had her lifted against his chest had he returned to a sense of himself. The madness of losing her had receded at once, and he'd found the surety through his exhaustion that holding her fragile body gave him. It was his place to cherish her, that much he knew.

But beneath the instinctive relief, the flooding sensation of all being right, there lay a nagging, painfully rational fear of what would come. His position was what all of his life had been working towards, and he would have to resign for this. The Muhtasib sheltering a drunk woman from punishment? Not even pausing to question witnesses but taking her away! His career was done. That alone did not frighten him. What scared him deep in his bones was that he did not care. He knew it; he accepted it. It did not matter. She mattered.

Who was he?

He was not a man who would put a woman ahead of the position he had worked for all of his youth. He pulled her closer and felt her body stir as she swam up against her unconsciousness.

"You're too thin," he told her, resisting the urge to crush her against him, risk hurting her just to feel her pressed to his body. "Too light."

He would have her fed when they got back. He knew it was not her capture that had made her this bone-thin. It was a lifetime not just of slavery, but of the forced need to remain 'beautiful.' Owners would prize her looks, so would customers at the bathhouse where she worked, but they should have prided her skill with hands and the body's aching muscles. They should have realised how competent she was at setting people at ease and organising a household.

He should have honoured her for that. He should not have taken one thing that she had done and been so afraid of his own name that he focused solely on that and not on the way she had transformed house and household into a home. That stupid fight over the ledgers might well have destroyed her trust in him. Guilt ached his heart, forcing the simple satisfaction of having her safe back into the recesses of mind and heart.

She raised her head, and he looked into her eyes for a moment, damned be the chance of falling flat on his face. The gold was dimmed by the wide pupils, blown by opium this time, not desire.

A dank, disloyal thought shot through his head. Was that why she had been sold on? Addiction? Had it followed her through her next positions? His mind recoiled in guilt, and he looked ahead, even though he could have walked the route home with his eyes closed. He could not suspect her and still be willing to give all to keep her safe, could he? He had spent less than a day without her, and it had gnawed him apart. Had he trusted her, she would not have gone in the first place.

"They tried to keep me from you."

He glanced down briefly, and the faith and trust in her eyes flayed him while his mind clung to this evidence that she had been taken against her will. Hearing his brother call, he slowed his pace until Khalid came alongside him.

"Is she hurt?" his brother asked.

For the first time, Khalid's presence did not soothe or reassure him because it could not banish the fact that for a moment, he had doubted her. Nothing had changed. He still did not deserve her. And he had not asked her if she was injured. He had been so concerned about getting her into his arms and against his heart.

"I'm well enough." Tison shifted in his hold, curling against him. She was so light. So thin. So quiet. "If the world would only stop lurching about. And the sun is too bright ..."

Who were 'they'? What had they done to her? Did she mean the people in the market, or was she truly innocent? Please, any angel listening, let her be speaking of some captors who had forced this on her.

Was Kanto right? Had she been taken for the brothels? Had they hurt her? Would she tell him if she was injured in such a way? Had she just snuck away to find release in coiling smoke?

A lifetime of intellect, philosophy, study of law and practice of it in the Qasbah and the markets was swept away and left him raw and animal. He wanted to find anyone who had hurt her and break them. No justice or mercy, just violence. He would smash them against the pale stones of Marrakech until they smeared crimson over the walls. Or had she lain in some other man's arms, dizzy with smoke, until she decided to return?

A shudder ran through him.

"He has been worried," Khalid told her.

Sabbah was both relieved and disappointed when she did not reply. Tension had returned to him. Guilt and fear banished the last of the sweet, heavy surety he had felt once he'd had her in his arms. He had doubted her. The words kept repeating themselves over and over, the most damning evidence that could have been presented.

He was not any more worthy of her than of his position. He had failed both in one day. He had ruined their ... their friendship over a slight to his reputation, and then cast it aside himself the next day. All for nothing. It was all for nothing.

"Did you call off the search?" Sabbah asked, and he could hear the misery in his own voice.

"Of course." Khalid, in turn, sounded concerned.

"Can I—" His voice dried, and he swallowed hard. Weight pulled his brow and slowed his steps. "Can I take her to your house?"

He felt her fingers touch his chest. He did not look down. He did not deserve her. Her trust, her faith, or her sweet, too thin but perfect body—perfect because it was Tison inside it. If she was in his house, he would let her love him; he could not resist her. He had to give her a better chance than that. If he let her come home, he would never let her leave him.

He loved her, but he had still been a jealous mess of a man. He did not deserve her.

"I will go ahead and let Jessamine know."

Reproach underlined the continued concern in Khalid's words. A clipped, military tone of tacit rebuke. He strode on, and Sabbah followed north, skirting the main streets. He could not cope with noise now. He needed to hear Tison's breathing. He needed to store it up. He held her tightly even when his arms began to ache.

"Sabbah?"

Heat made his eyes itch.

"Rest," he asked, pleaded. He could not stay strong if she asked for him.

"So serious, Important Man." She had tears in her voice, crackling her breath. "You will leave Kanto with nothing to do if you are serious."

'I love you' hung on his tongue. He felt it in his heart and in his spine. It was his skin and blood. But she deserved. He did not. He had thought she had gone off in anger to abandon her duties; he had not been worried at first. He had not thought she had been drugged; he thought she had indulged.

The street branched, and instead of taking her home, he carried her on to his brother's household. She would be safe from his failed love there, safe from her own.

"I knew you would come." Her voice was stripped of all the teasing humour he had fallen for. "I'm sorry about the upset. They ... the people in the market ... they wanted to take me away to keep me out of trouble."

Apologising to him. He was dirt.

Even if she would not be his, she was worth the loss of his position. She was worth anything. Everything. Even if giving it up meant the slaves in his household would be released and have to find places in new households. Even if it meant living in a single room someday, he would do that with Tison. But would he be with her? Would she be able to forgive his temper, his failure to make amends, his not coming and finding her? Would she ever forget that he had doubted her? Would he? And did it matter if he was trying to be noble anyway?

As they entered the gates, Khalid led his wife down the garden path towards them. Sabbah's arms tightened around Tison as his brother held out his arms to relieve him of his burden. A sweet burden whose hands closed into his linen tunic, gripping tight. Suddenly, he could not give her over. His heart would not allow it. It was attached to her, and if she was removed, it would stop beating. He felt a surge of jealousy that his brother would hold her.

"Let me take her." Khalid's voice was reassuring now, calm, and oddly bland. The voice of a big brother. Shame licked him.

"Sabbah?" Her fingers clutched his shirt, and only then did he hear the tears she had been crying all this time in his arms. He heard then saw her fallen tears. Her voice was twisted with emotion, and he felt a small warm, wet patch against his shoulder as her sorrow finally soaked through his clothes. "Please, don't leave me."

Her voice, her pain, made his decision for her. He loved her. He had to be worthy and free of his constraints before he could hope to win her back. She would not be safe in his household until he was certain of the loyalty of every slave, and until he was no longer Muhtasib, a target to be brought down at the expense of the most precious woman in all the world. He did not deserve her, would never deserve her, but he could not live without her. He just had to make himself a better man first.

Lifting her, he put her into Khalid's arms. The tears she had endured alone broke, and strong, mocking Tison sobbed. As her slight weight left his arms, Sabbah's heart broke, and he turned and walked away with splinters of it jabbing real, physical pain into his chest. He heard her weeping all the way to the gate, and it echoed in him all the rest of the day.

What frightened him was that he might never be good enough to come back.

THROUGH DIZZINESS AND cracking pain that reverberated in her head, Tison wept. She had been cast aside before, but never by a good man, and she was too tired, too drug-addled to try and control her pain. Or her grief.

His brother carried her into the house, past tear-blurred walls, deeper inside, farther from Sabbah's bowed head and retreating back. She cried through her throbbing head and the moment she was laid on another soft, raised bed. She cried herself sick and weak and aching. Every time she tried to stop, the sheer inescapable truth that he had left her came back, cold and crystalline, and she wept all the more.

She had known he would find her.

She had never imagined he would walk away from her when she was too weak to stand and chase him.

She drank water when it was offered. She felt someone near her, comforting, but they were not Sabbah, and that truth was killing her. She no longer knew who Tison was, except a mess of confusion who hurt, who bled from her heart and soul.

The room refocused. Through misery, nausea, and an agonising skull, she struggled through the effects of the narcotics that had smothered her senses. Jessamine, Khalid's beautiful wife, brought her food with her own hands. Drinking water and eating salted bread to aid her body's recovery, Tison felt herself form a crust of rational, sensible control. Anything could break it and send her into the magma beneath, but slowly, she stopped the deep, keening moans. Her heart, though, never stopped hurting, even as she sank into a deep, true sleep as the sun rose.

When she woke again, she was hungry, sorrowful, but finally had regained some sense of herself as more than emotion and pain. She would have risen if she had not heard Khalid and Jessamine on the other side of the room. They spoke more in murmurs than whispers.

"When she is not sleeping, she weeps. Were he not your brother, Khalid, I would be sending him boxes of scorpions!"

"He did not seem to have slept when I saw him." Khalid's voice was heavy with worry. "He ... is affected. Altered. But he will not answer me. He would not speak of it. All he would say was that Mother would be ashamed."

Tison's cracked heart clenched. Was he that ashamed of wanting her?

"Love is not always easy." Jessamine sighed. Tison heard the whisper of cloth as the noblewoman moved. "But I do not understand how the man who came for your help in finding her is the same man who just ... left her here!"

"Neither do I." More rustling, and his words became more muffled as they held each other close. "If you went missing, I would never leave your side again."

Tison's weary eyes stung, but there were no tears there to shed. She sat up, throwing back the sweat-soaked sheet and rising. Unsteadily, she walked to the window, looking through the cedar wood screen to the garden below. Now she could see that the couple were behind a screen, but though they had not seen her, they had heard her. Awkward silence emanated from them as she watched the birds picking half grown grapes and dates from the trees beneath.

"I— er—" Khalid had raised his voice in poor theatrics, a jolly, humorous tone to his words. "I should speak to her, be sure she has not done anything unforgivable."

She had.

She had fallen in love with another Master.

IN THE ABSENCE OF THE Caliph who was far in the north in Andalus, the Qasbah was a hive of rebuilding work. Hammering and shouting workmen surrounded him as he walked past cedar and ebony screens, piled into the corridors while work continued in other rooms and up above in the vaulted ceilings.

Approaching the Vizier's office, he felt bile twist his empty stomach and willed it still with little success. A strong smell of glues and paints surrounded him, but the bright colours of the craftsman's palette barely registered to his eyes.

"Ibn Abdella al Muhtasib!" called the Vizier's doorman.

Sabbah looked down into the face of Yahya ibn Abi Hafs, the Caliph's trusted adviser and friend, and his heart was heavy. He was here.

"Muhtasib!" Ibn Abi Hafs waved his hands, his sleeves rolling back to reveal strong, often scarred forearms. The man had been a warrior for many years, and his strength was as clear as his intelligence.

"Vizier!" He bowed his head. "I am here to resign my position."

For as long as he could bear, he kept his head down, his eyes on the table between them. The silence pressed on them. Finally, Sabbah found his courage and lifted his eyes. The

Vizier stepped around the table and passed him, going back to the doorman, and said,

"I believe you had already left, to enjoy your afternoon off."

"Indeed I had, exalted Vizier," replied the servant.

The door closed, and a friendly hand patted Sabbah's shoulder before he had even heard Ibn Abi Hafs move.

"Come." The voice was gentle. "Sit awhile, Muhtasib."

Frustration bubbled against the heavy crust of exhausted misery, but Sabbah obeyed, sinking onto a plush couch at the edge of the room. He had not relaxed into Ibn Abi Hafs' hospitality since he had been accepted as Muhtasib. There was an odd moment as he felt himself looking back at the nervous man he had been, sitting in this spot years before with the walls barer and the exquisite wooden screen over the window nothing but a plain shutter. He had been determined, vindicated, and hopeful.

He took a breath, but the Vizier spoke quickly across him.

"Did you find her?" he asked, pouring cold, minty tea into cups for them both.

Sabbah stared, dazed. The Vizier knew about Tison.

"She was found." He remembered with vivid clarity the way she had shivered in his arms. "Intoxicated."

"Was she drugged?"

And Sabbah once more dropped his eyes down.

"If she imbibed of her free will, I must resign, because this is a scandal which must not hurt the justice of the city."

The word 'justice' made a cold, clammy hand touch his neck as he thought of the Qadi. The judge would revel in his downfall. He would loudly and publicly remind everyone he had decided Sabbah would amount to nothing, his mixed blood and lack of political jockeying a clear sign of failures to come.

He could almost feel the weight of her, hear her cry for the Muhtasib, and the whisper of his name as she realised he was there. The fingers at his tunic. The tears as he gave her over to his brother. She had needed him, and he could not stay with her, or he would never leave. At least now, he could make a clean break with the city and return to her as himself.

"And if she was forced?" the Vizier prompted him as he fell into bitter silence.

"Then she was drugged to get to me." Sabbah felt violence in his blood once more, the longing to tear and smash and break. Unfamiliar but undeniable. He pushed it down. "And I cannot let her be hurt because of me. She could have been flogged. I should have flogged her—it was my duty because she came to the market intoxicated, willingly or not. Where she is concerned, there is no duty. As such, I am unfit to continue in my position."

Swallowing hard, he forced his eyes up to meet the Vizier's kind, avuncular smile.

"I have a harem of fourteen women," the older man said. "And still, I can only dream of such a love, Muhtasib."

He sat back, lounging on the cushions and stretching his legs, his smiling eyes making Sabbah feel like an ornate puzzle box.

"I cannot relieve you of your position," he continued, shrugging a shoulder. "The Caliph will return before winter. You will have to ask him. The trouble is, Ibn Abdella, that this is a clear sign that you are doing good. The city needs you, and I find it hard to believe a woman worthy of you would ask you to surrender Marrakech."

Sabbah shifted in his seat, tension bringing a spasm of pain to his neck and shoulders.

"This is not about ..." Tison—her name conjured her.

Her scent, her eyes, the particular sound of her breathing. He had known her less than a fortnight, and he knew her breathing. He knew her skin. He knew what made her sweat and moan and buck.

He clenched his hands together, trying to control his restless energy, his need to pace. He was exhausted, but still, not moving was driving him mad. "This is not about my housekeeper. It is about me. Even if the case was clear, I could not punish her. My integrity as Muhtasib cannot be questioned. Not now, with the coin problem."

But if he gave up the city, it would be a sacrifice enough to lay before her that perhaps he could stop himself remembering that he had doubted her. That he had not feared when he should; he had not trusted when he should. The stillness was pressing in on him, but the Vizier simply sat at ease. Smiling.

"Go home," Ibn Abi Hafs told him. "Speak to your housekeeper. Gather information. If you still think the city must lose you altogether, you may tell the Caliph when he returns. In the meantime, keep her close and safe, to prevent her being, as you said, hurt in your name."

They both stood, Sabbah springing to his feet and the Vizier rising with poise and focus and a controlled strength that Sabbah could not have summoned for the world. His frustration ground his teeth as he took formal leave of the empathetic but unwavering Vizier. Frustration and dread.

Dread filled him with suffocating silence, crushing his head from all sides as he walked down the corridors. No thoughts intruded, no words of advice from the more rational part of him, or challenging suggestions or excuses from his wants and desires. The entire long walk home, he stayed alone in his head with the feeling of ominous emptiness. The hubbub of the streets could not make him feel at home. The familiar faces and flagstones did not welcome him.

Sabbah returned to his house, to the fronds of palms and ferns with which she had filled the courtyard and the smells of food from the cook she had employed. He beckoned Kanto, who was already rising from his seat by the firepit.

Turning into his quarters, face aching from his jaw to his shaved scalp, Sabbah led the way to his desk. He opened the lockbox beneath it. Tison's bill of sale was still on the top of his other recent acquisitions. The other people in his home, for whom he was responsible, who would lose their positions if he surrendered the highly paid position of Muhtasib.

"How is she today?" Kanto's dragging stride crossed the room, heavier than usual after long hours of worry and searching.

"I don't know." Sabbah took ink and began to write, wincing as his porter cursed explosively.

"You have not seen her?"

When Sabbah did not turn, he received a bruising blow to his shoulder.

"What ... what game is this?" Kanto's voice roared from his throat, rattling Sabbah's ears. "You are not this man!"

Sabbah wished he was not. He drew a hand over his face, pushing off his head-covering. His scalp was stubbled. He remembered only too well the caresses of her hands as she had shaved close and smoothly.

If he could not give up the city, he had to give up Tison. He wished he was strong enough to tell her why. To face her. But he could not see those tears again. It would break him. She would be in danger so long as she was seen to be the woman he loved. And it would be clear now.

Chapter Thirteen

Tison barely remembered how it had felt to be so disconnected from herself. The last traces of the drugs they had given her had slid from her system painfully, and she was thankful the memory of the sensations had gone, too.

Now, she sat in a beautiful courtyard in the middle of Khalid ibn Abdella's house, wishing her grief had disappeared, as well. It was cool; she had slid her feet from borrowed slippers to smooth them against the mosaics. The green filtered light, glowing through vines and the trees that rose above the building surrounding the little Eden, soothed the last of her headache away.

Sipping her sherbet, she breathed the fresh, clean air and tried not to listen to her heart break.

She was strong. She would not care that he had not come to see her. She would not panic about her uncertain future. She would enjoy this very pleasant present. Fingers curling around the cold cup, she struggled to keep her back straight and her hands steady. The yawning abyss of possibilities aside, she could not stop hurting.

She missed him.

She missed his voice and presence. She missed his warmth and sweetness. She needed someone to talk to, but that someone had to be him. Only he would do.

Pathetic!

Into the quiet came the sound of a male voice. The low rumble made her stomach feel empty and her heart brittle. Then, she heard a shuffling step, and her shoulders dipped, but a wry smile folded her lips. Setting down her cool, empty cup, she rose to meet Kanto as he walked through the door into the courtyard.

"Serious Man." She smiled as warmly as she could, then she caught herself, gave herself a mental shake. Her smile softened, and she made herself meet his scrutiny, because he was her friend.

His eyes and brow were creased with sympathy. Kanto, whose face was usually so bland and even, looked at her with visible concern. He stood silently while she swallowed down the cracks that would have marred her voice.

"Come and sit," she suggested. "Before you make me uncomfortable with this melodramatic display of emotion!"

She was, however, grateful for his silence as they sat on ornately carved wooden benches in the small but perfect garden. She stared at the tiles on the floor without seeing their pattern. Her smile was strained and felt dry and twisted.

"Are you recovered from your capture?"

She relaxed a little. At least they knew that. At least, that much truth was understood. Sabbah knew she had not gone willingly.

"A bruised skull." Words seemed too difficult. She barely remembered her mother tongue, let alone the Arabic of the masters, at present. Because she had realised that if they knew— If he knew— If Sabbah knew that she had been captured, there was no reason for him not to come and get her, unless he did not want her back. The tension returned.

"Struck from behind?" Kanto asked, leaning forward on the bench to ease that sore back of his.

"I think so." She had intended to tell Sabbah face to face, but the danger had to be known. "A man in different coloured clothes approached me the first morning I was with you. Before either of you rose, I went to get water. He asked me to spy on—" Her Important Man. Sabbah. Only if he had not come, did she still have the right to his name? "On al Muhtasib."

She forced her eyes to remain steadily on her friend's face, forced her voice calm and the words to flow.

"He found me again the day I ordered the ledgers. He told me he wanted me to tell him what the Muhtasib's weaknesses were. He must have found me again when I returned to ..." The ledgers and the money seemed so unimportant now.

Kanto's jaw shifted, but then his eyes snapped up over her head.

"Describe him."

Khalid's steps had been silent, and Tison barely dared turn. She could hear the intensity in his voice, and it reminded her of a harsh, clipped voice that had torn her heart apart twice. He sounded like a Master, like the sort of trouble that made a slave lie and twist to avoid the glare of danger.

"I—" she swallowed. Her eyes were on the floor again. Strength had turned elusive and slippery.

"Hey, Tison." Kanto's voice was quiet. "They let you go. They won't come after you again. But they might still try again with the others."

She held her chin up with an effort. She could not let something happen to him, or to her fellows.

"Swarthy, but not pure Arab. Berber, maybe, or mixed. Hard to tell. I've only just come to Marrakech." She found the words flowing viscous from her tongue. "He wore lots of different coloured clothes. Bright colours."

Khalid came into her field of vision. He stood beside Kanto, watching her, arms folded and mouth grim beneath his moustached, stiff lip.

"Where they kept you. What do you remember of it?"

The saccharin, musty smell of the smoke drifted through her senses like a phantom.

"It stank. They brought incense. I think that's how they drugged me. But it stank. Like a thousand funduq alleyways. Worse."

Khalid nodded, rubbing thumb and finger over his well-trimmed beard.

"The tanneries. Coloured cloth and clothes sold off cheap. And the smell there is truly unbelievable to outsiders."

A twitch of added hurt licked across the inside of her ribs. Knowing did not mean anything was different.

"You need to talk to your brother, Ibn Abdella," Kanto said, his voice respectful and face bland. But when Tison glanced at him, she could see the tension, the anger, behind his eyes. "He went to the Vizier. Tried to give up his post."

"What?" Khalid spun, his back to her, but before he could hide the big Ghanaian completely, Kanto's eyes met hers, and she felt her face fall into a frown.

As Kanto explained, dry and factual, Tison had to hope. But in that hope lay a dark, nasty hook of selfishness. She could not take Sabbah from Marrakech. Even if it was the right thing to do, she could not deprive the city of such a good man. Even if it would not destroy him to give up his life for her, it would destroy her to watch him make such a sacrifice.

"How can I help you stop them?" she asked, interrupting them with no hesitation.

Khalid turned, still silent on his feet. His eyes were narrowed, his mouth a considering moue between moustache and beard.

"Bait," he suggested. "Draw them out. I'll send you into the tanning quarter with some of my men following. Look shifty, nervous."

"No!" Kanto rose. "Too much danger."

"I cannot leave him open to attack." She took a breath, holding Kanto's frowning eyes. "I needed him, and he did not come. He needs me, and I will go. For him. To him. And I will find a way to protect him."

"Tison ..." There was warning in Kanto's voice. "He was going to give up being Muhtasib for you. He ... he cares, stupid girl."

"I know." She felt her heart, deflated and sore, thumping away in her chest. "But he does not ... dare. He could give the decision to the Vizier, but he won't make it himself. He ... he won't protect himself, Kanto. If I can ... Important Man should not love me. He should marry some noble woman. But she can't help. I can. So I am trying to be noble, and not cry about all this."

Khalid took a breath.

"Don't make me regret liking you, Tison." He came toward her, standing over her. "I don't know why he hasn't come, but he loves you. I am sure of it. And I'd do what I can to bring him to realise that. It's a brother's duty. I'm not suggesting you should give up, but I will need your help. You are the only person who can identify this man for me."

She looked back to the now familiar mosaics.

"I was trying to be noble."

"So is he." Khalid lifted his hands helplessly.

She blinked. Possibility and potential began to seep back into her future.

"I'm going home." She rose smoothly, and Khalid stepped back as Kanto mirrored her behind him. "I cannot abandon my post as housekeeper."

She could see no emotion on Kanto's face, so she must be doing something right. "Send for me when you have suitable men to accompany me, Ibn Abdella. And thank you for your hospitality. Forgive my manners in not staying for the full three days, or taking my leave of your wife."

"That is quite all right, Tison." He smiled and then bent, bowing to her. "But do not run too quickly out of my house. We may be able to make things easier yet!"

ONCE AGAIN, SABBAH walked home through a darkening city. His house was more comfortable than it had ever been, and still, he knew it would feel empty. Just as it would be every time he stepped over the threshold. As he neared the white walls of his residence, he heard singing, a sweet voice singing a beautiful song.

He stopped, knowing it would end if he, the master, appeared into gateway.

The voice came in a language he did not understand. Since it sounded Slavic, he assumed it was Veta. That was as far as rational thinking took him. Even not knowing the words could not save him from the way her poignant voice sent an aching pain into his chest. He did not so much hear it as feel it through his heart.

How could he spend the rest of his life like this?

Without Tison.

The song stopped when the last light in the sky faded to darkness, and as applause and chatter broke the silence, the stars took command of the night. Heart leaden in his chest, he walked the last few steps and stood on the threshold to his home.

"There you are!"

He shuddered, head to foot, thrown off balance despite the flat flagstones.

"Tison?"

His chest felt cavernously hollow around his heart. The woman who had wept in his arms was gone. Instead was the Tison he had seen in the street, laughing with Tashfin the first time she had met him. Her hair was hidden from him, her body clad in a bright blue gown that concealed far too much of her perfect skin but revealed every curve of body and bone.

"Have you eaten, Muhtasib?"

Sabbah searched her face, his eyes flickering, looking for the bravery or tension he expected. His knees felt weak. For all his determination to set her aside, to keep her safe, he had not anticipated that she would face him so calmly. He had only been able to torture himself with the weeping creature in his arms, who had shuddered with grief and pain.

"Tison," he repeated, foolishness on his tongue, as he tried to make sense of her being there.

"No?" She bowed and gestured to the fire pit. "Sit, Muhtasib. Hudayda will see you fed."

Numb and desperate even if he was not sure what for, he sat. He should be on his knees, pleading forgiveness, but with so many witnesses, he simply could not. Besides, the frightened woman he had held to his heart was gone. This Tison was coolly professional and might not welcome such a display in her domain. Staring at her as she slid through the other slaves, men and women whose eyes he was too cowardly to meet, he wanted to let her pretend nothing had happened.

But she had been taken and drugged as a message to him. He could not let her be hurt again. Even though he wanted her, even though he was aware of a relief so strong it made his bones ache, he could not endanger her.

Something tapped his shoulder, and he reached up without taking his eyes from Tison's back and the long column of her neck. Parchment met his fingers, and he forced his hungry eyes down. It was a document. A mukharajah. Tison's.

Shaking himself, he tilted it to the light. Kanto had signed as his head of household. Khalid had witnessed it. A mukharajah. An arrangement to free Tison. Which he had wanted. Which now brought a slice of fear through his new gratitude for her return. His eyes scanned the words, unable to make sense of a language he had spoken all of his life.

"She will be your housekeeper at least until you are married." Kanto sat beside him on the bench. "The rest is minimum price she can be sold for, and conditions for whoever purchases her then if she has not met the requirements for her freedom."

His fingers spasmed around the parchment, creasing the edges, as the idea of another man owning her, abusing that ownership, flashed through his mind like glass in sand.

"She was safe with Khalid." His voice came out hoarse and cluttered. "I was doing the right thing."

He waited, but Kanto said nothing. Nothing to agree or argue with, or even to ignore.

Hudayda came to him with a plate heaped with grain and lamb and dried fruit. He was halfway through it before he realised it tasted good. The last two days, his cook's food had been as delicious as ash. He must have been punishing his faithless, deserving master.

Sabbah stared at the bowl in his hands. He was nearing having been awake for forty hours in the forty-eight. But this was not some sleep-deprived waking dream. Tison moved, adding a cheerful voice to the clamour of those asking Veta to sing again.

Tired and baffled into numbness, he sat and watched Tison sit to listen to the song. He did not know how they had learned that Veta sang, since she struggled so much with Arabic. What he wondered about, though, was whether Tison sang.

The noise settled as Veta started a song without any accompaniment. Hush levelled itself between the notes. Though he did not speak the language of the Slavs, the song was clearly one of heartbreak. His eyes did not leave Tison's face, even when she stopped his heart by meeting his scrutiny with a look that started as a challenge. As the song ached on, however, her brow relaxed, allowing an expression of questioning to tilt her eyes and tighten her lips.

I am sorry, he thought, doubting he would ever be brave enough to say the words aloud to those lioness eyes. *I should have come to you. I needed to be free, too, Tison, or you would not be safe.*

Safe was not as important as 'his.' Keeping her protected at his brother's house was not as important as spending the rest of his life worshipping at her feet. As she stared into his eyes, the world faded to grey, with nothing but a golden light around the face of the woman he loved.

Her golden eyes fluttered as she blinked rapidly. Still, she did not turn away, and he could not lower his gaze. She was so incredibly beautiful. Holding her eyes with his, though, he could still imagine her in his arms. Not laughing or gasping with pleasure, but shuddering, scared, and suffering. It was his fault she had been reduced to that bundle of fear and sorrow.

She was now always a woman who had been hurt for his sake.

Just like the Qadi's daughter.

Aisha.

As the song returned to its chorus, Sabbah watched the face of the woman he loved and thought of the woman he had intended to marry. A woman who had died because he had not been good enough for her father, because he had not achieved enough. And now, Tison was hurt because he had achieved too much. To look at her now, no one would believe she had been sitting in dust and dirt, clinging to the leg of a table, head turned away from the crowd while she waited for him.

What if he had not come?

Finally, he dropped his head, wrenching the invisible ropes between them. He felt as though he would feel her wherever she went. The trouble was, he knew that was not true.

With a final chorus, Veta finished her song. Kanto leaned towards him to murmur about her talent, but the cord was tightening, and he knew Tison was coming to him. There was no question he could ask that could make sense of this, so he raised his heavy head to stare at her.

She bowed her head.

"Is there anything else you need, Muhtasib?"

He waited, but no answer followed her polite, dutiful enquiry. His eyes stayed on her face, and he could not read her. After the scorching holding of her eyes on his while Veta's song broiled his soul, the peculiarly bland expression now left him feeling winded and dizzied. His heart was beating so hard, he felt it shattering, and he was too tired to conceal his own baffled hurt, because seeing her did hurt. Seeing her and knowing he would have to be a better man than he thought he could be, and leave her alone, crackled pain through him.

What do I do now?

"Tison." His voice crackled, too, rough and deep in the base of his throat.

She bent and filled a cup with a jug he had not even seen her holding. The movement drew his gaze, and he blinked at the smooth stream of water, still dazzled by her eyes but instantly fascinated by her even, unshaking hands.

Lifting his chin, he let his eyes go over her completely covered head, missing the curls he had discovered lay beneath. Only her earlobes could be seen, oddly intimate, bare of earrings that might have set off and emphasised her flawless, arcing neck. Exhausted, he could only let the tingling in his blood grow as he fought the urge to kiss her throat and then work up her jaw to that tantalising lobe.

Feeling the heat rush to his cheeks, he took the cup from her silently, trying to touch her deft fingers and failing. Still, he waited in vain for a wink, or a smile at the least, something to indicate that this was a show for the rest of the household and not how things would be.

He knew it was stupid. He knew that it did not make sense, that he was trying to see a future with her laughing at him and with him for the rest of his life, but at the same time forcing himself to consider the future where he kept her away from him, gave her a better life where she would not be hurt by men trying to damage his reputation.

Or by him being a complete idiot.

Tison bowed, and then, she walked away from him.

He had pushed her away. Whatever his intentions, his actions had to have wounded her deeply, to the core, to her heart, and yet, she had come back. He had given her an easy way to leave and have a new start in Marrakech, and she had returned to him.

"Tison," he murmured.

He supposed that was the only explanation. Dusty or bathed, weeping or laughing, commanding or pleading, she was unexpected and glorious. And he still did not deserve her, just because she was in his home.

Kanto shuffled beside him, and Sabbah inhaled sharply, wood smoke itching his eyes as he moved, the spell of Tison's gaze broken as he remembered his friend was next to him.

"You told me many times that we are friends."

The big man's voice was hushed. Since the courtyard was quieter since the end of Veta's song, Sabbah was grateful.

Quieter than usual. A fortnight ago, normal would have been totally silent. There would not even have been the whisper of night air against the fruit trees and palms Tison had used to fill the courtyard.

"We are friends," he replied. "At least, I will always be your friend, even if I have ... angered you of late." He turned his head, meeting Kanto's eyes.

"Frustrated me," he was pointedly corrected. "You know she would do anything for you. You have a chance here. A chance for love and joy. Nothing is more important than that. Not Marrakech or Morocco. Not even freedom. So love her, fool!"

"I do."

The words were out before he had even thought them. Once again, he found his eyes irritated by the aromatic smoke from the braziers as he gulped in a swallow of air as if he could force the admission back. She should have been the first to hear them, if anyone ever did.

"You think I don't know you do?" Kanto moved and then stood stiffly. "You know better than to help me walk when my back pains me. You know I'm stubborn. You know I'm prideful. But you are stumbling, friend. I tried to leave your pride be."

"You hit me," Sabbah objected, his humour withering on his tongue.

Kanto ignored him. "But you would hold me back from a cliff, so I have to hold you back from throwing yourself off, and tell you that she has been hurt before. She will not keep giving you chances."

"Loving her does not change who I am." An invisible weight pressed on his shoulders.

"This is not about you." Kanto set a hand briefly on his master's shoulder. "It's about her."

CHRISTIAN AND MUSLIM prayers, murmured and mouthed, whispered into the air of the women's dormitory. Tison found herself listening to Veta's quiet murmurs. The mellifluous tones of the Rus language might have been indecipherable to her, but they were soothingly musical. While she gave her own prayers to the angels, she honestly did not know if she would go to Sabbah or not. And the wondering devoured her peace. If she went, she would always be the one who went. Sabbah would likely mind not one bit, but she? She would mind. She would care.

He had not come to her in his brother's house.

She shook her hands, physically ridding herself of the insidious doubt and tension. Love or not, this was a good position. She was housekeeper to the Muhtasib. Was a man who had not kept her close and cherished her worth losing a good place in a rich household?

She jumped as Veta's hand closed around hers, squeezing tight. She had been fidgeting. That was not what a housekeeper did. A housekeeper was calm and inscrutable.

Tison squeezed back and turned her neck slightly to smile at her fellow Christian. Then she rose and left on silent feet, unconsciously gripping her sandals with her toes so they did not shuffle as others continued their prayers. She walked from the dormitory to the small room she had chosen for herself. She was grateful for a doorway that could close her in and away from sight, even more so for a bed of her own. Even if it was a silly, raised bed. She had picked up the mattress and put it back. She was a housekeeper. She would have to work hard to be respected if she was fool enough to love her master.

Though a woman would have to be a fool not to fall for Sabbah.

If only he could love her a touch as much as he loved his city.

Unwinding her headdress, wrapping it loosely around one wrist while she lifted her other hand to scratch her aching scalp, her flattened hair fell down her neck to her shoulders. Slipping off her shoes, she sat on the corner of her bed and slid them under the frame.

For a moment, she merely sat, flexing her toes and letting her hair writhe, snakelike, on her head until the curls fluffed themselves back into place. Calm descended on her, soft and sweet, and she sighed quietly, releasing the tension in her shoulders.

A shuffle of feet sounded outside her door, and the anxiety came rushing back, making her entire body shudder. The tap on the wall was gentler than she would have expected of him, but her heart refused to consider it was anyone else. Her hand shot to the curtain as she rose towards it. Then she steadied herself, and forced herself to open it slowly, and only once she had drawn herself to her full height and raised her chin.

Veta stood on the threshold.

Tison was not sure if she slumped or relaxed, but she saw the recognition and understanding beneath the pale, frowning brows.

"You ... good?" Veta asked, her deep voice decisive despite the broken Arabic.

"I'm good," Tison replied, reaching out and hugging the young Slavic girl. She squeezed her tightly for a moment and then released her only to hold onto Veta's hands. "We came a long way."

"You save my feet. You save my ... me." Veta looked around and gestured. "So I save ... you happy?" She frowned all the more over her struggle and then pointed vaguely towards the main house. "Him." She punched one hand into the palm of the other.

Tison was touched, and smilingly hugged her again. This girl who had been on the point of death by dehydration and heatstroke, whose feet were still bruised and bloodied from the long journey from Tunis, would challenge the Muhtasib for her.

"Thank you, Veta." She gestured between them. "You and me, we are friends. Forever friends. But now—" she smiled and pointed towards the dormitory, "—sleep!"

"Bah!" The Slav girl shrugged a slender shoulder and then flowed back to the dormitory just as someone extinguished the last lamp and cast the room beyond into darkness and shadow.

Leaning against her doorpost, Tison watched her friend go, and her smile lingered. She had made the right decision. Even if she could not be loved by Sabbah, she was not going to waste this chance and lose the people she had gathered. This time, she sighed not to calm herself, but with a sense of rightness. She might not yet be content, but she could feel a future once more. With that came a certainty, a trust in herself and her pride. She would not go to him. He would have to come to her.

Turning her head, she regarded the courtyard through the archway that led to it, listening for the shushing whisper of the ferns and palms on the night breeze. They hung dark and sleepy, their greens black in the night, the faintest silver sheen gliding off some of them where they reflected moon and starlight. She considered going to sit in the stillness, weighing the balm of those shining stars against the sensible need for sleep. Crossing her arms, she rubbed their bare skin.

Even though she did not feel cold, she was tingling, goose-flesh rising.

No. She would sleep. There would be a thousand more nights for sitting in the garden after everyone else was asleep. She turned slightly.

And saw Sabbah. He was standing down the corridor, beyond the garden archway. He looked baffled, and she guarded herself, reminding herself of the way she had felt when he had not come to her. She would not humiliate herself by imagining there was more there than attraction.

He shambled forward, each step lacking the drive and purpose she was used to seeing in him. The man who had once curtailed a fine stride so that she could keep up almost staggered. One of his hands reached out to graze the white wall at his side. His expression shifted as he drew closer. Confusion slid past pleading, and then his brows came together and his bearded cheeks twisted into a grimace.

"I thought we should talk."

His eyes were dark in the gloom, but his voice concealed nothing. She could hear his struggle, hear his plea, and hear the wry recognition of how much he seemed to be falling apart. That voice, barely more than a whisper, sent anticipation skidding on her skin, and her heart began to thump against her ribs, leaving her breathless.

"I wanted to—"

He stopped and stood looking down at her, and now his hands rose, lightly settling against her arms, not holding her, just barely touching her.

But though his voice had shaken to a halt, his eyes seemed to have reached clarity.

"I just had to see you," he whispered, his words a breath of surrender.

Chapter Fourteen

Does it make me weak that I want her this much?

Sabbah stared at Tison, his entire body exhausted. Feeling as though he wanted to fall into her arms and stay there for the rest of his life. She looked so achingly beautiful, even though she stood with shoulders slightly forward and head hanging a little, that his heart twisted with each pump of blood.

He found his hands moving to those hunched shoulders, rubbing his fingers and thumbs into tense muscles. He frowned, his head fighting instinct. All he wanted to do was wrap her in his arms and bring her close. She was still looking at him, and as he worked her shoulders, she managed to raise her head. She melted and seared him.

He saw pain. He saw disappointment. He saw a desperate need that matched his own. Most of all, though, he saw a begging plea for explanation. She did not know why he had rejected her, and she wanted to know.

All this passed without a word, and he wondered if he was trying to read what he wanted to see, but that question vanished as she closed her eyes and stretched her neck, breathing deep and tilting her head into his kneading hand.

She rubbed her cheek against his wrist, and he cupped her face, thumb stroking her perfect skin and fingers sinking into that mass of curls.

"Tison." He heard the settling contentment in his own voice. She took hold of his wrists, gently but still with a firm touch that burned his skin. He lowered his forehead to hers and breathed within her space.

"Sabbah," she replied, soft, barely audible at all, but still his name.

His heart flared, and he hated himself for trying to keep her away. How had he thought he could manage it? The deep dark of the last few days lightened. There was danger, but at least, she was here with him now.

She gripped his wrists tighter and pulled back. He swayed towards her for a moment and then righted himself.

"I let someone down by not being good enough." His tongue felt heavy and reluctant.

"I had my heart and life smashed—" she had stammered a little over that last word, "—by a master I loved. Thought I loved."

They stood together, and his breathing stirred the loose curl by his thumb.

"Come in."

She did not ask. She spoke as though it was simply something they said to one another, not a momentous gesture of trust. She turned her head, but backed into her room, holding his wrists between them. His fingertips missed the warmth of her hair, but he followed, because not going with her was unthinkable.

They went within, and they sat beside each other on the bed, the slight wooden frame feeling fragile beneath him. He looked at her and held one hand while he touched her face again with the other.

"Has it only been a few days?"

He found himself talking, found himself staring at her profile as his fingers stroked along her jaw. He dropped his hand. He was in her room, touching her skin—he was going too far. She deserved better than him, let alone having him satisfying his cravings for touch when she was hurt by him.

"Why did you leave me, Sabbah?" She was staring at the door, but there was a calm resignation to her now. Her shoulders were no longer taut with tension, and she was still holding his hand.

There was no easy way to explain without sounding either pompous or ridiculous. After all, he had thought he could go without her for her sake. *You were wrong there, weren't you! Thought you could go without Tison in your life?* It was what she had first said to him. He needed her in his life. She had been right. She still was.

"They took you because of me, Tison," he began, but she snatched her hand from him and turned her head sharply towards him, her eyes flickering with something very like anger.

"No, the truth, Important Man." Her voice throbbed, shook, and felt hard and harsh against his heart. "Tell me you thought I'd gone in a fury and bought enough drugs to collapse in a souk. Tell me you thought I was your Delilah."

"No." He did not try to take back her hand; he did not have the right, but he slid from the bed, kneeling at her feet.

She held herself tightly, knees together, hands in her lap, eyes following him. "Tison, I feared you had left me. Once I found you, I knew that even if you had decided to lose yourself in opium or hashish, I would not be able to flog you. I would not be able to cast you aside or sell you on."

Her eyes did not soften, but the pain in them was tempered with hope. Sabbah could see her wrestle with her fear. His own shoulders lost their tension. He sat back on his heels, looking up at her, and turned over her hands so the palms were upwards. They were work-roughened, and not as pale as his own were, and they were utterly perfect.

He bowed his head and kissed each palm, then he met her troubled eyes and lifted his shoulders in a helpless shrug.

"I love you, Tison." He looked for joy, but he was glad that he at least saw a gentle surprise, and strengthening of the hope. "I love you more than myself. More than the city. More than anything. I tried to resign my post the day you were taken, because I did not want you to be judged by others, because I could not be impartial with you. Always, I have known that if wrong was done, I could act. With you, I just cannot."

"Sabbah, we cannot be." She still looked hopeful, though, as though she was struggling to do the right thing.

The right thing was being his wife. Anything else was not possible now. He would marry her. He needed her. He just had to be sure she needed him.

"We can," he replied, simply holding her hands above his and staring up into her golden eyes.

"You left me with your brother." She broke eye contact, and her hands jerked as though she would pull them back but could not, even though his touch was light and his grip non-existent. "You did not trust me."

"I did not trust myself," he replied, his voice becoming a little desperate. He tried to suppress that, but panic shook him. She had not said she loved him in return, and he was not sure he would be able to convince her that he could protect that love. "Tison, I was holding you, and you were so hurt, so fragile. If you came with me, they could have come for you. They could have placed a spy within our home. They would not have one in my brother's. His people are of long standing, before even I became Muhtasib. He is my big brother. I knew he could protect you where I could not."

Even from myself.

Tison sighed softly and closed her eyes.

"You told me you wanted me." She sounded tired. "Now you say you love me."

"I do, Tison." Sabbah looked down at her feet. Her toes were curled. Even they were defensive, afraid of contact. "Tison, I wanted you to be free so I could have you as a free woman. Now I want you free so I can ..." he hesitated, fear and hope warring in his chest. "So I can marry you."

"Sabbah, no."

She pulled her hands away and covered her face. She shook, curling into herself again. He rose, sat beside her, and wrapped his arm around her, pulling her to him. Her hands dug into his tunic, and he rested his head on top of those glorious curls.

"Want to tell me I should marry a noblewoman?" he asked, trying to be funny, trying to be light and silly, and not really succeeding.

"Yes." Her proud voice was small, and he heard tears in it, roughening the words. "You should marry a Muslim, Sabbah. A beautiful, Arab Muslim whose children will be rich and happy."

Her voice broke, and she wept.

Not understanding why she cried, he merely held her tighter, bringing his other arm up around her and kissing her hair, nuzzling against it, whispering comforting noises without real words or sense to them. She swayed in his arms for a moment, then took deep, harsh breaths.

"Tison." He squeezed her hard. "I love you."

"Just words," she crackled out, muffled against his chest. One of her arms was around him, though, returning pressure.

"Truth," he countered. "I love you. I'll tell you over and over until you believe me, Tison, even if that takes years."

With a jolt, he realised that it could indeed be years before she had enough faith in him. He understood that. He accepted it with a slow blink, and then returned to laying kisses amid her curls.

"You did not visit me."

She lifted her head, and he forced himself to meet her reddened eyes. He deserved the pain that lanced through his chest and twisted his heart. He released one arm from its embrace and wiped the dampness from her face. Her cheeks had swollen a little.

"I did not think I could leave you there if I did. Look at us now. There is no way I could tell you to go back to Khalid's where you are safe. I need you too much to be that good a man, Tison. I thought I was the best of men, and I hurt you.

But I am not ... I am not like the man in your ledger, Tison. I am not going to sell you cheap."

She looked all around, her eyes straying from his face and roaming her small room. Then her face crumpled, and she began to cry again.

"He told me he loved me."

The words came out as a hard, choked sob, and she fell forward into his chest again. She sobbed, harsh and pained, against his chest. He could feel the wetness there now.

"I am not lying, Tison." He held her tight again. His arms were aching with how hard he held her, and how much he had to struggle against the urge to crush her to him. "But I understand why you do not trust me."

"That's not it." She took several deep, gulping breaths. "Damn it, Important Man, I was going to be cool and collected and calm and ..." She breathed deeply again, controlling herself as best she could. He waited. "It is not that I do not trust you. It is that I do, but I was wrong once before. I thought I was safe, too. Eight years passed, and then, he found me and ruined me again. I feel like something is going to ruin this. That those men who ... the men who took me. What if they take you?"

She was shaking violently now, and he rubbed his hands over her arms and back.

"What if they take me to hurt you and sell me where you cannot find me? I knew you would come eventually. This is your city, you would have found me."

His heart clenched, and his stomach turned over. He could not find the lead money—how would he have found her?

Sabbah blinked. With a surge of sudden understanding, his eyes went wide. The tanneries! The merchants who had been 'robbed' and had money replaced with lead purses had all lived in a ring around the tanneries. So if some thief had been caught, he could have run back there with ease before the scent dogs could hope to catch him. Once there, the poor hounds would be reduced to whining and pawing at their assaulted noses.

Someone in the tanneries was not just targeting him through Tison; they were targeting the Sayrafi through coin. The Muhtasib's woman being found drunk in a market, and him refusing to punish her suitably, was not just scandalous—it was proof he was not suited to his position. The Sayrafi allowing lead coins to pass into the markets was a sign he was corrupt or a fool.

Neither of them spoke to the Qadi if they could avoid it, but Sabbah wondered what they were doing to prove the judge was inept.

This was an effort to bring down Marrakech.

Anger rose in him.

Someone had used Tison, had hurt and frightened and drugged her, just to bring him down, and now, the woman he loved was doubting and too scared to tell him either that she loved him or that she could not.

She had stopped crying once more, and she looked back at the bed behind them.

"Sabbah."

Quiet and fragile, he wondered how hard it was for her to seem brave and strong all the time. He was wondering a lot. It was time to know.

"Does it hurt to be so cheerful all the time?" he asked. "Do you have to work at it?"

"A little." She glanced at him and shrugged. "I try so hard to be ... to be Brave Tison. Clever Tison. All I want to do is laze around, occasionally organise things, and ... and be with you."

His heart soared so fast, he felt dizzy. The conspiracy could wait until morning. She could not. He touched her chin, just beneath her lip.

"Sabbah, not tonight?" she asked. He did not like that she thought she had to ask. Then she continued, still plaintive, still hopeful rather than demanding. "Would you stay with me, though? Just stay and ... hold me?"

She loved him. He found a smile on his face, and he pressed a kiss to her forehead, forcing himself not to move on to her lips with an effort of will.

"Of course," he replied.

Shoes were kicked off, and he lay against the wall on the small, somewhat rickety bed, and then the woman he loved curled herself up against him, pulled his arm around her like a blanket, and they lay together. Her body was hot, and her scent, usually elusive, played with his mind, reminding him strongly of the time she had waited in his room.

The time he had nearly broken everything.

She lay there, and she breathed easier and easier, but his heart clenched with words unsaid.

"I'm sorry, Tison," he told her, whispering. "For being a jealous, stupid fool."

She found his hand and held it, weaving their fingers together.

"Hush, Sabbah," she murmured. "I don't want ... I just want you to be there. So shush."

The need for forgiveness roiled inside him, but he understood. He had a lot of proving to do, and tonight, he had to prove he could put her needs above his own. Perhaps she did not mean that, but he did. He needed to make up for his mistakes. Tomorrow, he would find ways to make amends.

And he would find out about how to go about getting the permissions needed to marry a Christian.

THAT NIGHT BROUGHT the first rain since she had been in Marrakech. First, the wind breathed against every door like a whisper from God making them lean and creak, and then, she heard the rattle across tiles as it brought the first droplets across the city. Soon, the wind had been replaced by the delicious sound of drenching rain.

Tison, warm and safe in the arms of the man she loved, listened to the sounds grow louder than his deep, steady breathing. She dropped a hand to the ground to feel the breeze rushing under her curtained doorway. Her fingers curled in the coolness, a tiny moment of relief from the sheer heat of the beloved man sharing her small bed. She loved Sabbah. She did not want to, but she did. She wanted to be angry with him still, but the moment she had seen him, she had known it did not matter.

Nothing had mattered so much as being past all the hurt and being together again.

She touched his arm, thrown over her chest, his hand limply fisted beneath her jaw. They had not had this the first time. They had not had tenderness. Every intention had been to rebuff him, to calmly explain to him that they could not be together, that he had been right at first to try and maintain a professional distance.

All of that had become empty words once she was looking into the eyes of a hungry, breaking man, who needed to be with her and was shattered at being yards away instead of chest to chest.

Or perhaps she had been the hungry one. Perhaps she had fed him questions because she needed the right answers. Whatever he had said, she would forgive him, because she needed to or she would never be able to love him. And the love was already there in her heart.

A heart twisting with pain, sharp wires of it shooting from shoulder to shoulder as she cramped with loving. She could have woken him, turned over into his chest, and cried a little until he comforted her. She did not.

He had tried to resign for her.

And if he had done that, the Wasp in Bright Clothes would have won. Whoever he and his people were, they would have beaten a good man so that a lesser one could take his place. Then they would start picking away at Marrakech, not killing the beast, merely drinking its blood a little bit every day.

The pain in her heart stopped being quite so sharp, and her brow furrowed as she tried to think. She had told Sabbah she was as clever as Solomon when they first met. It was time she proved that she was at least smarter than a man in garish clothing who'd hit her over the back of the head.

Slowly, she slid from her mattress to the floor, straightened the under dress down over her legs, and slipped from the room.

How was a woman supposed to think with a man apparently entirely comprised of elbow and heat?

A smile ghosted her lips, and she stored that remark away for when he inevitably discovered her missing and followed her out into the rain.

Within moments of stepping from the cover of the corridor to the courtyard, she was drenched from head to foot. Water ran down her chest to soak into the cloth of her tunic under dress. Her feet pushed through inches of silvery puddles, constantly roiling from the rainfall. It ran to drains to join the mountain water that came down in the stone tunnels beneath, but they could not pull it down quick enough to keep up with the deluge. Her scalp was the only thing still dry, as the water fought to sink through her thick curls.

Childishly, she raised her hands up to the skies and felt the purity of the clouds above her. Tison span, too quickly, making herself dizzy after a few turns, and grinned just for the sake of it.

Things will work out, she told herself. How could they not? *He is a good man; I am a good woman. We will work things out. As soon as he is safe.*

She went to sit on one of the stone benches, skimming the water away with one hand before she did even though she knew it would make little difference by the time she returned to bed. She took in a deep breath, tasting the cool raindrops on her tongue as they slid between her lips, and stretching her toes out, tapped them against the busy surface of the puddles by her feet.

The first trickle of cold at her scalp made her shiver deliciously.

Sleep had done her good, she realised. She felt less like life was too hard to handle, less like she was overwhelmed and out of her depth. Still, she supposed, at least she was thinking about Sabbah and Marrakech, and not Rafiq and Tunis. Apparently, all it took was getting thrown in a stinking cellar, being drugged, and then being abandoned in a stranger's house for three days.

Movement by the gate drew her eyes instantly to it, and she froze in place for a moment, until a hood was drawn back, and Khalid ibn Abdella looked at her through the blurring rain.

Speak of the Devil, and lo he appears.

Except that Khalid was more warrior angel, who was going to help her protect Sabbah. As such, he was raised as high as Kanto now on her list of friends. She smiled as she rose from her soaked seat, and her skirt smacked loudly against her leg and then stuck there.

Veta was her friend, too. She had friends again. They had been harder to leave behind in Tunis than the luxury and sense of *home*. She had had a whole bustling building full of people who liked her, appreciated her, and had been horrified that Rafiq had forced her sale.

But not one of them would have stood in front of a master like Veta had, and not one of them would have searched for her with a painful back, for hours, as she had learned Kanto had. Not one of them would have tried to give up their position in the bathhouse for her sake, but Sabbah had tried to give up one of the highest offices in the land because of her.

The cool bliss of the rain could only soothe so far. She could not let him be in danger.

Tison rested her hand against the metal of the gate while the fingers of the other raked through her sodden hair, pushing it over her scalp and tangling half way back. The weight of it was already aching her neck, but she stood without shame. Khalid had seen her when she was shaking and made of nothing but an aching head and pathetic body. He had seen her with dead eyes and a weary soul.

"You want me to fetch him?" she asked, fingers reaching to unfasten the gate.

"No."

Khalid's voice was hard and brittle with anger. Instant concern banished her own lethargic worries, and both hands gripped the metal.

"What has happened?"

"Tomorrow," he told her, sharp and harsh enough that her heart clenched in instant dread, not for him, but for that tone. The tone of a master promised pain if ignored or disobeyed.

"Something has happened?"

His eyes glittered in the light from the lamp over the door.

"Men are watching my house." Loathing dripped from his voice. "My house!"

Shock reverberated in her stomach. She felt pain and realised she was gripping the gate so hard, she was hurting her own knuckles. She opened her hands and forced them down.

"Jessamine has been warned?" Tison barely registered that she had spoken Khalid's wife's name, her 'ism,' as though they were equals. The idea of sweet, generous Jessamine being drugged and lost in the city made her feel sickly dizzy. She would rather be kept in that stinking cellar for a month than expose Jessamine to that.

"Yes." Khalid rubbed the water off his face, the movement eerily similar to Sabbah's.

"I am ready," she told him, offering a pitiful attempt at a smile, knowing too well that there was no reassurance for this. "I will meet you at the northern side of al Djemma." She thought for a moment. "There is a shop that sells fennecs and tame birds. It is loud enough to drown speech."

Khalid released a long breath, hands up on the gate where hers had been, and lowered his head, rolling broad shoulders as if shaking off after carrying a heavy weight. Then he looked up and searched her face. She kept the smile on her lips. She was unnerved, even afraid, but that smile had to remain. Perhaps it was because she was so frightened. Perhaps years of smiling at fear in the face instead of curling into a ball when threatened with violence or being sold into a brothel had finally paid off in that strained attempt and reassurance and confidence.

"I cannot make you do this, Tison." Khalid straightened, his eyes wary.

"Neither can I make you do it to save him." She felt the rain change, felt it lighten overhead. "But I will not insult you to think you would for a moment consider not helping me in this."

He gave a little exhalation, a sharp attempt at mirth.

"I will see you tomorrow, then, Tison."

"Tomorrow, Ibn Abdella," she returned, bowing. She watched him down the street, and then turned to go within again.

She barely breathed as she pulled aside the curtain to her room and to the gentle sound of deep, heavy breathing. She discarded her soaking shift, putting it down carefully to stop the smack of wet cloth on stone waking Sabbah. Tison regarded him for a moment and wrung out her hair. His arm was stretched over the place where she had been, his mouth slightly open, and though he was not snoring, the sound of him filled the small space.

She stood over him, and the smile she felt grow across her lips was no longer strained or false. He looked at peace, and her heart swelled in her chest, making her breathless.

Pressing a hand over the beating organ, she closed her eyes for a moment, overcome by the sweetness of watching him sleep. It was such a small, stupid thing to be emotional about, she told herself. Then she opened her eyes back up and once more felt a stab of feeling so strong, it physically hurt. She moved to the edge of the bed, lifted his arm, and slid under it.

He half woke, an undignified snort and half murmur all he managed.

"Hush." She moved against his chest, not caring that she was naked, only that she would be warm and safe in his arms.

People might watch the house, but they could not see them here, alone and together.

"Hmmm," he responded, sliding his other arm clumsily underneath the flat pillow and nuzzling into her neck. "'son."

"Sleep," she told him, ignoring the pounding of her heart and leaning into the heat she had got out of bed to escape.

Closing her eyes once more, she did not try to sleep; she merely enjoyed having him there behind her. For the first time since she was a little girl, someone held her, strong and comforting, keeping out the night. Surrounded by his warmth, she realised that she had not been stupid, thinking he was better than other men.

Chapter Fifteen

Sabbah woke slowly, sliding straight into smoky desire with a growing sense of joy. His arms were heavy with Tison. Emotion rolled over him, and as he blinked the last fogginess away, he could have wept just to have her there, despite his body's demands. He tried to tighten both arms around her, but the right one would not move. He smiled.

He had never had an arm go to sleep because another person was lying on it.

"Awake?" She sounded far too alert for how tired he felt. "Some Muhtasib you are, Slugabed!"

He thought he heard nerves there, beneath the teasing, but he was so grateful for her humour, he did not push her.

"Some housekeeper you are, still in bed when the master is awake," he retorted, before using his one good arm to hold her still. "And there you are, still not getting up. Tch!"

She gave a murmuring chuckle that sounded like a yawning cat being bounced.

"Hilarious!" she drawled, beginning to wriggle in his arms and turn over.

Ah, so that was her 'fake laugh.' It was not at all convincing. He was beyond joking, however, because she was now rubbing up against his body, trying to get comfortable. He swallowed, aiming to breathe through the jerking pleasure that his body was doing its best to encourage. He did not deserve to want her that way, not until he had made amends.

"Oh." She had stopped moving, and gave him the same look she had whenever he lost his tongue talking to her because of her agonising beauty. "Why, good morning, Little Muhtasib!"

"No!" He leaned back, nearly hitting his head on the wall behind him.

"Hmmm?" Her eyes, now visible in the growing light of dawn, were dark and tantalising.

"You are not calling my ..." He struggled against his upbringing, and lost. "... any part of me 'Little Muhtasib.'"

"Why not?"

She popped her eyes so wide, he could see right around the irises.

"It is wrong!"

He tried to pull his arm from beneath her, and she propped herself up on it, her hand nestling under the glory of her curling hair.

"Wrong?"

"Wrong," he repeated. "And possibly sacrilegious!"

She gurgled in amusement and bopped him on the nose with one finger.

"Tison ..."

"What?" she challenged, then she sighed, and the world settled into contentment, because the sigh was happy and replete. "Thank you for being with me. I have been so alone, Sabbah. Your fault!"

He touched her cheek and then put his arm around her again, holding her close and setting his head amid her soft curls.

"My fault," he agreed.

She ran a hand up his back, dragging her fingers over his skin. She did not answer. She did not have to; he knew he was in the wrong, that she could not forgive her abandonment.

"Why did you leave me, Sabbah?" She nuzzled against his neck. "Were you still angry with me?"

"No." His heart clenched. "I stopped being angry the moment I realised what I had done. I was ... stupid, Tison." He held her all the closer. He could not bear her eyes in that moment. "I was jealous. Mad with it."

Still, he did not ask for forgiveness.

"Jealous of Kanto?" She tried to tilt back her head, and he closed his eyes. "Really, Important Man? You thought so little of me?"

"I did not think." Her leg moved against his, and his arousal tightened once more. Despite his need to be sincere, his body betrayed him. "All I knew was that I had hurt you, was in the wrong. I ... did not react well. I was a child. A fool."

She traced her fingers over his shoulder blades and then swept her index finger down his spine.

"Say more like that," she said, and her voice was teasing again, and he could have wept for that, despite the mass of confusion his desire was causing. She shifted again, and he was certain she had done it on purpose.

"Ledgers don't matter." He realised that he could not open his eyes now, even if he wanted to, and his breath felt odd, as though he had to concentrate for each inhale. "Nothing matters as much as you, Tison, but I don't deserve you. And I do not deserve to be Muhtasib, when I love someone more than I honour my duties. I cannot have you, but I cannot have my position, and that frightens me. How can I support you with no work to bring in money for the house?"

Finally, he looked at her, and her face was twisted with shock and dismay.

"Sabbah," she sobbed, and kissed him hard.

He groaned against her tongue and surrendered to every little desire. He had wanted to nibble her lip, so he did. He had wanted to lose his hands in her hair and against her body, so he did, one burying into her curls, the other reaching down to stroke over the slight curve of her buttocks.

She whimpered into his kiss and tugged at his shoulders, rolling, and the small bed creaked as he rose over her, looking down at her pleading face and dying for the need he saw reflected in her eyes.

"I don't deserve you, either." She caressed his jaw with both hands, fingertips brushing against his beard and her thumb settling at his chin. "I'm just a slave."

"Oh, Tison." He shook his head and set his arms on either side of her, not wanting to crush her despite his need to touch her in return. "You are not just anything."

She let out a small, breaking sound and pulled him down to kiss her again. Hard against her body, he broke with every strangled noise she made and every ripple that went through her. Her hands left his face, and she began to push at his sleep-rumpled trousers. Between them, they won out against their clothes and the confined space.

When they were skin to skin, he was once again tortured by the worry of crushing her. She was so small, so slight. He knelt, and she murmured desperately as he pulled away, but gasped with excitement as he wrestled with her legs. He was still clumsy, still not used to handling a woman, let alone one he had hurt and needed to make amends with, but he managed to pull her legs to his hips.

Shifting, hoping vaguely that the bed would hold, he pulled her up so he could sheathe himself inside her. He moved as slowly as he could, and not entirely for her sake. He was shattering in her slick heat. She was wet, just from their kisses and closeness, and he ached knowing she wanted him so badly.

Slowly, he encased himself in her warmth, and every inch she gripped of him pulsing, needy. He grunted and stared at her as she squeezed him within her, and she grinned at him, sweat beading on her lip. She licked it away, and he thrust the rest of the way almost without thinking.

She threw back her head and arched, grinding up against him and tightening her legs around him. Her heels dug above his hips. He reached his hands down her legs, grasped her thighs. She was too slight, so thin he could almost pass his hands around her legs at their widest point.

He growled.

"I am going to feed you up." Not the most romantic statement, but all he could manage without mumbling about need and unworthiness.

She laughed, quiet and breathless, but utterly glorious. He had feared he had chased her laugh away.

"You are going to drive me mad if you just stay like that," she pleaded. He agreed, but still, he waited. "Sabbah!"

"What, Tison?" His voice was far from teasing, since he was still twisted with lust and admiration. He wondered if she would slip if he reached for her perfect breasts and her dark nipples.

"Sabbah," she begged. "Please don't make me wait. I can't ... with you inside me ..."

"Tell me, Tison," he breathed, shifting his hips slightly. She had teased him often. Maybe she liked it.

She groaned long and twisted, driving him just as crazed as she gripped his length inside her.

"Ah, saints alive!" She put her hands over her face and moaned into them, the sound muted and small when it escaped. "Sabbah, take me now, or I will start trying to please you!" She lowered her hands and narrowed her eyes at him. "You want me Tison, or you want me sultry and seductive?"

He withdrew and thrust into her, and she bucked.

"Please, yes!" She covered her mouth again.

"I want you, Tison." Hoarse and low, his voice rumbled in his own throat. Then he thrust into her again. And again.

Feeling her tightening around him reduced him to nothing but frenzied desperation. The bed rattled each time he slid into her, and she reached for a sheet and covered her beautiful face, moaning into it until she was crying out in earnest and came around him, climaxing so hard, she took him over the edge.

It had been faster than he would have liked. He would have wished to pleasure her all day.

Still moaning into her sheet, she let her legs go limp around him and groped with one hand for his. He slid from her and collapsed against the wall, shoving the bed a fair few inches from the cool stone. Tison threw the sheet aside and wrapped her arms around his head, kissing him and then biting at his collar bone and shoulder with weary ferocity, then licking the imagined wounds away.

A strangled groan left his own throat without his volition, and he held her close against him, putting his upper leg through hers as though he could weave them together.

"So much for keeping my distance," she muttered.

"So much for my honour," he replied, and she poked a curled knuckle against his neck. It was surprisingly painful.

"Stop it!" she told him. "I am not a smirch on your honour."

"No." His heart was still pounding hard, and it skipped in fear. "But I should protect you."

"A master should see to the needs of his slave," she reminded him, curling against him again. "And I need you, Sabbah. Just ... don't hurt me again."

He kissed her. He had earned a far harsher rebuke than that, but still, her simple request made his spine feel weak and his vaunted honour crumble to dust and nothingness.

"I promise I will never doubt you," he told her. "Even though you have heard empty promises before, even though I hurt you, even though I was a stupid, jealous fool, even though I thought you had left me because I am ..."

"Sabbah." She had uncurled her finger, and she rested it at the base of his throat. "Shut up."

"Yes, Tison," he murmured, and kissed her again, because he could, and that was a remarkable thing. All was well. He would speak to an imam about permission to marry a Christian. He was not going to let her think herself lesser ever again. Somehow, he would be worthy of her. Nothing was more important. He loved her.

He loved her.

ALL AROUND TISON, PEOPLE moved. Merchants and mercenaries, slaves and masters, black, swarthy, and ruddy all walked together, and all were unaware of the feeling of isolation amid them. She was utterly terrified.

The clamour of the birds at the stall behind her came in waves. They would quiet, cowed by the crowds or a sudden noise from one of the tiny, half-tamed foxes also sold at the stall, and then, one of them would shriek and set the whole cacophony going again. They also stank, for such pretty creatures. She shifted on her feet, exchanging a long look with one of the eyes of some soft-feathered grey thing with a bright red tail.

Am I mad? she asked it, silently. *He's big. He's the Muhtasib. He can look after himself, right?*

It began to eat one of the thin sticks of its cage.

What do you know? You're a bird!

She would do this, because he was trying to look after an entire city, and he deserved to have his brother and his Tison looking after him. Besides, these people had to be stopped. If they were brave enough to challenge the Muhtasib, they would not hesitate in breaking the lives of people with more ordinary jobs. She loved Sabbah, but stopping these men hurting him was more important than her. She was just a slave.

An excellent slave, she added, still watching the parrot nibble at its cage. She glared at it for good measure.

"Everything is ready."

She flinched, sucking in a gasp. Khalid stood close behind her, and dread slashed her stomach before the shock of hearing his voice had cleared. *Everything is ready. Am I, though?* For Sabbah, she had to be. She lifted her chin, eyes blind, and tried to think the plan through. Her brain stayed unhelpfully blank.

"Tison?"

She nodded.

"Ready," she replied, her voice steady even while her eyes were wild and her chest yawning with empty, frightened hollowness. Just because she would do this for Sabbah did not mean she was not afraid that she would be dumped back in that cellar, drugged, or merely killed because they saw through the subterfuge before Khalid's men could save her.

She waited a few more moments, staring blankly, and then she fluttered her eyes to a blink and moved away from the stall. A pair of veiled, giggling girls took her place to coo at the fennecs. Keeping her head down to avoid meeting the eyes of the surging masses around her, she found her breath coming in anxious gasps.

This will not do.

Just because she had decided she did not have to pretend with Sabbah did not mean she could go without pretending to the world. Yes, she had to appear nervous for the plan to work, but letting her own breathing choke her would only make her crumble at the first sight of true danger. She had to be brave. That was it. Brave Tison. Clever Tison. She had to be fierce as a lioness and just as protective while appearing to be a wounded gazelle.

Her breathing steadied. She ducked against a wall and let her head covering slip back a little, exposing her face to the hot sun. The air was moister than usual while the rain was burned from the streets. Only covered corners still had slickness to them or darker patches of earth.

If she played at fear, maybe she would not feel it so deeply.

So Tison looked around with exaggerated furtiveness and slid back into the flow of foot traffic. She knew these streets a little better now, but even if she had not, she could have followed the smell of the tanneries. In the moister air, the pungent stink was unmistakeable. Even here, delicate noses were covered with veils and scarves. Tison, needing to be recognised, did not have that luxury. Still, in all her long life, she had never encountered a worse smell than Marrakech's tanneries. They might be the reason the city was touted and admired, but they turned her stomach.

It was absolutely the smell, and not the memory of helplessness it evoked.

Moving aside for a cart pulled by a disgruntled donkey, she went on her toes to see how far she had to go before the street opened into the small market at the edge of the tannery quarter. All down the sides of the street were stalls selling cloth, leather, and pigment. Men and women who could not afford the taxes on the market itself set up outside workshops and homes. Off balance, she found herself pushed aside by someone going to greet a friend beside one of these dye shops, and for a moment, she was once again as afraid as she was trying to appear. The people around her all seemed so strong and determined.

The stink grew stronger, slamming through her nose and mouth, wrenching her stomach and invading every breath. She forced her way onward. Twisting through the slow-moving crowd, taking advantage of her slight form and lunging through gaps politeness dictated she leave free, she advanced down the street. Bright colours from the pigment stalls danced past her vision. Virulent greens and vibrant pinks tried to catch her eye. Rainbows of dyed leather shoes ranged alongside her. They were cheap here, far from the sweeter-smelling markets of al Djemma and the smaller souks around it.

With a hoarse whimper at the base of her throat, she stepped out from the cover of the street. Her hands shook, and the sky seemed far too big. She looked around her, knowing her eyes were too unblinking to be natural, but she could not see Khalid. She felt horribly alone and exposed.

She darted her eyes from face to face, looking for recognition. The only man she knew had worked towards her capture was the Wasp. The others were shadows in her memory. They would know her; she could not hope to know them.

She found a space in a cleared area of the market square and let her shawl fall further back on her head. Her hair was still wrapped up, and once the soft but worn cloth was about her shoulders, she was clearly visible to all. It was terrifying.

The hairs at the nape of her neck and on her arms stood on end, and her breathing kicked uneven again. This time, she found she could not manage even to try and fight against that feeling. She felt like a young girl, the first night sleeping as an owned creature, knowing her father was in the house but not where or whether he could help her if someone hurt her. With her skin prickling, she could assume she was being watched, but nowhere could she see eyes on her.

Twisting, she looked over her shoulder, eyes scattering through the crowd.

Then, with a wail, the call to prayer sounded from the first minaret. Soon, the sky was filled with the keening chant, and people around her were moving. Men were unrolling mats nearby, and she realised why that space had cleared. Feeling even more untethered, she made her way to the edge of the prayer area and then darted down a corridor of stalls. The Muhtasib's Christian woman interrupting men's prayer? He would certainly have to resign after that, and the city needed him. Tison might not be on close terms with Marrakech, but it could just owe her a favour. She was going to save him.

With the help of his warrior brother, whom she still could not see.

Icy realisation dropped on her neck like a handful of crushed ice.

Her chest rose and fell as her breath was torn from her and her body fell into total panic. She looked around. There were a few men and women still upright, non-Muslims watching stalls and waiting for their day to continue. Ritual words were spoken and murmured around her, and she found herself begging all the angels she knew the names of to watch over her, in a silent, gasp-broken litany.

She rounded a pair of stalls and started walking back towards the bowed heads of the praying men. She had walked half way back to where Khalid would expect her to be when she saw a flash of a vile purple and a grip like Toledo steel closed around her wrist.

"Didn't remember the prayers, did you!"

The Wasp grinned at her. She smelled cloves and sickly sweetness on his breath, and all her confidence left her. She looked from him to the burly, swarthy man at his side.

"Please, don't." She sounded so young to her own ears, like the child she had been, not the woman she had striven to become.

"Don't what?" He began to walk her backwards. No one came forward to help her. She did not look for help. A rabbit does not look around when faced with a cobra. His grip became painful. "Don't do what you hoped I would do? You think you and Ibn Abdella are clever? You think you can stop us?"

Stop you from what?

She looked down at the ground, stumbling as he shoved her onward. Then, she dug in her heels, pulling back so hard, she almost ended up falling to the ground. Her mind was scrambled. All of her life, she had been taught to give in to fear. Do not sleep too long, or you will be flogged. Do not love, or you will have your heart broken. Do not make noise, or you will be starved to remove your spirit. Do not try to move on, or you will be sold far away. From the petty to the life-altering, her fears had been the only response to a threat.

So Tison threw her head back and screamed, long and scratching and echoing. She lowered her chin to her chest, drew another breath, looked straight into the eyes of the man who was attempting to drag her past uncaring eyes so they could use her to hurt Sabbah once more, and screamed again.

Pain seared her cheek as she was backhanded, hard.

"Help me!" she roared with all the force of her voice straight at the Wasp's face. He turned and yelled to another member of his gang for aid, but she could see the movement beyond him. "Ibn Abdella! Help me!"

The Wasp dropped her wrist, but even as she gathered her balance, his fist crashed into her face. Pain splintered, hot and fleshy, from her other cheek, and as her head spun around, she was grabbed again and pulled hard against the wiry man's body. A blade kissed her throat. He cursed her, his breath hot against her ear, his voice growling and desperate, stripped of every hint of the bantering humour he had used on her over the past weeks.

They stopped with a jerk, and she guessed they must be up against a wall of some sort. Around them, men drew curved swords. Then Khalid ibn Abdella faced them down, a drawn bow in his hands.

The Wasp's head pressed against the back of her neck, just as Sabbah's had the night before, and she wanted to kick and struggle and hurt him for that. Far more than the pain throbbing and pulsing across her face, she wanted to end him for reminding her of Sabbah.

Strangely, she felt less afraid than she had moments before. An unearthly calm was settling over her though her hand shook when she raised it.

"Keep still," commanded her captor. He was tense, as still and unbending as a statue.

He was a dead man. The question was whether she would go before him. Though she was afraid, her stomach tensed with determination, and she planted her feet squarely. She was not going to die. She was going to walk away from this, and this time when she and Sabbah lay together, it would be with passion and desire, and he would not reject her afterwards.

"Were you taking me to the cellar again?"

She did not know why she asked. She just hated the arm pressing against her shoulder and neck, the wiry but solid body behind her, and the threat of the blade's edge against her neck.

"Keep silent," he growled against her ear.

She obeyed, staring straight ahead into Khalid's eyes as he lowered the bow and muttered an order to one of his men, who sheathed his sword and ran out of the market.

When he returned, he would have the Muhtasib with him.

THE DAY WAS WARM AFTER the rain cleared, and Sabbah was filled with a sense of hope and contentment that nothing could possibly break. He smiled at everyone who met his eyes, and when he prayed, he felt his heart in the words and not just his head. He only wished it was appropriate to use the time to thank Allah for the blessings He had bestowed and the second chances He had allowed.

Still, he considered as he rose from his prayer mat and rolled the woven fabric in his hands, there was the rest of the day for being thankful.

Tison had wept, but she had let him be her solace. He could still feel her warmth and the sheer, solemn power of holding her. He had a strong sense of hope. She would be back at home now, teaching the slaves, reasserting her position after her absence. Strangely, the image that came to mind was not a recent one. It was of the first night he had come home, when she was sitting amid jars, taking stock and preparing to make changes.

It was not her long, brown legs he imagined. It was the look on her face, concentration, excitement, and that hesitance. The moment of wondering whether or not he would let her continue. Wondering whether she could overrule him.

"Muhtasib!"

Sabbah recognised one of the merchants from the row to his left who had an ongoing rivalry with the leather seller across from him. He set Tison into his heart and focused on his work.

"Salaam Aleikum." Sabbah inclined his head, and the man's swarthy skin reddened.

"Ah, yes, Waleikum Salaam, al Muhtasib, but please, you must come! That jackal has spilled my wares all over the ground and refuses to clear them up! Tell him, Muhtasib!"

Sabbah followed with him, one of his agents coming alongside as they reached the scene. On the way to or back from prayer, the tabletop had been collapsed, and leather books of middling quality had been scattered into the street. As they approached, the other merchant came puffing up.

"Muhtasib, this man is blaming me for his own clumsiness! See how he blocks the street, and all to attempt to drag me down to his level!"

He looked between them and then found himself mentally shrugging. Yes, they were causing a disturbance in the markets, but if he tried to judge this seriously, he would start laughing and offend them. So instead, he bent and began gathering up the books. He tucked them against his chest and held them with one arm until it was toppling, and rose to set them on the table.

Both merchants were red-facedly helping by the time his agent had straightened out the table, and Sabbah left them with the last twenty or so, and simply inclined his head silently and walked away. His agent trotted alongside, and Sabbah turned to see a grin on his face.

"That was brilliant." The lad's voice was tense with controlled mirth. "Ah, Muhtasib, you shamed them without a word. Those two have been poking at each other for weeks."

"How's Ibn Yusuf's back, do you know?" He tried not to grin at the memory of Ibn Yusuf, on the floor with a large woman sitting on his back with her arms folded and a truculent expression on his face.

Had he told Tison about that? He would. And about today. He could imagine her laughing until she clutched her sides. He owed her laughter after all the tears he had forced on her.

He was turning the end of the row, looking for the next problem, idly keeping an eye out for men in brightly coloured and ill-matching clothing, when one of Khalid's sergeants came pounding towards him.

Sabbah shuddered. His brother's life was dangerous—it was something he understood at his core, but as the man reached him, he found his stomach twisting with the fear of living without his big brother. The man skidded, breathing deeply but not needing to collapse.

"The commander says you have to come at once!"

The knot in his stomach loosened, and relief began to sink through him. Khalid was alive. Then the man continued:

"Your slave Tison is in danger. At the tannery souk."

Shock once again slapped him hard across the face, and he almost buckled with denial. Tison was at home. Tison was safe and would not put herself in danger again for anything.

She would. For you.

He ripped his head covering from his head, clenching it in one fist, and began to run back the way the man had come. No one knew this city like he did. His toes pounded the cobbles and paving slabs, his arms punching the air at his sides.

She would not die. He would not let her. Khalid would keep her safe. Khalid would get a black eye if he had known she was putting herself in danger. He would never forgive him. Or her.

He leapt over a cart, vaulting it with a speed he did not know he still possessed. Two years as Muhtasib had softened him. He no longer had to run to a crisis, because he had agents to do that. He no longer had to run from attackers, because he was Muhtasib of Marrakech.

He pushed himself, ignoring muscles that objected to such an abrupt need for exertion, begging his legs to keep going. Khalid's sergeant pulled ahead of him, but Sabbah peeled off to the right behind a cork-seller's warehouse and climbed over a wall, bruising ribs and breaking his stride, but giving him two streets worth of gained time. He reached a crowded street and bellowed with all his might and the words he had never intended to use:

"Make way for the Muhtasib!"

They melted away, hugging walls as he pelted onward, lungs beginning to strain and calves now screaming their pain.

The stink of the tanneries reached his exerted lungs, and he saw the market square up ahead. The souk at the edge of the tanneries. Just a little more. Perhaps he would get there and Khalid would wave a hand, and all would be well. Tison would be ruefully apologetic for leaving the house, and everything would be fine.

"Move!" he shouted, and the command in his voice parted the ring of morbidly curious onlookers.

He saw a woman being held with a knife at her throat, and looked for Tison. Then, the world upended itself as he realised it was her. She was the one bending backwards, pulled to protect her attacker. There was blood in the dust. A man's body with arrows through the throat and face. Flies buzzing around fresh blood. Sabbah stared at it, looked up again, and met her eyes.

Calm sank into him.

"I take it you have all been waiting for me," he intoned, his voice low and quiet.

He learned something about himself all at once. He learned what he had thought he would never do was more than possible. It was definite. He would kill a man to protect Tison, and he would not hesitate or regret it.

"Absolutely, Muhtasib," Khalid replied from his left.

Sabbah did not take his eyes from Tison's face.

She stood, stoic and unblinking, mouth a little down-turned, yet her eyes clear and focused. But as he held her gaze with his, trying to silently reassure, he saw a ripple cross her expression. Just for a moment, he saw an unholy fear there. A fear he remembered from when he had found her, drugged and desperate, in this very souk. Worse, the fear was followed by a pleading look of apology. He wanted to reassure her. He wanted to beg for her release.

What frightened him most was that he did not know what would get her killed. He did not know what would make the knife slide.

He watched Tison's lips move, and her assailant shook her. His hand was tight around her arm, pushing the skin into deep dimples.

Sabbah did not know how he maintained his calm. Iron control somehow remained intact, and he folded his arms and tilted his head. He still felt it, though, felt that touch and the clenching of rage and the desire to beat and kick and break the man who dared touch his Tison.

"So, I'm here. You have my attention." He took a step forward. The man was so hidden behind her that he could not see an approach, but he would hear Sabbah's movement in his voice.

He looked down at the end of a bright purple trouser leg, the cuff frayed and whitened by dust and wear. The shoes were a virulent green.

The Wasp. The man in bright clothes who had followed her. Tried to turn her against him.

"I hear you were angry about the way I perform my duties." He turned his head, counting Khalid's archers. Then he met the eyes of one of his own men. "How about we clear some of the innocent people around us, so no one gets hurt?"

Bustle sounded. Stall owners would not go, but perhaps if some of the foot traffic was gone, giving chase would be easier. He felt the after-effects of his sprint from Djemma. His calves had started to burn, and he could have used a long drink of water and a bath. The sweat on his skin smelled acrid with fear, even if his voice remained even and as imbued with authority as he could manage.

"He disturbed prayers, too," Khalid added, his voice hard and crisp.

"Oh, well, Allah, forgive me for disturbing the peace." Tison's captor's voice was bitter and dark, with a hint of a Berber accent. "You can act calm all you like, Muhtasib, but if I cut her throat, you will weep and scream like a real man."

"And then you will be dead."

Sabbah's heart had started to even out after his sprint, but it began to pound again. He straightened his stance and put his head covering back over his scalp. His movements were slow, but for some reason, he could not work out how to be quicker. He smoothed the lines of it down to his shoulders.

"What do you want?" Khalid spoke again. He was fiddling with the fletching of an arrow, nocked to his bow but held with the point downwards. His brother was a good shot.

The cold fact of it helped keep the steady calm that had descended, blocking out a screaming part of him that wanted to rage and take the Wasp apart with his bare hands.

Once again, he raised his eyes to Tison's. She did not move, but as they stared at one another, she scrunched her nose up and rolled her eyes. A moment of forced levity that cost her some of her control over her fear, but he understood it. Tison trusted him.

He had to prove her right this time.

"It's going to be all right, Tison." He took another step forward.

"You cannot promise her that."

The Wasp sounded strained, and Sabbah saw him adjust his grip on his knife. His hands were probably slick. Fear was not good. If he decided there was no way out, he would take Tison with him just to bite back as he died.

"I can." He felt a ripple go through him as the man in him fought the Muhtasib once more, demanding violence and blood from the one who was threatening Tison. "You have not killed her yet. You did not kill her when you took her before."

"You think I lack the guts?" Still, the man hid behind her, not even attempting to make eye contact. He was too smart to be tricked into exposure.

"No." Sabbah contemplated another step, but was unsure, so he remained where he stood. His fingers tapped the side of his own leg spasmodically. *Kill him. Kill him so no one ever dares touch her again. Right here in the street. Rip him to pieces.*

"Then what?" Her attacker's voice dripped with mockery. "You just think you can order the world to obey, Muhtasib?"

He spat Sabbah's title.

"Not me." Sabbah swallowed silently, and then continued. "Someone holds your leash. They did not want her dead. So this is how you get out of this alive. You take me to whoever told you to make a fool of the Muhtasib. You take me to whoever put lead coins in the Sayrafi's purses. You do that, and my brother's men will not shoot you."

Tison shifted on her feet, and he could feel her stare as she tried to get his attention. She did not want him going into danger. He understood. He knew just how she felt.

Because if he did not get the knife away from her throat, he was going to lose everything that made him an honourable man.

"Your brother walks away before I do." The Wasp's voice had changed. He was considering the exchange.

Hope slicked across the back of Sabbah's neck.

"Tison goes free before he moves," he countered.

Now he could see Khalid in the corner of his eye. Standing straight and like Tison, trying to get his attention. They did not want to agree. They did not want him going anywhere. He knew that they had conspired, and with that solid, granite calm, he set aside the knowledge for later. Being angry with them for trying to save him would achieve nothing now.

"I do not think so, Muhtasib." The Wasp finally lifted his head. He knew he had his out now, that Sabbah wanted something other than his death. He was smart, and that could well be what saved Tison's life. "She is the one thing between me and an arrow in the back the second we start walking. So we go to a funduq, you, me and your housekeeper."

Sabbah's stomach contracted, and the urge to rip and tear brought cracks into the wall of control in his head. He tapped his fingers against his trouser leg again.

"And your leader will be there?"

"By the time we get there, yes." The Wasp removed the knife from Tison's throat, and relief buzzed in Sabbah's head. "I am going to need your word, Muhtasib who is so very noble. Your word your brother will not shoot me the moment I lead you away."

Sabbah cast him a mocking look. This man who had tried to undermine that honour, a man who held a woman hostage to coerce the man who loved her, now relied on his word.

"I give my word, as Muhtasib of Marrakech, and on my father's name, that my brother will not kill you today."

A crackle of tense laughter came from behind Tison. Then her head was jerked back as her assailant grabbed a handful of her hair through her head covering. The scarf was pulled back to expose scant inches of her hair above her brow. A few curls sprang loose.

Sabbah's hands shook. His stomach was tensed so hard, an arrow could surely not have pierced it.

Khalid strode to him, shoulder to shoulder, leaned in, and slid a knife into the protective curl of his prayer mat, which hung as ever by his side. Sabbah did not have to look to know. What else would his brother do? What else would he conceal in the mat? A treatise on peace?

"You are an idiot." Khalid's voice was tense with anger and fear.

Sabbah felt the press of people around them for the first time since he had bellowed his way through the crowd.

"These men attack the position of Muhtasib," he said, loud enough for people to become witnesses. "They attack Marrakech. They do this not because I am corrupt, but because I am not. The same goes for the Sayrafi, Abou Saal. The lead coins in the officially sealed purses, this is their doing. His doing. This is not acceptable, brother."

Khalid stared at him, worry and fury battling in his dark eyes, then the fight left them, and he nodded.

"Do not die," he commanded, and Sabbah's heart clenched as his brother thumped him hard on the shoulder.

Then he wondered why he was not frightened. He should be. There was no way he could win in a knife fight. He had trained to defend himself with one long ago, but as Muhtasib, he rarely used any sort of violence except in brief self-defence before his agents pulled an attacker away.

For Tison, though, he could have no fear. She needed him to be strong, and so he was. There was simply no alternative. His body might be reacting, tension and sweat. But his mind was granite hard.

"Try and keep the crowd from following." He saw Khalid's instant objection. His brother had intended to go after him.

Then Sabbah finally let himself walk to Tison. She had lowered her eyes, and each step stretched as he peered at her worried, frightened face. She looked older when she frowned like that. When she wept, she was tiny and small and in need of protection. At the moment, she looked beyond help. She looked distant, and he did not like it. His every bone ached with the need to banish that frown. She had taken violence with no expression, but him being in danger creased her beautiful brow.

"Shall we go?" He looked over her shoulder and met the eyes of the man she had called wasp-like. Cold, taut dislike returned his inspection.

"Oh, yes, shall we?" The man's nose quivered into a sneer.

"Yes, and let go of her hair, or we shall have a crowd and your leader will stay away."

"We are not cowards," the wasp replied, but he let go, taking a fist of her dress at the small of her back instead. It pulled her gown tight around her, but at least, she could stand straight. It was a small victory.

Sabbah wanted to soothe the skin at the nape of her neck with his hand. Afterwards, he promised himself. Afterwards, he would soothe every inch of her.

"Then lead on."

Chapter Sixteen

Hot breath on the back of her neck. Cramp in her toes where she had curled them away from the body of the Wasp's companion. The angry buzz of flies around his rapidly browning blood. And the twist of her neck as she was pulled against the whipcord lean man behind her.

Tison had feared for her future and her body many times, but she had never feared for her life so much as she did while waiting for Sabbah to arrive. The whisper of the blade was terrifyingly sharp. She had prepared enough meals to know a honed blade when it touched her. She had tried to talk to the Wasp. She had tried to be brave and negotiate, but he had ignored or rejected her attempts. So now, she merely stood in fear.

Stay calm. Stay calm. Stay calm.

She was wholly dependent on Sabbah.

That did not frighten her. She would not worry about herself once he arrived. She just repeated her instruction to herself over and over. Her mind was beyond her control. She could not stop it smelling the death, feeling the pain, hearing the breathing and the buzzing. The terror that she was going to die disappeared even while the knife was still there.

Her fear melted, and she felt the air change. Her eyes scanned left, and she saw his head as he emerged from an alleyway. Her ears roared with blood. Sabbah would not let her die. She knew that with an instinct as strong as the one that kept her breathing. What frightened her now was not that she might die.

It was that he might.

If they killed Sabbah, her life would be utterly broken. She could not even fully contemplate a tomorrow that he was not a part of, and she had not felt that since she had been separated from her father as a child. She wanted to hold his hand.

He spoke, and her disordered mind could not understand a word. She felt the Wasp behind her curl into a vicious thing, and she stared at Sabbah, wanting so much to be near him.

No, she wanted to throw herself against his chest and beg for forgiveness. This was her fault. She had walked too far from the praying men to give them space, and that had exposed her to attack.

Stay calm. Stay calm. Stay calm.

And she barely knew how she had gone from standing, watching his slow approach, his eyes blank and his face set, to being forced down back streets she did not know. She and Khalid had tried to save him, and instead, here he was, walking into a meeting with someone who had tried to humiliate him.

Who might try to kill him.

A shiver went through her body, quivering her arms and making her steps feel sluggish. The hand gripping her dress tightened again.

"Frightened, are you? You should be!"

The Wasp was desperate. He seemed a different man than the one who had bantered menacingly. He had lost that dark, threatening manner and seemed now little more than a common thug. A nasty thug with a sharp knife and a hold on her that went beyond his fingers. She was not much of anything, but she was all the support Sabbah had.

She lifted her head and stared blankly at the street ahead. She blinked. Yes, she was dependent on Sabbah to save her, but he? He needed her, too. The narrow alleyways of the stinking sector of Marrakech were full of people, and not all even noticed she was being led against her will.

"Oh, I was just thinking about how much work I have back at the house." She steadied her voice as she spoke, ending with an evenness of which she was quite proud. "Muhtasib? I am thinking of purchasing a cat!"

The Wasp breathed heavily behind her, but after a pause, Sabbah answered. His voice soothed her, and she gave up trying to be her own woman once more in favour of drawing strength from him.

"For the mice?" He was close behind them, within reach.

"Well, you know how we dislike vermin." A higher pitch sang in her voice like struck glass, and she swallowed, trying to control it.

"Oh, yes." Sabbah, on the other hand, dropped his voice low.

Now it was he who menaced, he who threatened. Tison had never heard that tone before. She realised then just how little disapproval he had shown over the stupid ledger mistake. If this was how he sounded when angered, she had escaped with a light scold. Even denouncing her in his jealousy, he had not been able to make her feel like a hunter who falls and comes face to face with a lioness. "We do not tolerate vermin."

"I am no mouse to be hunted," the Wasp muttered against her neck.

"Whatever do you mean?" She reached for her most vapid and irritating voice and won a puff of annoyed breath at her back. She felt giddy and possibly crazy.

"I think he assumes that just because we require a cat to kill mice, we will not find a way to swat him when the time comes." Sabbah came alongside her captor and reached out, touching her arm.

His hand was hot, his fingers strong. Her heart felt stronger just from that contact.

"We never had trouble with mice in the bathhouse." She felt dizzy all of a sudden. She wondered if shock was incredibly delayed or she merely could not be touched by him without going deliciously numb. "But the houses before, we always had cats. Oh! Or when I was a child, there was a mongoose. For the snakes, you see."

"I think we should start with a cat," he recommended. "Although, we risk the birds. They are very tame. Don't pretend you don't feed them seeds and grains."

"Oh, good point."

She stared around her, and only his fingers at her arm connected her to earth. Then the Wasp jerked her away from her Sabbah. Her gown tightened at her armpits and across her collar, and she winced as the strong linen drew a line across her chest.

"Be quiet!" he ordered. "This is not a trivial matter. You will pay me respect."

"And why should I do that?" Sabbah asked, his voice still low and hard. "A man who tried to bribe my slave into betraying me. A man who kidnapped and drugged her in order to force me to flog her in the street. A man who even now has a knife in one hand and my housekeeper in the other. Give me a single example of respect you have earned, Wasp!"

Tison's heart flared with pride. That was her man. She might be completely owned by her love for him at present, but that meant she got to boast. In her heart, she crowed at the Wasp, who remained silent. Even if he got angry and killed her, at least she would die knowing that her man was the best man in the entire world.

She still felt terror ripping at her stomach, but her heart beat strong and steady. Her feet walked blindly, ankles and knees weak, but her chin was once again high. Unfortunately, that combination caused her to slip on the dirt street more than once. The stench of the tanneries intensified, the quality of the streets worsened, and she stopped hearing people whisper Sabbah's title around them.

It was not that no one paid them heed; it was that no one would admit to having seen them. They looked anywhere but at the trio moving through their streets. For the first time, Tison felt that she had been sheltered from the hardships of life. She had not lived in such a place since she was an adolescent. Even after Rafiq had cast her aside, she had been sold to a family in a decent, safe part of Tunis. She had skills. She had never been truly poor.

As she moved through dusty, grimy, stinking streets, she wondered how anyone living here would not choose to sell themselves to slavery and a life of protection. The uncertainty these people must feel each day made her deeply aware that, even with a knife at her back, her life was safer than theirs.

She thought of the Mukharajah she had signed with Khalid and Kanto.

She thought of the terrifying possibility of freedom, when Sabbah tired of her and his wife wanted her removed. It would always be a future that could become her present. If she had not been found by Sabbah, she might have ended up here in the tannery quarter, or just outside the city walls as a whore. The angels had been watching for her. She hoped they watched for him, too.

"In here." The Wasp yanked her sideways, and there was a small, crunching rip as one of her seams finally started to come loose.

"Careful!" Sabbah commanded, coming alongside her at last and supporting her elbow so she did not fall.

She groped for his hand and squeezed it tight, drawing comfort and hoping she gave it, too. His thumb gently rubbed against her index finger, giving her warmth and an odd feeling around her heart, as if he had tugged on a cord from her skin to that nervously beating organ.

Her breasts hurt from the pressure of the taut cloth against them, and she knew she would have a purple line at both armpits come morning. She had been manhandled before.

Somehow, though, this felt worse.

She had been pushed around by her owners when she was younger. Once or twice, she had been slapped by a mistress or shoved by a man at the bathhouse until the guards came forward and the customer was reminded that damaging the property of the business was not permitted. She had always been Tison, but the blows had been meant for the slave.

The Wasp wanted to hurt her. He was desperate, like a cornered, rabid dog. She could not let him hurt Sabbah, but she was still afraid. She felt blind, and had she been asked to retrace her steps, she could not have. All she knew was the discomfort and pain of her captor's grasp, fear, and a roaring love for Sabbah that kept her going.

She feared what other pain might follow. It iced her veins and made her steps unsteady. It made her cling to Sabbah's fingers for as long as she could. She did not want to be drugged or hurt again. Her mind was by turns completely blank and full of the most inane trivialities that she wanted to gabble. She wanted Sabbah to know how many chores had been done, how much he needed to do, which of the women might possibly make a good housekeeper. She wanted to know that if she died, he would find happiness, and at the same time, she needed him to say he loved her, and would only ever love her.

"Here!"

The Wasp pulled her away from Sabbah and past a bench of old men drinking from wooden cups, eyes on the ground and jaws set with the determination that had seen them reach their years.

She was pushed into darkness; her eyes flaring and her vision going vaguely green as the sun was robbed and the gloomy, brazier-lit funduq slowly came into view. It was mostly empty, being a working day, but the owner did not come to greet them. The Wasp shoved her towards a table, and she righted herself, catching her balance on the aged surface and then smoothing her clothes, blinking rapidly.

"I'm here."

Sabbah came behind her, his heat even stirring her skin in the already hot sitting room. She turned to face him, chest to chest. For a moment, she looked up into his eyes, breathing as evenly as she could and digging her short nails into her palms, but then, she felt the fear quivering around her heart, and she forced her eyes down in case he saw her weakness.

"Tison." He reached a hand up and touched her cheek, moving a thick curl of her hair aside. "I am sorry for this. Please forgive me."

Her head jerked back up again so fast, she felt her neck twinge. Now when she blinked, it was in sudden confusion, not blindly like an owl at daybreak. He was apologising. He thought it was his fault.

"I am sorry that I am not as brave as I pretended to be." She swallowed hard, trying to bring the truth back from her lips. "I want so much to be that Tison. To be—"

"Come on!" The Wasp broke across her, silencing whatever wittering explanation she might have given Sabbah for not being as good as he deserved. This time, though, when the Wasp reached out for her, Sabbah shifted on his feet and blocked his way.

"You do not touch her again."

His voice was calm, low, a murmur of command which stilled the warm, smoky air like a desert wind cutting through incense and the ever-present stink of the tanneries. Tison's heart thumped, and pride and triumph filled her despite her fear, and despite the aching worry about her lover. He had said that for her. He was protecting her.

And it was the most beautiful thing she had ever heard.

Still, the fear remained, and she found herself unable to dredge up Strong, Sassy, or Brave Tison. She was just herself, and she knew that would not be enough. She had to remember how to be the clever one, or Sabbah would have no decent ally in this.

As ever when scared, her mind started to fix on daft, little details she did not need. She noticed the smoke scorching one wall where a fire must have broken out and been extinguished. She noticed the customer near the door leaving with his head down, and a serving girl cleaning the table nearby so she could listen in on the conversation.

The girl had bruises on one wrist and favoured it slightly. She leaned over and smiled.

"A hot cloth now and then will help the bruises heal." She gave the girl a slight shrug, seeking empathy.

The girl looked at her and gave a snort of derision, before turning away. Tison blinked. Of course, she was wearing a fairly rich gown, and she was clean and protected by her master. Envy was a bitter snake to hold close, but she could not fault the girl. If she had to live in the tanneries, she would be bitter, too.

"Follow me!" The Wasp's voice was beginning to take on a tone of nervousness not even arrows pointed at him had stirred. "Now."

"You should say 'if it pleases you'," she suggested, peering at her enemy around Sabbah's broad shoulder.

"If it pleases you," ground out her former captor.

Taken aback, she found herself blinking. He was afraid. Not of Khalid and his men finding them, but of whomever he had brought them to meet. She felt her heart quail a little. Someone who frightened a man who carried knives and snuck like a cat would squash her without a thought. What would such a person do to Sabbah? She had to find a way to keep him safe. He should not have come.

She scanned the rest of the room, looking to the curtained doorway at the back. The cloth was moved aside, and a pair of young men came out. She recognised them at once, and they recognised her. It was the two from the slave pens, the two who had come from Tunis with the man who had brought her here, who had tried to pretend to be Muslim-born to trick themselves free. Both stared at her, with venom and a smugness that frightened her further.

Once again, Sabbah moved, ready to protect her.

"Strange to see the mighty Muhtasib here," one of them muttered to the other, loud enough to be heard, quiet enough to be insolently denied.

The other turned his head and mimed spitting on the floor.

"Come on then, Tison."

Sabbah's voice settled into her skin, and she breathed and went with him, not seeking his hand now. She ducked her head as they passed the pair, remembering the weeks of travel while they plotted and stood aside, ignoring the other slaves as they struggled through the mountains. She wondered if they were the reason the Wasp had known her name. She wondered how fast these people had helped them escape their new masters.

She wondered if their hate for her had been passed on to whoever waited behind the curtain.

She wondered how she was going to keep Sabbah from sacrificing himself for her sake, if it came to a fight.

THE FUNDUQ'S CEILING was low for him, and as they walked through to a back room, Sabbah had to duck his head to avoid cracking his brow in the doorway. The smell of the tanneries was masked in incense the moment he crossed the threshold. The room was dark but for the orange glow of the brazier where the scented salts and roots burned. A curtain fell with crumpled quiet behind them, and the Wasp scuttled to one side, sitting on a cushion on the ground. The room was full of them.

Sabbah felt no urge to sit.

He was too caught by staring at the woman in the gloom. He could not judge her age, would not be able to point her out in a crowd, but he still allowed himself to be surprised. He had not expected a woman.

"I suppose it is an honour to meet you at last, al Muhtasib." Her voice was deep and crackled with undeniable charisma. She devoured words as she spoke them. As her head moved, there was the rattle of beads in her hair. Her

Arabic was flawless, and though he could tell she was African, he could not see any one nation in her features. Her nose was too narrow to be pure Ghanaian, like his mother had been, but her cheekbones lacked the height of the Eastern nations.

"Salaam Aleikum," he replied. She might be mysterious, but she had also orchestrated corruption in the markets' coinage. And she had had Tison captured and drugged. Being a woman would not spare her from his anger. "Why?"

She laughed, a soft, dry series of chuckles. And she moved, her hair clacking and her shadow drawing close on the edge of her cushion as she leaned into the dim light. Her eyes reflected the embers. Sabbah felt the hair on his neck prickle.

"Why do you have slaves, Muhtasib?" she asked, not pausing for a response or complaining that he had eschewed courtesies. "Why do you live in a nice big house when others live in squalor or on the streets themselves? Why do you flog people in the street?"

"Because they break the law." Guilt crawled over his skin, though, at her first questions.

"The law needs to be broken, Muhtasib," she answered, urgent now and filled with vigour. "Marrakech needs to be broken. Only then can she be free. Free of Caliphs and Muhtasibs. Free of imams. Free of masters."

He waited for more. There was more. She had been a slave, of that he was certain. The way she curled her mouth around the word 'master' made that uncomfortably clear. She had been mistreated perhaps, and was bitterly angry with what she saw as an entire caste of abusive owners.

"I understand that you want to break the three offices beneath the Vizier." He wanted her to know she had been on the verge of being caught. They had been close to finding the source of the lead coins. All of a sudden, he remembered the report from the old man in the tanneries and his lists of comings and goings. He wondered if she was in that report, or if she was always in shadows. "And that the Caliph is in the north, giving you a chance at a weakened city."

"Of course you do. You are not a child." She leaned back into gloom again and crossed her legs. She had an anklet, woven leather, above her foot. "I almost wish you had been stronger, Muhtasib. Watching you whip a woman you are obsessed with would have been entertaining."

Rage surfaced. An instinctive flare that made him want to wrap his arms around Tison and growl like a beast at his antagonist. He stilled himself with an effort.

"You want me to lose my temper," he observed. "Do you want to fight me?"

"It has occurred to me," she replied. "I would win, after all. I wanted you to be disgraced, but you have not quit your post or been forced from it. Proof of the corruption that remains."

"Here I thought you wanted me to be more corrupt." He was aware of how quiet Tison was.

He wanted her to be powerful and brave, and he was worried that she was letting herself be small. She was better than this woman. Stronger. If his Tison was trying to bring down Marrakech, it would already be a smoking ruin.

"It would have made my job easier," she admitted.

"Your job? You see this as a calling, do you? Destroying my city?"

As he had hoped, the use of 'my' made her move, agitated and angry. She got to her feet. She was tall, almost as tall as him, and with the brazier beneath her, she was fearsome in shadow and fire.

"This city—" she spat out the words, her upper lip curling above her teeth, "—is not yours. It is not the Caliph's. The people of Marrakech own their city. I will make it so, and there is nothing you can do to stop me, Muhtasib."

For a moment, they stared at one another, and he felt nothing but dread. He imagined Khalid finding his body, and the bloody aftermath that would follow in the streets of the tannery quarter. He imagined Tison, broken and bleeding, and something else began to surface. He was not going to let her be killed. He was going to take her home. He was going to make her his wife, and he was going to keep on doing his best for the city, whether it wanted him or not.

"If I am killed here, my brother will raze the tannery quarter to the ground in retaliation." He kept his voice even, protecting himself by imagining burying his face into Tison's soft hair. "It will take decades to rebuild. In that time, Marrakech's leather trade will crumble. Other cities will take up the load. There will be soldiers on the streets everywhere, and merchants will begin to feel unsafe here and stay in Cairo, in Tunis, in Alger. You are a woman. He will not hurt you, but you will have your broken city. You will have families starving, and you can move them into the big merchant houses, but that will not bring grain from the north or cloth from Cairo. We will be as empty as Chellah."

She stared at him, eyes glittering.

"So much for the kind man everyone adores." She sounded defeated, and he pushed his advantage.

"Adores?" The image of men nervously tidying their counters and bowing obsequiously flashed in his head. "I can count the friends I have on one hand since I became Muhtasib. The ones who would mourn my death. But you did not meet with me to kill me," he told her, hoping he was right. "If you wanted to break me, you would have killed Tison and left her body to be found. So let us talk. What injustice do you want me to right?"

Silence stretched, his feet ached on the uneven floor, and Tison's breathing quickened and slowed as she fought her own control over her panic. He would get them out of this. He knew that. He hoped she knew it, too. This was no different than facing a madman with a knife in the market. This woman's weapon was fear itself, but she was just as crazed in her way. She was dangerous, but not invincible. She sat in darkness and swathes of scented smoke while he strode abroad in the markets. She was merely a shadow.

"Slaves come to me when they run away," she told him, sitting back down, crossing her legs and leaning forward. One of her knees clicked as she settled herself. "They tell me of beatings and hardship, and then they come to live in the stinking part of the city. I want masters who complain of runaway slaves to be investigated for cruelty. Surely, men of your faith understand that."

He knew at once that a meeting with the Qadi would be unavoidable, and he cringed away from the thought. It was not a bad suggestion, though, and he could only hope that the Qadi would see past their differences for the good of those converts in slavery if not for People of the Book.

"I want you to stop putting lead coins in people's coffers," he returned. "It does not just undermine the Sayrafi. It undermines Marrakech as a centre of trade. Even if you get what you want and the Caliph and all his officers leave, you will need trade to survive."

He felt his fingers move as he tapped the side of his leg, waiting for her next demand.

"That is your big request, Muhtasib? To protect the Sayrafi, and not yourself?" She gave one of her dry chuckles. "All nobility."

It was not a compliment.

"I can look to myself," he answered her. "Money cannot guard itself. How did you get the seal so perfect?"

She laughed, and of course did not answer. He had a feeling he and Abou Saal would wonder about that for the rest of their careers.

"You are welcome to approach me if you have further things to bring to my attention." He swallowed as quietly and subtly as he could. "I ask that you do not approach or threaten my housekeeper. A new slave to the city, drugged and captive for her master's morals? How do you justify that?"

"I do not have to," she replied, drawing farther back into the shadows. "I could do the same to you, Ibn Abdella al Muhtasib. I could have you stripped and left in the markets, naked and rambling drunk."

Almost lazily, he stepped forward, allowing himself to be lit further by the brazier, so she would see his face and know his intent.

"So long as you do not touch Tison, you can try whatever you want with me," he told her.

His new nemesis regarded him from shadow, and then gave a mutter of amusement.

"Rich men can afford love." She curled her lip at him like a wild dog, the brazier light glimmering off her teeth.

She was too dangerous to pity, and Sabbah wondered if being fearsome was as lonely as being incorruptible. He stared down at her where she sat and wondered if she was as lonely as he had been before Tison.

"Anyone can afford love." As Tison spoke, Sabbah felt his skin prickle. "Even when the cost is your entire life. I had a master I loved. He used me, cast me out, and then eight years of missing him later, he came back into my life just to ruin it again."

She stepped forward, and he turned his head, looking at his beloved with an ache in his heart and anger in his head. Three coppers. If he ever met her once-master, he would not be able to stop himself going mad.

The woman in shadows gave a dismissive noise.

"Such men should be flogged," she snarled.

"Perhaps." Tison reached to him and took his hand, curling her fingers around his. "But that did not stop me loving again. Al Muhtasib is a good man. He owns his mistakes, and he will help you so long as the markets are not threatened and you do not harm or interrupt the devotion of others. How is that something you should oppose?"

The clack of the woman's beads came faster as she shook her head.

"A good man. But one who controls others. No one has that right."

"Do you?" Tison's fingers went tense and rigid. "Did you have the right to punish me for his sake? His agents wear livery and help people every day. Yours threaten and kidnap."

The woman laughed again, a deep mutter of noise.

"You think I want to be good? I do not." She rose to her feet and waved her hands. "You're thinking because I am a woman, I am really sweet and gentle on the inside?"

"I might have." Sabbah wished he could shield Tison somehow. It was grinding on him that she was here at all. Maybe that was the point the woman was making. "My religion encourages men to protect their women. But this woman, this woman you threatened and hurt, she has opened my eyes more than you ever could. So I am not dismissing you. I know you are a threat. I know that, more than this, you are right about the corruption and mistreatment of law and people. I know that you are the one who has begun to undermine Marrakech. And because you are a woman, I know that you can think in ways I cannot. But do not think that I will spare you punishment. I did not spare her because she is a woman. I spared her because she is the most important thing in my life. You do not have that distinction."

The shadow of a woman tilted her head, and for a moment, he barely breathed.

"Go then, Muhtasib," she said eventually. "I will not give up my war, but if you ensure men are questioned when a slave runs away to me, I will keep lead coins out of the city's money."

She rose and came close, holding her hand over the fire. Sabbah barely hesitated, his upbringing still marking how he felt about touching a woman's hand.

He shook it firmly.

"Oh," he added, the words flowing as the certainty formed in his mind. "One other thing."

He turned, finally letting his anger bloom from his control. He advanced on the Wasp, seeing the man's eyes flare in instant fear. Before he could scrabble out of reach, Sabbah picked him up by his tunic, lifting him to his feet, and then struck him backhanded.

The smaller man staggered and then drew a knife. As he lunged, Sabbah punched him hard in the jaw, putting all of his rage and fury and frustration into the blow, all of his love for Tison and his need to keep her safe. The hated man fell to the ground, breathing hard and spitting blood. It might be years since Sabbah and Khalid had sparred, even longer since he had actually trained, but for once, he took full advantage of his height and weight.

"Leave my city," he told him. "Get out by tomorrow. Because if I or any of my people see you again, I will have you flogged to death. To death."

The woman sat easily back down behind him. Apparently, she was willing to sacrifice her flunky for peace with the Muhtasib. Good, because he wanted with every inch of him that was a man to kill the one who had hurt Tison. All that kept him back was that he was hers, and he did not want her to see him kick a man to death in front of her.

"Salaam Aleikum." He inclined his head to the shadowy woman, but she waved it aside and did not respond.

He put an arm around Tison's back and guided her out, once more ducking through the doorway. He heard her give a satisfied little grunt as they stepped past her fallen assailant.

"It's strange to be near Quiet Tison," he remarked, letting the rage bleed out behind him.

She took his hand and pressed it against her heart. He felt it there, hammering against her chest, the slight softness of the top of her breast not disguising that beating terror.

"I couldn't help." She clasped his hand and lowered it, and they walked again toward the street. She spoke over his denial, his poor attempt to remind her that her speaking out had changed the direction of the conversation for the better. "I don't like not being able to help. Also ..."

She twisted and kicked his calf.

"Ouch!" He looked at her, confused, breaking out of the icy calm that had kept him from either panicking or raging. He blinked at her.

"Do not ever put yourself in danger for me!" she snapped as they stepped into the sunlight and the stink of the streets assaulted them once more.

He withdrew his hand from her and folded his arms, looking at her, staring into her golden-brown eyes and waiting patiently. Her cheeks darkened.

"Oh, you are—" she cleared her throat delicately, "—you are perhaps wondering what Khalid and I were doing in the market."

"Do not—" he tried and failed to keep the intensity in his voice quiet, "—put yourself in danger for me." He took a breath of stinking air. "You are too important, Tison. I cannot lose you. I simply cannot."

He looked around. Men whose eyes had been curiously fastened to the ground stared amazed, no doubt that he had emerged alive and unbloodied. "If we were not in a crowd, Tison, I would kiss you. I would hold you against me and not let you go."

Her eyes softened, and he read the love there and felt it soothe his fears.

"Maybe I do not need to wait until we're alone," she began, beginning to close the distance, beyond his will to stop her. She had said she loved him, simply and without demanding a response from him. She had merely said it, because it was true. He was going to hold her and kiss her senseless.

Only then, Khalid dropped from above them, grunting as he landed and wincing as he rose from the resultant crouch.

"You were not in there long." His big brother unstrung his bow and slung it back over his shoulder. "I had not even decided to come in after you."

Tison was staring at him in evident confusion.

"The roofs?" Sabbah barely had the energy to be surprised that his brother had followed over the tops of the houses. He was tired, and he had half a day to go before he could take Tison to bed and make amends to her for just being himself and not someone better.

"Did you think I would actually let you two go in alone?" Khalid looked behind them. "Where is that—" he bit off his insult, deferring to Tison's presence, "—creature?"

"I gave him a day to get out of the city," Sabbah assured his angry brother. "Or I will kill him myself."

Khalid grinned, bloodthirsty for a moment.

"I am so proud of you." His brother's grin dropped. "Now come on, the pair of you. I am tempted to lock you both into Sabbah's fancy house and just not let you out of my sight!"

"Poor Jessamine," Tison replied.

But when Sabbah turned to grin at her, he found her still staring at him with that dewy softness. A glisten to the gold. It heated him despite the foul-smelling street and the undercurrent of danger he now knew for certain ran through his city.

His heart clenched.

"I will agree to part of that." He drew himself up and set both hands on his brother's shoulders. "Find my men. Tell as many of them as you can find that I will be at my house for the rest of the day, recovering from this. They are to go to you for anything that requires authority, and only to come to me in case of absolute emergency. Tomorrow, they will meet me at market open at my office, and we will discuss how to deal with this threat."

Khalid grinned, his relief showing in his relaxed shoulders.

"You'll owe me one," he countered. "And an explanation."

"You let the woman I love use herself as bait to draw out a man who captured and drugged her in the past," Sabbah said smoothly, and with as little bite as he could manage.

"Fair point." Seriousness crossed Khalid's face, and then he turned and winked at Tison. "We tried to keep him safe, Ti!"

"Thank you, Khalid." Tison's smile was almost sleepy in its slow, quiet softness. "Please, if you do not mind, give my best to Jessamine."

They were out of the tannery quarter and walking through the backstreets of the city, through walkways and under vines, surrounded by colour and sweet smells, before he finally realised what her words had meant. Khalid was long gone, but Sabbah still frowned and looked down at the slender creature beside him.

"Why would he mind, Tison?" he asked, ready to clarify.

There was no need, and she gave him a look that was somewhat reproachful.

"Muhtasib, please, do not make me think serious things now," she asked. "I am enjoying this."

"Tison, you will not be a slave long," he told her, and when she closed her eyes, he felt the pain that showed on her face.

"Sabbah, please." Her voice was quiet and scared, and so unlike Tison, it hurt him.

"Tison." He stopped her and pulled her alongside bright, coloured glass and metalwork that was not as beautiful as her, and never could be. "I am going to marry you. You and Jessamine will be sisters."

"You cannot." She looked so sad. "Please do not make promises you cannot keep. You will break my heart, and I am so very tired, Sabbah."

He took her hands in one of his, his arm around her, and he pulled her against him. She did not struggle, but she sighed.

"You see how bad I am for you?"

"You see how good you are for me?" he countered. "Tison, I love you. Even if I did not, do you not see how much you have done for me? Do you realise how lonely I was before you? Do you realise how much I need you?"

"I did nothing today." She dropped her head, and he was glad that her headscarf was long gone, so he could inhale the scent of her hair, olive oil and something floral. "I caused trouble again."

"Trouble? Tison, you were captured, held at knife point, and you came with me into certain danger to face a woman who had tried to get you to turn from me first with promises and then with fear. You are brave and true, and I want no other for my wife. No other as the mother of my children!"

She jerked in his arms.

"Children?" She looked up at him suspiciously. He preferred it to the hurt sadness.

"I was thinking of boys, as I grew up only with a brother, but I would be happy with daughters if they were like you. Life is not easy for girls, but with a mother like you, I know they would be safe."

"And Christian?" she reminded him.

"Perhaps we let them choose their own faith, Tison," he suggested. "In ten years or so. I am more concerned with getting you to marry me. To be my wife. My first and—"

"And only?" she finished, the suspicion still strong.

"And only," he promised.

"Good." She worried at her lip with her teeth. "Because I am not having some noble Arab woman's children supplanting mine."

"Tison," he interrupted before she could work herself up into hatred of that imaginary woman. "Marry me. Please, marry me."

"If it will not spoil your standing with the Caliph and Vizier," she insisted. "And we must ask Kanto."

"Ask ... you want me to ask Kanto for permission to marry the woman I love. Love, Tison. Not would make a convenient match, not would make a useful alliance. Love. You need to say yes, Tison, because I cannot live without you at my side."

"I would make a good mistress," she suggested, still worrying away at that lip. "I would not leave you."

"Come home where I can kiss you," he asked. "Because I need to stop you making stupid comments somehow."

He started propelling her up the street.

"Stupid?" she objected, her voice a warning. "You be careful, Important Man. Else I will fight you."

"Fierce Woman." He grinned. Then he took her hand once more, public display be damned. "Important Woman."

Epilogue

Tison sat on a bench, hands slick with oil while she taught Veta to make olive soap. The day was hot, even to her, so they remained shaded by the palm and fig trees, and she had forced so much water into Veta, the Slav girl might well start to float. They were experimenting, as she had never made soap with clay before, and she had bought a jar of it from the mountains to mix with the wood ash and oil. Hands slippery, she frowned, hoping the ash would measure up against the Natron she was used to in the north.

"Is good?" Veta set a mould aside, next to the hand-formed cakes.

"We will see," Tison replied, frowning at the pale reddish mixture of the clayed soap. She had not even begun to add scents yet. This project would go on until she was satisfied. In other word, until she had created the Perfect Soap.

Soap worthy of her Important Man.

She raised her head as Sabbah rounded the corner. She had not heard him; she had just known he was there. She stood instantly, rubbing her hands clean of soap and ash and stepping clear of their work. He met her by the fountain and gestured to it. They sat together on its side.

"So tell me." She grasped his hand, squeezing hard.

"Can you not read my face?" he teased, his expression the one he used in the markets. She narrowed her eyes at him and stared him into submission. "Oh, very well, Tison! I am to continue as Muhtasib."

Relief swamped her, and she leaned back, perilously close to the water, looking up to the firmament and thanking every angel for helping her Important Man.

"Pho!" she said, indistinctly. "And so ..." She straightened, and tightened her fingers around his again. "I am glad."

"So am I," he mused aloud. "With all that has happened, I still feel as though this is what I am meant to be. Especially since I no longer have to make a choice." He raised her hand up and kissed her palm. "The Caliph has given me permission to wed my Important Woman."

Tison's heart quivered like the half-set soaps she had been making.

"Sabbah, you do not have to—" she stopped, cowed by the flat look on his face. "I know, but I had to say it. I love you, Sabbah."

"And I love you," he told her, pressing another kiss to her wrist. "Even though you have turned my life upside down and shaken my foundations."

"You are never going to stop throwing that in my face," she bemoaned. "But truly, Sabbah, we are to marry?"

"You have not once said that you want to, you know."

His eyes were on her hands, and she felt her quivering heart strengthen. So she shook her fingers free of him and then took his face in her hands. His beard tickled her palms, and she brushed her thumbs alone the bones beneath his eyes.

"I want to marry you, Sabbah," she said, firm but quiet, her shoulders feeling as though they were floating, so free of burdens. "I want to open myself up to be hurt, but know that you will not hurt me."

"I won't." He turned his cheek into her hand. "I promise, Tison, I will never, ever try to keep you safe."

She laughed at him.

"Well, maybe safe, but certainly not in ignorance." She put her arms around him and pulled him close. "And I will never again team up with your brother or Kanto to keep you safe."

"Please," he said, flat enough to make her laugh again. "So you'll marry me?"

His arms closed around her, and she felt exactly where she was supposed to be.

"Yes," she told him, and she kissed him, courtyard or not, and her heart soared as he kissed her back.

A thought tickled into her mind, and she drew back. "Oh, and we must start redecorating the women's quarters! I have so many ideas!"

He laughed and growled, kissed her again, and Tison knew she was home.

Thank you for reading Her Golden Eyes by Holly March. Please leave a review on the site of purchase.

This is the first book in the Heart of Gold series by the same author. Book 2, Her Golden Touch is out November 2024.

Subscribe to our newsletter[1] to keep up-to-date with all Love Africa Press book releases.

---

1.   https://www.loveafricapress.com/newsletter

ABOUT THE AUTHOR

Holly March has been telling stories all her life. She owes a great debt to the girls in the dorms, her RPG friends, and of course her family, who listened to her blather and read her fanfic. She lives on the welsh border and breathes the 12th Century. She did not discover she was autistic until she was 30 but has spent the years since saying 'yeah, that makes sense'. She lives with her parents, her familiar, and the other pets.

OTHER BOOKS BY LOVE AFRICA PRESS

Pharaoh's Bed by Mukami Ngari
Love and Hiplife by Nana Prah
Be My Valentine Anthology: Volume 2
Bound To Liberty by Kiru Taye/Kai Tyler
Fine Wine by Emem Bassey
Revelations by Lauri Kubuitsile

CONNECT WITH US

Facebook.com/LoveAfricaPress[1]
Twitter.com/LoveAfricaPress[2]
Instagram.com/LoveAfricaPress[3]

SIGN UP TO OUR NEWSLETTER

https://www.loveafricapress.com/newsletter

---

1. https://www.facebook.com/LoveAfricaPress

2. https://twitter.com/LoveAfricaPress

3. https://www.instagram.com/loveafricapress/